9-06

THE ELAGIN AFFAIR

The Elagin Affair

And Other Stories

Ivan Bunin

TRANSLATED FROM THE RUSSIAN,
WITH AN INTRODUCTION,
BY GRAHAM HETTLINGER

Ivan R. Dee
CHICAGO 2005

THE ELAGIN AFFAIR AND OTHER STORIES. Copyright © 2005 by
Ivan R. Dee, Inc. English translation copyright © 2005 by Graham Hettlinger.
All rights reserved, including the right to reproduce this book or portions thereof in
any form. For information, address: Ivan R. Dee, Publisher, 1332 North Halsted
Street, Chicago 60622. Manufactured in the United States of America and printed
on acid-free paper.

www.ivanrdee.com

Library of Congress Cataloging-in-Publication Data:
Bunin, Ivan Alekseevich, 1870–1953.
    [Short stories. English. Selections]
    The Elagin affair and other stories / Ivan Bunin ; translated from the Russian and
with an introduction by Graham Hettlinger.
        p. cm.
    ISBN 1-56663-641-8 (cloth : alk. paper)
    1. Bunin, Ivan Alekseevich, 1870–1953 — Translations into English. I. Hettlinger,
Graham. II. Title.
    PG3453.B9A239 2005
    891.73'3 — dc22   2005012806

For Mila, who made this possible once more

Contents

Acknowledgments

ONCE AGAIN I am grateful to Angela Brintlinger and Terrence Graham for their insightful reviews of earlier drafts of several of these translations.

I would like to express my heartfelt thanks to my colleagues Alissa Bibb, Darya Shakhova, Vladka Shikova, and Margaret Stephenson, who generously took on extra work in order to give me time to finish this project.

Finally I wish to thank my wife, Mila Medina. This book would never have been completed without her careful review and thoughtful corrections, her rich insights into the author and his work, her great help in researching the notes, and her tireless emotional support. In many ways these translations are hers as much as they are mine.

G. H.

Introduction

DESPITE his great stature in Russia, Ivan Bunin (1870–1953) remains relatively unknown in the West. After fleeing his homeland near the end of the civil war that followed the Bolshevik Revolution, he began a life in exile in France. Throughout the 1920s he wrote prodigiously, producing some of his best-known works, including the autobiographical novel *The Life of Arsenyev* (1927–1928) and the novellas "Mitya's Love" (1924) and "The Elagin Affair" (1925). During this time he was read and admired by the large Russian emigré community (which in France numbered roughly 400,000) and a relatively small circle of European writers and critics that included D. H. Lawrence, Thomas Mann, Rainer Maria Rilke, and André Gide. When in 1933 Bunin became the first Russian writer to receive the Nobel Prize for Literature, his fame grew considerably, and translations of his work began to circulate more widely in the United States and Europe. That year the author was something of a celebrity in Paris—two thousand guests attended a congratulatory dinner held in his honor, strangers hailed him in the streets, and the Russian emigré community feted him as one of its leading figures.

Yet by the time Bunin published his last book of stories, *Dark Avenues*, in 1943, he had been all but forgotten. Widely recognized today as one of his greatest works, this final volume received little critical attention when it first appeared, and it earned the author almost nothing. (One of the only payments he received for the book was a three-hundred-dollar advance for its translation into English, though a complete translation is still to be published in the West.) Bunin was soon reduced to asking friends and admirers for financial support in order to survive. The increasingly severe health problems that afflicted both him and his wife, and the mounting bills for their treatment, made his final years a misery. "I've begun my 79th year and I am so poor that I simply don't know how and on what I'll exist," he wrote in a letter in 1948. Five years later he died penniless in Paris.

Bunin was already an acclaimed writer when he left Russia in 1920. He had twice received one of the country's most prestigious literary awards, the Pushkin Prize, for his poetry and translations (most notably of Longfellow's "The Song of Hiawatha"). His novellas "The Village" (1910) and "Sukhodol" (1912) had been widely praised for their startlingly honest depictions of life in the Russian countryside, and his short story "The Gentleman from San Francisco" (1915) had been hailed as a masterpiece both in Russia and abroad. Russian literary figures as diverse as Maksim Gorky and Aleksandr Blok listed him among Russia's best and most important authors as early as 1901.

His intense opposition to the Soviets made it predictably difficult to find new editions of Bunin's work in Russia after the revolution, and in the 1930s the state began a violent effort to eradicate all traces of the author from recent history: his books were removed from libraries and destroyed, and it became a punishable offense to mention Bunin by name. (Varlam Shalamov, author of *Kolyma Tales*, was reportedly sentenced to ten years' forced labor for stating publicly that Bunin was a great writer.) But Bunin remained among Russia's most deeply loved authors, and after Stalin's death he returned to prominence, despite the unease of some Soviet critics who continued to view him as a dangerous and decadent figure. Today the Russian public's relationship to literature is changing profoundly, but one can say with certainty that older educated readers know Bunin as well as they know Anton Chekhov or Ivan Turgenev, perhaps even Lev Tolstoy.

Given his critical stature and widespread popularity in Russia, it is difficult to say precisely why Bunin has not become better known in the West. Many of his most famous works (including those presented here) focus on the themes of love, sex, death, and memory—topics with an undeniably universal appeal. But the importance of theme in Bunin's prose is never completely equal to the importance of style. Or perhaps it is more accurate to say that the meaning of Bunin's stories often derives from the movement and unfolding of their language. Whereas Tolstoy could be said to reveal important philosophical truths that are capable of surviving, at least to some degree, the inevitable disfigurements of translation, Bunin's most important accomplishments are invariably linked to form: how he says something is usually as important as what he says. For this reason he is widely ranked among the greatest Russian stylists of the twentieth century. His often elaborate sentences move with a rhythmic, fluid grace that few have matched, and his accounts of sensory experience are sometimes staggering in their musicality, their detail, and their sheer intensity. Here, for example, is a short passage taken at random from *Sukhodol*:

> *He opened the door and sniffed deeply: a bitter, almost astringent scent of autumnal decay still rose from the bushes, but now it was mixed with a winter freshness. And everything was motionless,*

calm, almost solemn. The sun was just rising over the village, and it lit the tops of the birches that lined the main path to the house like a painting, revealing a subtle, joyful lilac tint that the azure sky created as it gleamed through the white, half-bare limbs and branches still flecked with golden leaves. A dog ran to the cold shade beneath the balcony, its feet crunching sharply over the brittle grass, which seemed to be laced with salt. That crisp sound reminded him of winter, and a shiver of pleasure ran through the old man's shoulders.

This passage is typical of Bunin's style. All the reader's senses are engaged—smell, sight, sound, touch, even taste by association with the frost that resembles salt on the grass. The elaborately detailed description of the light that hangs among the birches is also typical. For Bunin this light is specific, unique, and recognizable: it is *the* light that appears in Russia when a few golden leaves, sunlight, and azure combine. If any of these components had been altered—if there had been no leaves on the trees, if the sky had been slightly darker, if the sun had already been shining for hours— the light would have been altogether different. The details are not simply decorative, in other words, they are a vital part of accurate description. In the original these nuances are delivered with an easy grace; they emerge in a series of rhythmic sentences, each detail slightly recasting those that preceded it. The author's language operates almost like a camera lens being focused with increasing precision.

It is this fluid, nuanced style that often suffers badly in translation. How does one preserve the music of a Russian text when one can no longer use Russian words? How does one replicate the elaborate structure of a Russian sentence when rebuilding it within the confines of English grammar? Struggling to preserve Bunin's style, one understands all too well Werner Winter's statement that "We may compare the work of a translator to that of an artist who is asked to create an exact replica of a marble statue, but who cannot secure any marble."

In the translations that follow I have sought to strike a balance between the demands of "literal"—that is to say, denotative—meaning, and the importance of style and form in Bunin's work. In doing so I have weighed not only what a phrase or sentence means but also how it moves and sounds in Russian, how it resonates with other words in the original. In trying to preserve some of these components, I have allowed myself to redistribute the weight of the original Russian when rendering it in English. For example, the flexibility of Russian syntax often allows Bunin to rely heavily on adjectives and adverbs to add depth and complexity to a descriptive passage, whereas more brittle English sentences tend to collapse under the weight of so many modifiers. Therefore I have sometimes tried to find verbs and nouns to carry some of the descriptive weight that Bunin builds into his often elaborate chains of adjectives and adverbs. At other moments I have allowed myself to break up sentences altogether and rearrange their wealth of detail, again in order to preserve some modicum of the graceful movement one feels when reading the original, and which, if rendered in literal exactitude, becomes overwrought and stilted in English.

Even before his emigration, Bunin had a deep fascination with Russia's people and their customs. In "Sukhodol" and "The Scent of Apples," for example, he delves with an ethnographer's interest into faith healing, religious wanderers, peasant customs, and the plight of petty landowners. And later, longing for his homeland, he developed in his writing an even stronger fascination with Russia's flora and fauna, its cathedrals, its weather, its restaurants and city streets, its ancient history, its unique words and customs. Indeed, reading Bunin's later works, one wonders at his ability to recall and capture Russia's smells, the textures of its light, the behavior of its birds with such precision. It seems that through memory and language the author was almost able to transport himself to that country he had left so long ago and missed so desperately throughout his life. Many of Bunin's best stories may be seen as attempts to preserve

INTRODUCTION

the past not as a historical record but as a living, pulsing memory—
one so vivid it can whirl its reader back to a place long since
"plowed over and seeded."

Bunin's fascination with Russia and its customs may have also
served to limit his audience in the West, for like the music of his
prose, these details are often resistant to translation, and the author
has no particular interest in explaining them to anyone. He writes
to other Russians. He assumes his readership feels the roots of its
language in Old Church Slavonic, that it listens apprehensively
when a cuckoo calls from the woods, that it eats *blini* before the
spring fast, that it knows the history of Tatar invasions, Old Believers, warring monks, country gentlemen, and serfs. Western readers
who have not studied Russian culture may be thrown, at times, by
such references. But I am confident that any reader will be able to
recognize the lyric beauty of Bunin's stories, regardless of the historical and cultural details that give them pitch. And I would argue
that those references that make us pause and wonder are in fact another reason to continue reading this author, for they show that
Bunin's portraits of his homeland are truly unlike anything we've
read before.

THE ELAGIN AFFAIR

Mitya's Love

T HE NINTH of March was Mitya's last happy day in Moscow. So it seemed, at least, to him.

Katya and he were walking on Tverskoy Boulevard. Winter had suddenly given way to spring, and it was almost hot in the sun. One could almost believe the larks had returned, bringing warmth and joy. Everything was melting, glistening, wet. Water dripped from all the eaves while yardmen hacked ice from the sidewalks and flung damp, sticky snow from the roofs. All the streets were crowded and alive. The high clouds had dispersed, transformed into a delicate white smoke that drifted in the sky's damp blue. In the distance Pushkin's statue rose, pensive and benevolent; the domes of the Strastnoy Monastery gleamed in the sun. The fact that Katya was so winsome, so engaging—this was best of all that day: everything she did expressed a kind of easy, natural intimacy. Repeatedly she took his arm and peered up at him with childlike trust,

[3]

studied the happy, slightly condescending look on Mitya's face as he continued walking, taking such long strides that she struggled to keep up.

"You're so funny," she said unexpectedly when they were near the Pushkin monument. "When you laugh with that big mouth of yours, there's a kind of awkward, almost boyish way you stretch your lips. It's terribly endearing. . . . Don't be hurt—I love you for that smile! . . . that smile and your Byzantine eyes. . . ."

Mitya tried not to smile as he overcame a feeling of both secret satisfaction and slightly wounded pride. "When it comes to looking like children," he answered amicably, looking at the statue that now towered above them, "I think it's safe to say that you and I haven't grown very far apart. And I resemble a Byzantine about as much as you look like the empress of China. It's just that you're all crazy about these so-called Byzantines, these children of the Renaissance. I really don't understand your mother!"

"What would you do in her place—lock me up in a tower?" Katya asked.

"Not a tower, no. But all of these supposedly artistic Bohemians, all of these future stars from studios and conservatories—I wouldn't let any of them through your door," Mitya said, trying to stay calm and keep a friendly, casual tone. "You told me yourself that Bukovetsky already asked you to dinner at the Strelna, and Yegorov asked to sculpt you naked in the form of some kind of dying sea-wave—an honor, of course, that you find terribly flattering."

"I won't turn away from art. Even for you, I won't do it," said Katya. "Maybe I am depraved, the way you often say I am," she continued, although Mitya had never said this. "Maybe I am ruined. But you'll have to take me as I am. I don't want to argue anymore. Stop being jealous over me—at least for now, on such a wonderful day. . . . How can you not understand that you—regardless of all else—you alone are best of all," she said with soft insistence as she looked into his eyes, her expression now deliberately composed to be alluring. "A drowsing secret lies between us," she recited, drawing out the words as if deep in thought. "A soul gave a soul a ring."

These last words, this verse, hurt Mitya deeply. In general, much was painful and unpleasant—even on that day. The joke about boyish awkwardness was unpleasant. He'd heard many such comments from Katya before, and they were far from accidental: she quite often revealed herself to be more adult than he in certain aspects of their intimacy, and quite often—unwittingly, which is to say completely naturally—she brandished this superiority above him while Mitya took it as a painful sign of her secret and depraved experiences. The phrase "regardless of all else" (regardless of all else, you alone are best of all) was unpleasant too, as was the fact that she suddenly lowered her voice to speak these words. And more than anything, that poem, its mannered reading—this was particularly unpleasant. But later, when he looked back at the ninth of March, it would seem that on that last happy day in Moscow he'd endured quite easily both the poem and its reading, despite the fact that this, most of all, reminded him of that artistic set that was robbing him of Katya and therefore sharply stirred his jealousy and his hatred.

Returning from Kuznetsky Most that day, they stopped at Zimmerman's so that Katya could buy several works by Scriabin, and there, in passing, she began to speak of Mitya's mother. "You can't imagine how afraid I am of her, even now, long before we meet," she said, laughing.

Throughout their affair, for some reason they'd never touched on the question of the future—had never asked where all of this would lead. And now, suddenly, Katya began to talk about his mother, began to talk as if there couldn't be the slightest doubt that they would join as one family.

II

After that day, nothing seemed to change: it all continued just as before. Mitya accompanied Katya to the actors' studio at the Moscow Art Theatre, to concerts, and to literary evenings; sometimes he visited her at home in Kislovka until two in the morning, taking advantage of the strange freedom granted her by her mother, a kind, appealing woman with bright red hair who never stopped smoking and always wore rouge. She had long ago separated from her husband, who now had a second family. Katya also stopped to visit Mitya in his student's rooms on Molchanovka, and these meetings almost always passed in the deep, narcotic haze of their kisses. But Mitya had a gnawing sense that something terrible had been set in motion, that some change had taken place—and now was taking hold of Katya.

It had passed quickly—that easy, carefree time when they'd just met, when they'd barely grown acquainted, and suddenly both felt that nothing could be better than to sit alone and talk (sometimes from morning until night), and Mitya found himself inside that made-up world of love that he'd been waiting for since his childhood and adolescence. It was December—frost and clear skies, each day decorating Moscow with heavy rime and the dim, red disk of the low sun. January and February seemed to spin Mitya's love in a whirlwind of happiness and small joys that had either come to life already or now, right now, would burst into the world. But even then, something had begun to cloud that happiness, to poison it—and this would be the case more and more often. Even then it often seemed as if two Katyas existed: one for whom he'd felt a stubborn and insistent need from the first minutes of their acquaintance, and another who was real, pedestrian, and painfully impossible to reconcile with the first. And still, what Mitya went through then was nothing like his current state.

It could all be explained. Spring had begun with all its feminine concerns, its purchases and orders, its endless alterations.

Katya often had to go with her mother to the tailor's, and soon her exams would begin at the private drama school where she studied. Her preoccupied, distracted state of mind was therefore only natural. Mitya tried repeatedly to comfort himself with these thoughts, but they were little help; the utterances of his suspicious heart—its refutations of those equitable thoughts—were far more powerful than reason, and everywhere his doubts were confirmed with growing patency. Katya's inner disregard for him grew steadily, and with it rose his jealousy, his grim suspicions. The director of her school filled Katya's head with praise, and she couldn't keep from sharing this with Mitya. The director had told her, "You, my darling"—he called all his pupils "darling"—"are the pride of my school," and then, in addition to his regular classes, he began to work with her individually during the spring fast so that she could pass her final exams with particular distinction and add to his renown. It was a well-known fact that he debauched his students, taking one of them every summer to Finland, the Caucasus, or abroad. And now it entered Mitya's head that the director had his sights on Katya. Of course she was not to blame for this, but Katya likely felt and understood the director's intentions and thus already shared a secret, foul relationship with him. This idea tortured Mitya more and more as the apathy that Katya felt for him became too obvious to deny.

In general something seemed to be distracting her from Mitya. He couldn't think calmly about the director. But he was not the only problem! Something larger—some new set of interests now seemed to dominate her love. What was it? Who was it? Mitya didn't know, and thus he was jealous of everyone and everything, fearing above all else some secret life that he imagined she'd begun to lead without him, and which, he was convinced, she kept from him deliberately. It seemed that she was being pulled inexorably away from him—drawn, perhaps, to something he found too terrible to contemplate.

Once, when her mother was present, Katya said to him half jokingly, "You, in general, Mitya, think of women in keeping with the *Domostroy*. You'll become an absolute Othello! I wouldn't want to fall in love and marry you!"

"I can't imagine love without jealousy," her mother countered. "He who feels no jealousy, I think, also feels no love."

"No, mama," said Katya, with her habit of repeating other people's words. "Jealousy is disrespect for the person whom you love. . . . You could say, 'If I'm not trusted, then I'm not loved,'" she added, deliberately not looking toward Mitya.

"I'd say just the opposite," her mother responded. "In my opinion, jealousy is love. I even read about it somewhere—an article that proved this point very well. It even used examples from the Bible, showing God himself is jealous, vengeful. . . ."

As for Mitya's love, it now expressed itself almost entirely in jealousy alone. And Mitya believed it wasn't ordinary jealousy but some particular strain. Although he and Katya had not yet breached the final bounds of intimacy, they allowed themselves too much during those hours spent alone, and Katya at times grew even more passionate than she'd been before. And now this stirred suspicions, roused in him a horror. All the feelings that comprised his jealousy were terrible, but one among them was most terrible of all—and Mitya couldn't sort it from the rest, couldn't see it clearly, couldn't understand. It was rooted in those passionate displays: when he and Katya shared them, they were pure and sweet, blissful, almost divine. But when Mitya thought of Katya and another man, those same displays seemed foul beyond all words, seemed to violate the laws of nature. At those moments Katya aroused in him a sharp hatred. Everything he allowed himself with her was steeped in virtue and celestial pleasure, but the moment he imagined another man in his place, everything changed, became utterly indecent, and stirred in him a violent urge to strangle Katya—strangle *her* and not his phantom rival.

III

Katya's exams were finally conducted during the sixth week of the fast. And that day seemed to validate all of Mitya's suffering, all his agonizing doubts.

She didn't see him, didn't notice him in the least that day. She was completely alien to him, completely public.

She enjoyed great success. She was dressed all in white like a bride, and her nervousness made her charming. She received warm, affectionate applause, and the director, a self-satisfied actor with sad and shameless eyes, made only occasional comments in order to inflate his own pride. He spoke quietly from his seat in the front row, but in such a way that the unbearable sound of his every word was audible throughout the hall.

"Less reading," he told her, his voice calm and grave—and so authoritative that Katya seemed to be his personal possession. "Don't act, experience. Feel," he said distinctly.

It was unendurable. That performance which elicited such warm applause was simply unendurable. Katya flushed hotly, her small voice broke, her breathing faltered—and all of this was touching and charming. But she read in a meretricious, singsong voice, the false and stupid notes of which were taken for high art in that milieu that Mitya so despised and that Katya already occupied in all her thoughts. She didn't speak. She declaimed. With a kind of languid passion, she delivered every line like some objectless entreaty, a belabored, ardent plea on behalf of nothing. Mitya didn't know how to hide his eyes in his embarrassment for her. Worst of all was the mix of angelic purity and prurience that seemed so evident in her, in her small, flushed face; in her white shoes and white dress, which seemed shorter now, as everyone was looking up at her on the stage; in the white silk stockings stretched taut across her calves. "A girl sang in the church choir. . . ." With excessive and contrived naiveté Katya was reading about some other girl, supposedly as innocent as an angel. And listening, Mitya felt that keen sense of closeness that always comes when you see a loved one in a crowd. He felt bitter enmity. He felt proud of Katya when the thought passed through his mind that she was his, despite all else—and then he felt a tearing in his chest: "No, she isn't mine . . . no more. . . ."

There were good days again after the exam. But Mitya didn't trust them as he had before. "You're so silly," Katya said to him, remembering her performance. "Couldn't you feel it? Couldn't you tell that it was for you—just for you—that I read so well?"

But he couldn't forget what he'd felt during the exam, and he couldn't admit that those emotions hadn't left him. Katya seemed to sense his secret feelings and once shouted in the midst of an argument: "I don't understand why you love me if you find everything about me so repulsive! What do you want from me? What, really— what is it that you want?"

He himself didn't know why he loved her, but he felt that, rather than subsiding, his love was growing stronger with the incessant, jealous struggle he now fought against someone, something because of her, and this taxing love, which gathered greater strength each day, grew more and more severe in its demands.

"You love my body—only my body, and not my soul," Katya once told him bitterly. And again these were someone else's words, some bit of theatre. But trite and shallow as they were, they touched on something painfully insoluble. He didn't know what he loved her for. He couldn't say exactly what it was he wanted. . . . What in general does it mean to love? Answering such a question was made all the more impossible by the fact that Mitya hadn't come across a single word in everything he'd read and heard about love that could come close to offering a definition of the subject. Everything in books and life seemed bent on speaking only of an utterly discarnate love or something known as sensuality and passion. His love resembled neither. What was it that he felt for her? That abstract love, or passion? Was it Katya's body or her soul that almost made him faint, that stirred in him the bliss one feels before death as he undid the buttons on her blouse and kissed her breasts, that immaculate, exquisite flesh laid bare with a submissiveness that stunned his soul—laid bare with all the shamelessness of utter innocence?

IV

More and more she changed.

Her success on her exam explained a great deal. But there were other reasons too.

The arrival of spring seemed to transform Katya into a young woman of high society: an elegant girl in a constant hurry. Soon Mitya felt ashamed of his hallway whenever she arrived—she always came by coach instead of walking now—and hurried down its dark length with her silks rustling, her veil covering her face. She was invariably tender with him but also invariably late, and ever prone to cutting short their time together with the excuse that she had to see the tailor with her mother yet again.

"We're possessed when it comes to clothes!" she told him, her shining eyes round with happiness and surprise. She knew full well that Mitya didn't believe her, but there was nothing else to say, nothing more to talk about. She rarely removed her hat anymore, rarely let go of her umbrella as she sat on the edge of Mitya's bed and drove him almost mad with glimpses of her calves in tight silk stockings. And then, before she rode away again, before she told him once more that she would not be home that evening—she had to see someone with mother!—she always acted out the same small scene, obviously designed both to make a fool of him and to offer compensation for his "silly worrying," as Katya called it: glancing at the door with affected secrecy, she slipped down from the bed and brushed her hip against his leg, said to him in a hurried whisper, "Quickly—kiss me!"

V

Near the end of April Mitya finally decided to give himself a rest and leave Moscow for the countryside.

He'd tormented Katya and himself to the point of exhaustion. Its apparent lack of any cause or reason made their suffering all the more unbearable: what in fact had happened? What was Katya guilty of?

"Go, yes—go to the country! I don't have the strength for this anymore!" she told him once, with the finality that follows despair. "We need to be apart for a little while. We need some time to make sense of this relationship. . . . You've gotten so thin my mother actually believes you have consumption! I can't do this anymore!"

And so Mitya's departure was decided. But to his great amazement Mitya found himself almost happy as he prepared to leave, despite his overwhelming grief. Everything they'd had in better days came back the very moment they agreed on his departure. He still struggled to resist the dreadful thoughts that plagued him day and night, and the slightest change in Katya was sufficient to convince him that everything had changed for the worse between them once again. But her passion and her tenderness seemed to grow more genuine, seemed to lose all traces of affectation—he felt this with the flawless sensory perception that a jealous nature seems to spawn. Again he stayed in her room until two in the morning; again they had things to talk about. And the closer his departure drew, the more senseless their impending separation seemed, the more pointless any attempt to "clarify" their relationship. Once, Katya wept— she'd never cried before—and those tears seemed to make her part of Mitya's flesh and blood; seeing them, he was pierced with tenderness for her and vaguely troubled by a sense of blame.

Katya's mother was leaving in June to spend her summer in the Crimea; Katya was to join her in Miskhor. They decided that Mitya would join them there as well.

And Mitya continued to prepare for his departure. He walked around Moscow in that strange delirium that comes when a man continues cheerfully with all his ordinary duties while knowing that he's gravely ill. He was ill, drunk with grief and sorrow, yet at the same time he was filled with a sickly happiness, elated by Katya's renewed intimacy and her concern for him (she'd even gone with him to buy packing belts for his trip, as if she were his bride or wife), deeply moved in general by the return of almost everything he'd experienced when they first fell in love. And everything he encountered was charged with these emotions: houses and streets, the people walking past, the people riding in their coaches, the typically cloudy spring weather, the smell of dust and rain, the churchlike scent of poplars opening their buds behind the fences in the alleys: everything spoke of the bitterness of separation and the sweetness of his hopes for summer, their meeting in the Crimea, where nothing would hinder them, where everything would finally be realized (though he still didn't know what, exactly, "everything" entailed).

On the day of his departure, Protasov came to say goodbye. Among university students and older boys in grammar school, it's not unusual to find a few who've perfected a demeanor of endless, genial derision and subsequently act as if they're older and more experienced than anyone on earth. Such was Protasov, one of Mitya's closest friends and his only confidant: despite Mitya's general reticence, Protasov had learned all the secrets of his love for Katya. Watching Mitya strap his suitcase shut, he noticed that his hands were trembling, and he smiled with melancholy wisdom.

"You're just children, God help you," he said. "And yet, it's time for you to understand, my dear Werther from Tambov, that Katya is, above all else, an embodiment of the feminine—she's a feminine essence, and even the chief of police is powerless to change this fact. You are a male essence, and so you climb the walls, present to Katya all the high demands of instinct—all those stipulations that she propagate the species. Of course, all of this is in keeping with the law—to some degree it's even sacred. The body is superior to the intellect, as Herr Nietzsche rightly pointed out. But it's also in keeping with the law for some to break their necks when they set out along this sacred course. After all, there are certain individuals in the animal world who must pay for their first and final reproductive act with their very existence. But that requirement is probably not mandatory for you, so you ought to be careful. Use your eyes. Look both ways. Try not to hurry. 'Junker Schmidt, it's true—summer does return.' The world's not held together by a single thread, and it doesn't ride only on Katya's shoulders. . . . But I can see from your efforts to strangle that suitcase that you don't entirely agree—and those shoulders for you are all too dear. Well, forgive me for dispensing advice that you never asked to hear. May St. Nicholas and all his cohorts keep you safe!"

After Protasov pressed Mitya's hand and left, a student of singing who lived across from him—and practiced from morning until night—began to test his voice. Mitya had his window open to the courtyard, and as he bundled up his blankets and his pillows, the words to "The Asra" boomed into his room.

Then Mitya began to hurry with the packing belts. He fastened them haphazardly, grabbed his hat, and left for Kislovka to say goodbye to Katya's mother. The words and music of the student's song played so insistently inside his head that he walked without seeing the streets or passersby, feeling even more intoxicated than he had the weeks before. As a matter of fact, it did seem that the world rode only on those shoulders. And Junker Schmidt was quite prepared to shoot himself! Well, what can you do? If it rides on those shoulders, it rides on those shoulders, he thought to himself, and went back to the song again: how the sultan's daughter who is "radiant with beauty" wanders in the garden and meets a dark-skinned slave who stands "as pale as death" beside a fountain; how she asks him who he is and where he's from, and when he answers her, his voice is menacing but restrained, filled with sad simplicity: "My name is

Magomet"; how his voice then builds toward a kind of howl, an ex-
ultant, tragic wail: "I'm descended from the wretched race of Asra:
If we love, we die."

Katya was getting dressed in order to see him off at the station.
She called out tenderly to him from her room—that room in which
he'd spent so many unforgettable hours!—promising to find him on
the platform before the first bell. Sitting alone and smoking, the
kind sweet woman with bright red hair looked at Mitya very sadly:
she'd probably understood everything long ago, had probably
guessed it all. Flushed and trembling inside, he kissed the soft, slack
flesh of her hand and bowed his head before her like a son. With
maternal tenderness she kissed Mitya on the temple several times,
then made the sign of the cross above him.

"Oh darling, live and laugh," she said, quoting Griboyedov
with a timid smile. "Well, Christ be with you. . . . Go now, go on. . . ."

VI

Mitya finished the last few chores at his lodgings and with the help
of the house attendant loaded his possessions onto the crooked bed
of the cart he'd ordered, then awkwardly climbed in among his
things and started his ride down the street. The moment the cart
began to move, he was struck by that sensation that so often comes
with a departure: *forever, a chapter of your life has ended.* And together with this realization came an unexpected lightness, a hope
for the beginning of something new. He grew calmer as he rode,
began to watch the passing streets more cheerfully: at times it almost seemed he'd never looked at them before. It was over.
Farewell to Moscow! Farewell to everything that happened here! A
fine rain fell from the overcast sky, and all the alleys were deserted;
the dark cobblestones shone like iron; a sadness hung around the
dirty houses. The cabbie drove at a painfully slow pace and repeatedly forced Mitya to turn his face away and struggle not to breathe.

They passed the Kremlin and Pokrovka Street, then started down the alleys once again, where a crow shouted hoarsely at the evening and the rain—and still it was spring, the scent of spring was in the air. Finally they arrived, and Mitya ran behind the porter through the crowded station, down the platform to track three, where the long, heavy train stood ready to depart for Kursk. And in the great, chaotic mass of people assaulting that train, among the countless porters shouting at the crowd to let them through as they wheeled their roaring carts of luggage to the platform's edge, instantly he picked her out—a being who was "radiant with beauty"—solitary, somehow, in the distance, as if something held her separate not just from the crowd but from all the world. The first bell had already rung—this time it was he instead of Katya who was late: she'd touchingly arrived before him at the station, waited there, and now rushed forward, again as caring and attentive as a wife or bride.

"Darling, hurry—find a place. The second bell's about to ring."

And after the second bell she even more touchingly stood on the platform, looking up at him as he stood in the doorway of a third-class car that was already jammed with people and beginning to stink. Everything about her was enchanting: her small, endearing face; her delicate figure; her freshness and her youth in which the childlike mingled with the feminine; her raised and shining eyes; her modest blue hat and the alluring, elegant curve of its brim; even her dark grey suit, the cloth and silk lining of which Mitya could almost feel as he looked at her admiringly. Skinny and un-gainly, he stood there in an old coat with worn-out, tarnished but-tons and a pair of heavy, clumsy boots he'd put on specially for the trip—and still Katya was looking at him with genuine love and sor-row. The third bell rang so unexpectedly and struck so hard at Mitya's heart that he leapt onto the platform like a madman. Terri-fied, Katya rushed toward him as if she too were mad. Mitya pressed his face to her gloved hand, jumped back onto the train, and began to wave his hat ecstatically, watching through his tears as Katya

clutched her skirt in one hand and began to fall away with the platform, never lowering her eyes from him. Katya fell farther and farther back, the wind blew with growing force through Mitya's hair as
he held his head out the window, and the engine gathered speed:
relentless, ever more impervious, it demanded open track with a
disdainful, menacing roar—and together with the platform, she was
torn away.

VII

Dark with rain clouds, the slow dusk had fallen long ago; the conductor was passing through the corridor, collecting tickets, placing
lit candles in their holders as the heavy car rumbled through cool,
bare fields where spring had begun later than it did in Moscow—
and still Mitya stood before the rattling window, the scent of Katya's
glove still perceptible on his lips, the last moment of their separation still burning like a sharp flame. The long Moscow winter that
had changed his life now stood before him with all its joys and ago-
nies in a new light. And Katya—she too stood in a stark new light.
Who is she?. . . Yes—what is she?. . . And love and passion, the
body, the soul—what is it all? None of it exists. None of it is. There
is something else. Something absolutely other. Here: the scent of
her glove—is this not love, not Katya? Not body, not soul? And the
mouzhiki on the train, the woman who now leads her ghastly child
to the lavatory, the dim candles in their trembling stands, the twilight in these empty spring fields—all of it is love, is soul, torture,
inexpressible joy.

Morning found him in Oryol. He changed to a local train on
the far platform. And Mitya felt how simple this world was, how
calm, how much more a part of him than Moscow, which now had
drifted into some imaginary, distant kingdom with Katya at its center—Katya who seemed sad and lonely now, the object of mere tenderness. Even the sky, streaked here and there with pale blue clouds

that promised rain, even the wind was calmer, simpler. . . . The train moved unhurriedly from Oryol, and Mitya slowly ate a Tulsky Pryanik while sitting in the almost empty car. Then the engine gathered speed and the car began to rock, lulling him to sleep.

He woke up only in Verkhovye. The train had stopped. The station was crowded and quite busy, but it felt remote. A pleasant smell of cooking smoke and charcoal rose from the kitchen. He ate a bowl of cabbage soup, drank a bottle of beer with pleasure. And then he dozed again: a heavy tiredness had taken hold of him. When he stirred, the train was already racing through a familiar forest of spring birches that stood before the final stop. Again there was a spring cloudiness to the dusk; the air that streamed through the open window seemed to smell of mushrooms and rain. Although they were still completely bare, the trees reverberated with the roaring of the train more distinctly than the fields, and the small, sad lights of the station blinking in the distance once more revealed the change of season. There it is—the signal light burning green! It is lovely in this kind of dusk, this twilight from the bare birches. . . . With a knock the train began to switch its track. . . . My God, how forlorn he looks on the platform, the worker waiting for the owner's son—for me, the *barchuk*—to arrive. . . . Poor. . . . Endearing and forlorn in that way only country people have.

The dusk and rain clouds thickened as they drove from the station through the big village, already grimy with spring. Everything sank into the remarkably soft twilight and that profound silence that comes when a warm night blends with the vague darkness of rain clouds hanging low in the sky. And again Mitya was seized by joy and wonder: how calm and simple it was, this wretched countryside, these small, chimneyless huts with their heavy scents, everyone gone to sleep long ago—good people who leave their lamps unlit after the Annunciation. . . . How good it is—the warm, dark world of the steppe! Their *tarantass* plunged up and down the muddy hummocks of the road. Beyond the courtyard of a rich *mouzhik* stood several massive oaks—completely bare, unwelcoming, rooks' nests blackening their branches. A strange man stood beside a hut and peered into the twilight: he looked like something from ancient history with his bare feet, his tattered, heavy coat, his long, straight hair beneath a sheepskin hat. . . . And then a warm, sweet-smelling rain began to fall. . . . Mitya thought of the girls, all the young women sleeping in those huts, thought about everything feminine to which he'd drawn so close with Katya in the winter—and all of it merged into one: Katya, the girls in the huts, the night, the spring, the smell of rain and turned earth ready for the planting, the smell of the horse's sweat, the scent of her kid glove.

VIII

Life in the country began with sweet and peaceful days.

During the night when he rode from the station, Katya seemed to dissipate, seemed to fade and dissolve into everything around him. But this sensation wouldn't last. It would seem this way for only a few days while Mitya caught up on his sleep and rested from his journey, grew accustomed to the stream of childhood impressions that now returned to him as if completely new—impressions of the house where he was born, the village, the countryside in spring, the bare and empty earth prepared to bloom again, ageless and pristine.

The estate was modest and the manor house was old, lacking ostentation, and as its maintenance required only a small staff, a quiet life began for Mitya. His sister Anya, a second-year high school student, and his brother Kostya, a teenage cadet, were both still studying in Oryol and would not come home before early June. His mother, Olga Petrovna, was always busy running the estate, assisted by a single steward. She was often in the fields all day and went to bed as soon as it was dark.

Having slept for twelve hours after his arrival, Mitya came scrubbed and spotlessly clean from his sunny room—it had windows on the garden and faced to the east—and roamed through all the other rooms of the house, feeling an acute calm within them, a kindred, peaceful simplicity that put his mind and body at ease. All the rooms had been cleaned, all the floors washed before his arrival, and now everything stood in its customary place, everything smelled as familiar and pleasant as it had so many years ago. Only the dining hall, which joined the foyer, remained to be washed. A girl covered in freckles—a day worker from the village—was standing on the windowsill near the balcony door, stretching to reach the upper squares of glass which she wiped clean with a whistling sound, her dark blue, seemingly distant reflection hanging in the lower panes. The maid Parasha pulled a large, steaming rag from a bucket and walked barefoot through the water that had been poured across the floor, her delicate heels and white calves exposed.

"Go and have tea," she said, running her rapid words together with friendly familiarity. "Your *mamasha* left before sunrise for the station with the steward. You didn't hear a thing, I'll bet."

At that moment Katya asserted herself powerfully in his memory. For a moment Mitya had found himself looking with desire at the girl on the windowsill, the freckled skin of her outstretched arm, the curve of her figure as she extended herself upward, her skirt and her full, sturdy legs—and suddenly with joy he felt Katya's power, her ownership of him, her secret presence in all the morning's impressions.

And that presence became more and more perceptible with each new day, grew ever more enchanting as Mitya returned to himself, settled down, forgot that ordinary Katya who had failed so often and so painfully in Moscow to correspond with the Katya created by his desires.

IX

For the first time he was living at home as an adult—an adult with whom even his mother acted differently than before. But most important, he lived now with a real love inside his soul. And it was giving life to everything he'd waited for, everything his core had sought since childhood, since adolescence.

Even during infancy something had stirred—secretly, transcendently—inside him, something inexpressible in words. . . . Somewhere . . . At some moment . . . It must have been in spring as well. . . . He was still a very small child, standing in a garden somewhere, near a lilac bush—he recalled the sharp scent of blister beetles. . . . A young woman was nearby. His nanny, probably. . . . Suddenly something before him seemed to fill with a celestial light—the woman's face, perhaps, or the *sarafan* covering her heavy breasts. And a surge of heat passed through him, seemed to stir inside him like an infant in its mother's womb. . . . But all of it was like a dream. . . . And everything that followed—his years of childhood, adolescence, school—this too was like a dream. There were moments of intense delight—each distinct and unrepeatable and utterly unique—brought on by some young girl or other who would come to visit on some children's holiday with her mother—a secret, all-consuming curiosity he felt for these small, intriguing creatures who resembled nothing else with their dresses, their small, delicate shoes, and the silk ribbons in their hair. He developed a much more conscious fascination with a girl from grammar school, later, in the major town of the province. It lasted almost the entire fall. She would periodically appear in the evenings in a tree beyond the fence of the neighboring yard: her exuberance, her taunting, the round comb she wore in her hair, her brown dress, and her dirty hands, her laughter, her pleasant shouts—all of this made Mitya think of her from morning until night, and suffer bouts of sadness, even weep from his relentless longing for something from her. Then it somehow finished on its own, faded from his memory—and there were new, secret fascinations that transported him—some brief, some more sustained. There was the knife-edged joy, the grief of falling suddenly in love at high school dances. And there was a languor to his body, a dim presentiment—a vague expectation in his heart.

He was born and grew up in the countryside, but during secondary school he was forced to spend the spring in town, with the exception of one year—the year before last—when he fell ill while home for *Maslenitsa* and had to stay there for all of March and half of April. It was unforgettable. For some two weeks he lay in bed and did nothing but look out the window, study the snow, the garden's trunks and branches as they changed each day with the earth's growing warmth and the sky's increasing light. He saw: now it's morning and the room's so bright, so warm from the sunlight that already flies have stirred, begun to crawl along the window panes. . . . One day later, in the hour after lunch: the sun's behind the far side of the house, its light is falling through the western windows. And here the spring snow's so pale it's almost blue. Big clouds are hanging in the treetops, drifting in the clear, deep sky. And after one more day: bright clearings have emerged in the cloudy sky. A glistening sheen on all the bark. A constant dripping from the roof above the window. One cannot see enough. One cannot feel enough joy. . . . And then began warm mists and rain. The snow was eaten away in a few days. Dissolved. The ice on the river broke. In the garden and the yard the earth began to bare itself, to show its joyous black. . . .

For a long time Mitya remembered a day at the end of March when for the first time he went for a ride in the fields. The sky wasn't bright, but it gleamed with freshness and vigor in the pale, flowerless trees in the garden. A cold wind blew across the fields; the stubble of the cut plots was rough and overgrown, a reddish brown like rust. They were planting oats, and as they plowed, a primeval force seemed to rise in the rich, clumped soil, the almost fatty blackness of the fields. He'd ridden right across those plots of stubble and turned earth toward the forest, which he could see far off in the clear air—small, bare, its entire length visible from start to finish. When he reached it, he rode down into the forest hollow, and his horse's hooves rustled loudly through the deep beds of last year's leaves, wet and brown in places, dry and pale as straw in others. He crossed ravines where leaves were scattered lightly over the rocks, and the snowmelt was still running in streams. And suddenly a woodcock rose with a sharp crack from the underbrush, its cloudy, dark gold body bursting into flight beneath the horse's legs. . . .

And what had it been for him, that spring—that day in particular when a fresh wind blew in his face and his horse breathed heavily, its nostrils flared as it strode hard through the boggy fields of cut stubble and black plowing, snorted from its depths, bellowed with the majesty and power of some wild, untrammeled force? It seemed then that the spring itself was his first real love—that spring and all its days of artless love for every girl in school, for every girl on earth. But how distant those days seemed to him now! What a boy he was then—so innocent and simplehearted, so limited in his joys, his hopes and sorrows! That aimless and incorporeal love now seemed to be a dream—or, more accurately, the memory of some lovely dream. Now there was Katya. Now there was a soul that embraced the world—reigned over it, and everyone.

X

Only once in those early days did Katya make him think of her through something sinister.

Late one evening Mitya went onto the back porch. It was dark and quiet, and the air smelled of damp earth from the fields; stars hung above the vague, black outlines of the garden, glistening like tears as the night clouds streamed across them. Something in the distance suddenly erupted into shouts, a wild and devilish shrieking followed by strange barks and squeals. Mitya flinched and froze, then carefully descended from the porch into the dark avenue of trees, which seemed to hold themselves inimically, as if on guard against him. There he stopped again and waited, listening. Where was it? What was it? What would fill the garden with those awful shrieks so suddenly at night? A *sych.* A screech owl with a mate— nothing more, he thought, going completely still, as if he could feel the devil's invisible presence in the darkness. And again it wailed from somewhere near him; Mitya's soul convulsed as the voice sent up another howl, followed by a rustling and cracking in the trees. Soundlessly the devil moved to some other perch in the garden, where he began to bark, then whine and cry in a child's beseeching, plaintive voice. He beat his wings and screamed with tortured plea- sure, squealed, then broke into hysterical, mocking laughter like a lunatic being tickled violently. His entire body shaking, Mitya peered into the darkness, strained to hear the slightest movement. But the devil had suddenly stopped, choked off its jabbering. It split the garden's darkness with one final cry—a call containing all the lassitude of death—and vanished, as if swallowed by the earth. For several minutes Mitya waited in vain for that amatory horror to re- sume, then quietly returned to the house. And all night he was tor- mented by the same pernicious thoughts and poisonous emotions that had fouled his love in March in Moscow.

But his suffering quickly dissipated in the morning sun. He re- membered how Katya had wept when they decided firmly that Mitya should leave Moscow; he remembered how ecstatically she'd seized upon the idea that he too would come to the Crimea at the start of June; how touchingly she'd helped in his prepara- tions for the trip; how she'd seen him off at the station. . . . He took out her photograph and for a long time studied her elegant hair and delicate features, struck by her forthright, open expression and the clarity of her slightly rounded eyes. . . . He wrote her a particu- larly long, emotional letter expressing his faith in their love—and then, once more, he began to feel her radiant and loving presence, her unfaltering participation in everything that brought him life and pleasure.

He remembered what he went through when his father died eight years ago. That too was in the spring. Bewildered, horrified, Mitya had passed timidly through the hall where his father's body lay on a table the day after his death. He was elaborately dressed in a nobleman's full uniform, his large pale hands folded over his elevated chest. His nose was white; the blackness of his sparse beard seemed deeper than before. Mitya went onto the porch and glanced at the huge coffin lid wrapped in gold brocade that leaned near the door, and suddenly he felt it: death is in the world. It's in everything: the sunlight, the spring grass in the yard, the garden, the sky. . . . He went into the garden and down the avenue of lindens, where everything was mottled with bright sunlight and shade, then turned onto a side path where the sun was even stronger. He looked at the trees and the first white butterflies, listened to the first tender songs of the birds—and he recognized nothing: in everything there was death, that terrible table in the hall, that long lid wrapped in gold brocade, leaning on the porch. The sun shone differently now. The spring grass had changed. There was something else, something new in the way the butterflies settled and went still on the sunstruck tips of its blades. None of it was the same as it had been a day ago. It seemed that everything had been transformed by the close proximity of the world's end. Now the eternal youth of spring and all its charms seemed only pitiful and sad! This sensation lasted for a long time—lasted the entire spring, just as that terrifying, sweet smell seemed to linger in the house even after they had scrubbed the floors and aired the rooms repeatedly

Now a spell held Mitya in its thrall again. But it was of a different order. This spring, the spring of his first love, was unlike any other. Once more the world had been recast; again it was filled with some new and unfamiliar element. But it was not a horror. Just the opposite: inexplicably, delightfully, it seemed to coalesce with all the youth and joy of spring. And this new element was Katya—or, more accurately, it was something Mitya sought from her—that sweetness, that loveliness to which nothing in the world compares. Now the intensity of his demands grew proportionally with each spring day that passed, and in her absence Katya was replaced by an image — an image of a woman who did not exist but who was earnestly desired — and thus she didn't stain the purity, didn't break the charming spell of what Mitya sought from her, and with every passing day he felt her presence more acutely in everything he saw.

XI

He was joyfully convinced of this during his first week at home, when spring seemed just about to break open. He would sit with a book near an open window in the living room, looking past the trunks of pines and firs in the front garden to the muddy river in the meadow and the village on the hillside beyond it: as they do only in early spring, rooks still shouted ardently in the bare branches of the ancient birches on the bordering estate, exhausting themselves in a ceaseless, cheerful commotion that lasted from morning until night. There on its hill, the village still looked grey and lifeless, its only color confined to a yellowish green spreading through the willows. . . . He would walk in the garden: it too was stunted, bare, transparent. Only the glades were going green, specked with small turquoise flowers, and the acacias near the avenue were coming into leaf; in the hollow that formed the garden's southernmost edge, the cherry trees alone had released their pale, thin blooms. . . . He would walk out to the fields, where all the land was still empty, damp, and raw; where the stubble of the cut wheat still bristled in the barren tracts; where the dried-out mud of the uneven roads among the plots was still a deep red-blue. . . . And it was all a rich display of stark anticipation — youth laid bare, exposed. . . . And all of it was Katya. He only seemed to be distracted by the girls who came to work during the day on the estate and the laborers who lived in the servants' quarters, by his reading and his visits to the *mouzhiki* he knew in the village, by his conversations with his mother and his trips in the fields on a *drozhky* with the steward—a hulking, crass, retired soldier.

Then began another week. One night there was a pounding rain, and in the morning the sun turned hot, came into its own. The spring lost its pallor and reserve; everything in sight began to change—not by the day but by the hour. They began to plow, turning the dry stalks and stubble of last year's cuttings into black velvet; the borders of the fields began to green; the grass turned succulent in the yard; the sky took on a brighter, fuller blue. A soft fresh verdure spread across the garden like a cloak; the lilac went from grey to a rich, reddish blue and began to scent the air while large black flies massed on its lustrous, deep-green leaves and in the spots of hot sun that dappled the small roads, their bodies glinting with a metallic, dark blue sheen. The limbs of pear and apple trees were still visible beneath the slightly grey, unusually soft small leaves that they'd just begun to release, but their nets of crooked branches wound beneath the other trees with a milky whiteness, a dusting of snow that grew lighter, thicker, sweeter-smelling every day. During that remarkable time Mitya observed with joy and close attention all the changes taking place around him. But Katya was not lost among them—just the opposite: rather than receding, she took part in everything he witnessed, added herself and her own flourishing beauty to the spring blooms, to the luxuriant white of the garden, to the darkening blue of the sky.

XII

And so it was that one day, as the late afternoon sun sloped into the dining hall, Mitya came to tea and was surprised to see the morning mail, which he'd been waiting for in vain, lying near the samovar. He went quickly to the table—Katya should have answered at least one of his letters long ago—and a tasteful envelope, its address written in a familiar, touching script, flashed before his eyes with terrifying irrefutability. He snatched it up, bolted from the house and down the avenue, then entered the garden and walked into the hollow that descended from its far side. There he stopped, looked around, and quickly tore the envelope open. The letter was short, only a few lines altogether, but Mitya's heart was pounding so violently that he had to read it several times before he could understand. "My beloved, my one and only" he read over and again, and the earth began to swim beneath his feet with those fervid exclamations. He raised his eyes: the sky seemed to shine with triumph and joy, and beneath it the garden's white petals were as bright as snow. Already sensing the approaching chill of dusk, a nightingale chirped sharply and distinctly among the fresh green leaves of the distant bushes, its notes filled with that sweet selflessness that drifts so often in the songs of nightingales. The blood drained from Mitya's face; a shivering swept through his body.

He walked home slowly. His love was like a cup filled to the brim. And for several days he continued to carry that cup carefully within him, quietly, happily expecting a new letter.

XIII

The garden varied its attire.

The huge old maple that towered over its southern corner, visible from all directions, seemed to grow even larger and more imposing in its coat of thick fresh leaves.

The trees of the central avenue also seemed to rise and grow more striking. Mitya studied them constantly from his room. He could still see through the tops of the old lindens, but their new leaves were thick enough to form a bed of pale green lace above the garden in the distance.

A leafy covering spread beneath the maples and the lindens. It smelled sweet; it curled like ivy; it was white as cream.

And all of it—the huge luxuriant maple, the pale green bed above the garden, the bridal-white blooms of the fruit trees, the sun, the deep blue sky, all the riotous growth in the garden hollow, all the bushes and burgeoning shrubs along the small roads and secondary avenues, all the sprouting plants at the base of the southernmost wall of the manor house—the lilac and black currant, the burdock and acacia, the wormwood, the nettles—all of it was staggering in its vitality, its abundance, and its youth.

The green open space surrounding the house seemed to grow smaller as the blooms and new leaves pressed in from all sides; somehow this made the house too seem smaller, and more becoming. It seemed to be waiting for someone to arrive; for entire days all the windows and doors were left open in every room—in the white hall; in the old-fashioned parlor with its dark blue decor; in the small den where the walls were also dark blue and decorated with small pictures and lithographs in round frames; in the library, which formed one corner of the house—a large and sunny, often empty room with old icons in one corner and low bookshelves made of ash along the walls. Everywhere the encroaching trees glanced buoyantly before the windows with their pale or dark green leaves, the bright blue sky visible among their branches.

But there was no letter. Mitya knew that Katya had no faculty for writing, that she had trouble sitting down at a desk, finding a pen and paper and an envelope, buying a stamp. . . . But rational thought was little help once more. The happy certainty and unflagging pride with which he'd waited for several days for a second letter had vanished: now he was increasingly despondent and alarmed. It stood to reason that a letter like the first would soon be followed by something even more delightful and uplifting. But Katya had gone silent.

He went less often to the village and the fields. He sat in the library, leafing through journals that had dried and yellowed on the shelves for decades. They contained many fine works by old poets, their exquisite lines almost invariably consigned to the same subject—that subject which has driven almost every poem and song since the beginning of the world, that subject which now gave life to his soul, and which, no matter how a given work described it, he could always link, in some way or another, to Katya and himself. And so for hours on end he sat in an armchair near the open shelves and tortured himself, reading and rereading:

Find me, dearest, in the darkened garden
Now, while everyone's asleep
And only stars look down on us. . . .

It seemed that all of these affecting words, all of these appeals were his alone—and all of them were dedicated to just one listener, she whom Mitya found in everything, saw everywhere. Sometimes they seemed almost threatening:

The water's like a mirror
Until the swans unfold their wings,
Then the surface swells and trembles:
Come now to me! While stars still shine,
While leaves stir softly in this wind,
And storms assemble in the night.

Closing his eyes, growing cold, he repeated this plea, this entreaty from a heart unable to contain the force of its love, a heart driven by its need to triumph, to satiate its longing. Then he looked for a long time into space, listened to the deep silence of the countryside surrounding the house—and shook his head bitterly. No, she would not respond to any supplication. Somewhere far off in the distance she shone, somewhere in the foreign world of Moscow. And again tenderness welled up in his heart! Again that threatening call, that slightly sinister invocation, resounded in his mind:

Come now to me! While stars still shine,
While leaves stir softly in this wind,
And storms assemble in the night.

XIV

Having dozed after lunch, which they ate at noon, Mitya left the house and walked unhurriedly to the garden. Girls often worked there, digging around the apple trees—and they were there today. It had already become a habit of sorts for Mitya to sit and talk with them.

It was a hot, quiet afternoon. He walked in the transparent shade of the avenue, surrounded by tendrilous white branches that in the distance resembled snow. The pear tree blossoms were particularly thick and full, and their pallor mixed with the bright sky to tinge the shadows violet. Together with the blooming apple trees, they scattered white petals on the upturned earth around them while their sweet, tender scent mixed with the smell of manure warmed by the sun in the cattle yard. Occasionally a small cloud drifted overhead, the sky turned a lighter blue, and those smells of growth and decay turned even sweeter and more delicate. All of the warm, fragrant air was filled with a contented, soporific buzzing as bees and bumblebees buried themselves in those curling leaves of snow laced with the scent of honey. The intermittent songs of nightingales drifted in the distance and nearby, their notes filled with the afternoon's blissful tedium.

The alley ended at the gate to the threshing barn; in the distance to the left, a black grove of fir trees rose from one corner of the garden. There two girls in bright clothes stood out sharply among the apple trees. Mitya turned when he was only halfway down the avenue, as he usually did, and began to make his way toward them through the trees. The low splayed limbs brushed against his face as gently as a girl's hand when he pushed past them, inhaling their scents of honey and lemon. One of the girls, a thin redhead named Sonka, began to laugh wildly and shout the moment she saw him.

"Oh, the owner's coming!" she yelled with mock alarm, jumping up from the bough of the pear tree on which she'd been resting, and hurrying toward her shovel.

[31]

The other girl, Glashka, acted as if she hadn't noticed Mitya in the least. Wearing short, black felt boots—the tops of which were filled with white petals—she planted one foot firmly on the iron blade of her shovel, calmly drove it down, and turned the fresh-cut turf. As she worked, she broke into a loud song, her voice strong and pleasant: "Ah my garden, my darling garden, whom are your blossoms for?" She was a strong, somewhat masculine, and always serious girl.

Mitya took Sonka's place on the thick pear bough that rested in the fork of another tree. Sonka looked at him conspicuously.

"Ah, just got out of bed? Be careful not to oversleep. You might miss something!" she said loudly, trying to sound casual and blithe.

Sonka liked Mitya. She tried hard to hide this but never knew how, and wound up holding herself awkwardly or saying the first thing that came into her head whenever he was near her. She often hinted at her vague but persistent suspicion that Mitya's constant lassitude had no innocent cause: she believed he was sleeping with Parasha—or at the very least aimed to do so. Jealous, at times she spoke tenderly and looked at him with a kind of languor, hinting at her feelings—while on other occasions her words and tone of voice turned sharp and cutting, and her stares expressed a cold hostility. All of this gave Mitya a strange kind of pleasure. There was no letter. There was no letter, and it seemed that he no longer lived, only passed from one day to the next in a state of constant expectation, feeling more and more oppressed by his desperate hope and his inability to speak with anyone about his secret love and his misery, about Katya and his hopes for the summer in the Crimea. It was pleasant therefore to hear Sonka hint at his involvement in a nonexistent love affair, for at least these conversations bore some connection to the hidden cause of his despondency. And her obvious affection excited him, in part because it meant that she now suffered some of the same emotions that tormented him and thus shared secretly in the afflictions of his heart. Indeed, he even felt, at times, a strange hope that he might find a confidante in Sonka, or even, somehow, a replacement for Katya.

Now, unknowingly, Sonka once again touched on Mitya's secret. "Don't oversleep! You might miss something!" He looked around. The solid, dark green grove of firs seemed almost black in the brilliant afternoon, and the sky that hung between the sharp tops of the trees was a rich, magnificent blue. Shot through with sun, the fresh leaves of the lindens, the maples, and the elms spread a cheerful, lambent canopy over the entire garden, flecked the grass and small paths with spots of shade and brilliant light. The hot, sweet-smelling blossoms turned even whiter beneath that canopy, flashing and gleaming like porcelain where the sun fell unencumbered through the leaves. Mitya smiled against his will.

"What could I sleep through?" he asked Sonka. "That's what's so regrettable—I have no affairs to oversleep!"

"Fine, fine—I'll take your word for it. Just don't cross yourself or take God's name to make me think it's true. I'll believe you as it is," Sonka shouted in a crude, happy voice, pleasing Mitya with her skepticism about his lack of love affairs. Then she began to shout again. A red calf with a few white curls on its head had wandered out from the firs and slowly approached her from behind to begin chewing on the flounce of her blue calico dress.

"A fainting fit for you!" she shouted, waving it away. "Go find a mother somewhere else!"

"Is it true—what I heard?" said Mitya, not knowing how to continue the conversation but not wanting it to end. "Are there plans for your wedding? They say his family's rich, and the groom himself is handsome. But you keep refusing him, won't listen to your father."

"Rich, but not too bright. Dusk starts early in his head," Sonka answered playfully, slightly flattered. "Besides, I might have someone else in mind."

[33]

Glashka, taciturn and unamused as ever, shook her head. "Words run out of you like water from the Don," she said softly without pausing in her work. "You bark out anything that comes into your head. But just wait until they hear your barking in the village—you'll be famous then!"

"Oh, stop clucking," Sonka shouted. "I've been weaned already."

"Who do you have in mind, then?" Mitya asked.

"You think I'd tell you?. . . All right—I'll go ahead and confess it all, just because you ask: I've fallen in love with your old shepherd! I see him and my thighs get hot—my legs burn right down to my heels. I'm just like you—I like a good ride on an old horse," she said provocatively, hinting at the twenty-two-year-old Parasha, who was widely considered an old maid in the village. As if her secret feelings for the *barchuk* entitled her to such bold behavior, Sonka suddenly tossed her shovel aside, sat down on the ground, and stretched out her legs, displaying a pair of mottled wool tights and coarse boots. Sitting with her legs slightly parted, she helplessly dropped her arms to her sides.

"Oh, I haven't gotten anything done—but I'm all worn out," she shouted, laughing. She began to sing in a piercing voice, "My leather boots are worn and broken," then broke off, laughing again. "Come and rest with me in the hunters' shed," she called out. "I'll do anything you like."

Her laughter enticed him. With a large, awkward smile, Mitya got up from the tree limb, lay down on the ground beside Sonka, and put his head in her lap. She pushed him away, but he rested his head against her thigh again, thinking of a poem that he had read again and again during the last few days:

Oh rose,
The potency of joy's made manifest
When you unfurl this tiny scroll
That has no end,

When you unfold the folded petals
Folded past all reckoning,
When you expose these whorls
Rich and redolent beyond all reason,
And they turn damp with dew. . . .

"Don't touch me," Sonka shouted with genuine fear, trying to lift his head and move it away. "I'll shout so loud the wolves come out of the woods! I don't have anything to give you now. That little fire's all burned out!"

Mitya closed his eyes and didn't speak. Broken up by the pear trees' leaves and branches, the sun fell in narrow shafts, warmed his face in little specks of prickling light. Sonka pulled at his coarse black hair with both tenderness and scorn. "Like a horse's hide," she shouted, and covered his eyes with his hat. The back of his head touched her legs—that most frightening thing in the world, a woman's legs!—then brushed against her stomach; he inhaled the scent of her cotton skirt and blouse—and all of this mixed with the blooming garden and with Katya, mingled with the near and distant chirping of the listless nightingales, the steady buzzing—the voluptuous and drowsy hum—of countless bees, the warm and honey-scented air. Even the sensation of earth behind his back created in him an acute and overwhelming desire, a painful longing for a strain of joy that lay beyond all ordinary human experience.

Suddenly something rustled in the grove of firs, chuckled as if gloating, then rang out: Ku-ku, ku-ku. . . . It was so close, its call was so distinct, so sharp and startling, that Mitya even heard the wheezing and trembling of its small, sharp tongue as the cuckoo began to wail. He was seized again by a longing for Katya, seized by an almost violent demand that she provide him with the superhuman joy he craved. And this longing took hold of him so violently that Mitya suddenly got up and strode off through the trees, to Sonka's absolute astonishment.

Together with a wrenching, furious demand for joy, that voice that sailed out of the fir grove and resounded with such terrifying clarity above his head—that voice that cleaved the spring calm to its core—also stirred in Mitya a stark and absolute conviction that nothing more would come from Moscow: not another letter. Something had happened there—or would at any moment. And he was lost. Destroyed.

XV

Entering the house, he paused for a moment before the mirror. "She's right," he thought. "They're Byzantine eyes. Or just the eyes of a lunatic. . . . Gloomy eyebrows. Like something drawn with charcoal on a sack of bones. Black hair. A horse's hide—isn't that what Sonka said?"

He heard the quick, light padding of bare feet and turned, embarrassed.

"You must be in love—looking at yourself so much," Parasha said, gently teasing him as she hurried past, carrying a heated samovar toward the balcony. "Your mother wants to see you," she added as she placed the samovar with a flourish on the table set for tea, then turned and looked at him intently.

"They've all caught on. They know everything," Mitya thought. "Where is she?" he forced himself to ask.

"In her room. . . ."

Slowly descending into the western sky, the sun sloped across the roof and flashed as if reflected by a mirror beneath the needled branches of the pines and firs shading the balcony. The shrubs and staff trees beneath them also gleamed with a summer glassiness. Covered with a limpid shade and patches of hot, bright light, the tablecloth seemed to shine while wasps hung over the basket of white bread, the cups, and the cut-glass dish of jam. All of it spoke to the joys of summer in the country, the countless possibilities for happiness and contentment. Hoping to convince her that no great weight was burdening his soul, Mitya decided to approach his mother before she came to him.

He left the hall and walked down a corridor that led to his room and his mother's as well as those in which Anya and Kostya lived during the summer. Dusk already filled the corridor, and a dark blue shade had gathered in Olga Petrovna's room, which was comfortably crowded with all the most antique furniture in the house: old wardrobes and chiffoniers, a large bed, and an icon stand, before which, as always, a lamp was burning, though his mother had never demonstrated any particular religiosity. Beyond the open windows a wide shadow lay across a neglected flower bed before the entrance to the main avenue; beyond it the green and white garden blazed cheerfully in the last full light of the sun. Paying no attention to this familiar view, Olga Petrovna sat in an armchair in the corner, wearing eyeglasses and crocheting rapidly. A tall, thin woman in her forties, she had dark hair and a serious, slightly dry disposition.

"You asked for me, mama?" Mitya said, standing in the doorway to her room.

"No, no—nothing important, really. I just wanted to see you. It seems I hardly ever do anymore, other than at lunch," answered Olga Petrovna without interrupting her work. Her manner seemed inordinately nonchalant.

Mitya remembered how Katya had said on March 9 that she for some reason feared his mother—remembered the delightful, secret hint she meant to deliver with those words.

"Well, perhaps there was something you wanted to tell me?" he muttered awkwardly.

"No, nothing really. Just that, lately you've seemed a little sad. A little at loose ends," said Olga Petrovna. "Maybe it would be good for you to take a little trip. Maybe visit the Meshcherskys, for example. There's a crowd of young ladies in that house," she added, smiling. "And they really are a very nice family."

"I'll be very glad to visit them one of these days," Mitya answered with difficulty. "But come and have some tea. It's lovely on the balcony. We'll talk more there," he said, knowing that his mother's sensitivity and tact would keep her from returning to this pointless conversation.

They sat on the balcony almost until sunset. After tea his mother continued crocheting as they talked about the neighbors, the farmland, Anya and Kostya. Again Anya had to retake an exam in August! Although he listened and responded periodically, Mitya felt intoxicated, delirious from some grave illness throughout the conversation, just as he had before departing Moscow.

In the evening he paced ceaselessly for some two hours, walking back and forth through the hall, the living room, the den, and the library, where he marched right up to the southern windows, which opened on the garden. Through the windows in the living room and the hall he saw the sunset's soft red glow between the branches of the firs and pines, heard the laughter and the voices of the laborers gathering to eat their dinner near the servants' quarters. Looking down the row of adjoining rooms, he could see the library windows and a pink, motionless star suspended in the evening sky, which was such a constant shade of blue it seemed to have no color at all. Against that backdrop, the landscape seemed particularly picturesque, with the massive green crown of the ancient maple and all the blossoms in the garden, so white they made one think of winter. And still he marched back and forth, no longer caring in the least how everyone would talk about him in the house. He clenched his teeth so hard his head began to ache.

XVI

From that day on he stopped observing all the changes brought on by the approaching summer. He saw them everywhere he looked, even felt them, but they had lost all independent meaning. He could enjoy them only as a source of torment: the lovelier they were, the more suffering they caused him. Katya occupied his mind to an absurd degree; she haunted him like a phantom: anywhere he looked, he saw her—she was in everything, behind everything. And as each new day confirmed even more terribly than its predecessor that Katya no longer existed for him—that she was already in someone else's power, that she was already giving herself and her love to someone else, despite the fact that both were meant exclusively for him—as each day proved these facts more cruelly than the last, everything in the world seemed to grow increasingly useless: all the earth's beauty, all its charm only made more savage its gratuity.

He hardly slept at night. And nothing could compare to the beauty of those hours when the moon was out and the silence of the milky garden seemed deliberate, as if every leaf and stalk were intent on keeping still. The nightingales could barely stir in their exquisite languor; they sang cautiously, deliberately—each trying to produce a note that had no equal in its delicate precision, its intricate and absolute sonority. Reticent and tender, the pallid moon hung low over the garden, invariably accompanied by a bluish strand of clouds that spread below it like a ripple on the surface of a lake, its charm beyond all words. Mitya slept without any curtains on his windows; the garden and the moon peered constantly into his room, and the moment he opened his eyes on that white disk, Mitya uttered in his thoughts the word "Katya," like a man possessed—uttered it with a degree of ecstasy and agony that he himself found frightening; why should the moon bring her to mind? What possible connection could there be? But it was something visible. How strange! He saw something in the moon that made him think of her. At other moments he saw nothing at all. Memories of Katya and everything they had shared in Moscow would sometimes seize him with such force that he trembled as if consumed with fever and begged God—alas, always to no avail—to let him see her, now, here in bed with him—if only in a dream. Once he'd gone with her to the Bolshoi Theatre to see Sobinov and Chaliapin sing in *Faust*. Everything sent him into raptures that night—the vast, bright hall that opened like a brilliant chasm below them, already crowded and warm and richly scented with perfume; the gold and red-velvet tiers of box seats that could barely hold their scores of stylish occupants; the soft, nacreous glow of the gigantic chandelier that hung above it all; and then, from far below them, as the conductor waved his arms, the overture rising, streaming up into the air—at times roaring and demonic, at others sad and tender beyond words: *"There was a King of Thule. . . ."* Afterward he walked her home to Kislovka through the night's heavy frost and bright moonlight, and then stayed especially late, her kisses more than ever like a drug. When he finally left, he took with him the silk ribbon that she used to tie her hair at night, and now, during these torturous nights, he couldn't think of that ribbon, which lay on his writing table, without shuddering.

During the day he slept, then rode on horseback to the village with a railway station, where there was a post office. The weather stayed fine. Rain fell, thunderstorms passed through, and again the hot sun beat down, continuing without a pause its rapid work in the gardens, woods, and fields. The garden bloomed, dispersed its petals, then continued to grow, turning a luxurious dark green as its leaves thickened. The forests seemed to be sinking beneath countless flowers and tall grasses; the calls of nightingales and cuckoos never stopped rising from their green, sonorous depths. Rich and varied shoots of wheat now covered the fields that once seemed so barren and exposed. For entire days he disappeared into those fields and forests.

It was too embarrassing to linger all morning on the balcony or in the courtyard, waiting in vain for the steward or a worker to come with the mail. And neither the steward nor the workers necessarily had time to travel eight *versts* for such trivialities. And so he started to make the trip himself. But he invariably came home with nothing but an issue of the local paper or a letter from Anya or Kostya.

His torments grew extreme. The beauty of the forests and the fields through which he rode weighed on him so heavily that Mitya felt a physical pain in his chest.

Once, just before evening, he was riding home through the empty estate next to his mother's. It stood in an old park that merged with a surrounding forest of birches. He was riding down the main avenue, known by the local *mouzhiki* as Table Road. Its broad surface lay between two rows of huge black firs that led all the way to the old house. The avenue was covered with a slick layer of pine needles the color of rust, and a magnificent gloom hung between the trees. The sun was setting to Mitya's left; its reddening light sloped peacefully between the trunks of the firs and flashed like gold among the thick covering of needles. Stirred only by the intermittent, solitary songs of nightingales rising from the far ends of the park, the silence that reigned over the land seemed so spellbound and transfixed, the smell of the firs and the jasmine bushes growing thickly around the house so sweet, and the happiness that others must have shared there, long ago on that estate, returned to Mitya now with such intensity that he felt his face go tight with a morbid pallor when Katya suddenly appeared before him, appeared in the image of his wife on the huge, decaying balcony among the jasmine, appeared with utter, terrifying clarity.

"One week," he said aloud, his voice carrying through the woods. "I'll wait one week. And if no letter comes, I'll put a bullet in my head."

XVII

He got up very late the next day. After lunch he sat on the balcony with a book on his lap, looking at the pages covered with print and stupidly asking himself, "Should I ride to the post office or not?"

It was hot. White butterflies drifted in pairs over the warm grass and the staff shrubs, which shimmered like glass in the sun.

"Ride to the post office or finally stop—finally break this ridiculous habit?"

The steward came over the hill on horseback, paused at the gate, and glanced at the balcony, then rode straight toward it.

"Good morning," he said, stopping his horse before Mitya. "Still reading?" He grinned and looked around, then lowered his voice. "Your mama still asleep?"

"I think so," Mitya answered. "Why?"

The steward was silent for a moment, then spoke in a serious tone. "Well, *barchuk*, what can I say? Books are good. Fine things, books. But everything has its time. Why live like a monk? No girls, no ladies for you?"

Mitya lowered his eyes to his book without responding. "Where were you?" he asked, not looking up.

"I was at the post office," said the steward. "And of course there wasn't a single letter. Just a newspaper."

"Why do you say 'of course'?"

"Because they're still writing you a letter—a long, long letter that's not quite done yet," the steward answered with crude derision, insulted by Mitya's refusal to maintain the conversation. "Take it please, here," he said, extending the newspaper to Mitya. Then he spurred his horse and rode off.

"I'll put a bullet in my head," Mitya told himself with conviction, looking at his book and seeing nothing.

XVIII

Mitya knew that nothing more insane than this could be imagined: to shatter your own skull; to stop the beating of a young, strong heart; to eradicate all thought and feeling; to extinguish every sight and sound; to vanish from a world that had only recently revealed itself to him in all its glory and now defied all human language with its beauty; to reject—instantly, inexorably—this life that contained

Katya and the approaching summer, sky and clouds, sun, warm wind, wheat in the fields, villages and towns, girls, mama, the estate, Anya, Kostya, poems in old journals, and somewhere in the future—Sevastopol, the Baidar Gates, those lilac-colored mountains with their forests of pine and beech in the blazing heat, the still and heavy air of the blinding white highway, the gardens of Alupka and Livadiya, scorching sand by the brilliant sea, children and bathers tan from the sun—and again Katya, in a white dress beneath a white umbrella, sitting on the pebbled beach, sitting right among the waves that blind you with their glare and make you smile reflexively from a happiness without cause. . . .

He understood all of this. But what was there to do? How else could he break free from this vicious cycle in which the better anything became, the more savage and unbearable he found it. It was this that he had no more strength to endure—this happiness with which the world crushed him, and which lacked some vital element at its core.

When he woke up in the morning, the first thing he saw was the cheerful light of the sun; the first thing he heard was the cheerful ringing of chapel bells in the village, a sound he'd known since childhood, rising there, beyond the garden with its dew and deep shade, its birds and flowers and flashes of sun; even the yellow wallpaper in his room—that wallpaper that had been fading since his childhood—even it was cheerful and close to his heart. But momentarily another thought cut into his soul with ecstasy and horror: Katya! The morning sun was shining with her youth; the freshness of the garden came from her; everything lighthearted and buoyant in the pealing of the bells played with her beauty, her image, and its elegance; the old wallpaper became a stark demand that she share in the rural life that was so much a part of Mitya, that life his father and his grandfathers had lived and died on this estate, inside this house. And so it was that Mitya—young and thin, long-legged, strong, still warm from sleep—threw off his covers and leapt to his feet in just a nightshirt with the collar unbuttoned, yanked open his desk drawer and pulled out his cherished photograph of her, then fell into a stupor, staring at her with greed and wonder. Everything that was alluring and graceful in a woman, all the mysteries, radiance, and charm that a girl could possess now appeared in her small, slightly serpentine head, in the arrangement of her hair, in her inviting yet completely innocent expression. But it was impenetrable, that look. It answered him with an enigmatic, cheerful silence that nothing could disturb—and where was he to find the strength to endure it now, that expression which was so close to him and yet so distant, that look which once revealed to him the ineffable happiness of life and which now, after deceiving him with such a terrifying lack of shame, might be forever alien?

That evening, when he rode back from the post office through Shakhovskoe—that old empty estate with an avenue of black firs—he let out an unexpected cry that almost perfectly expressed the exhausted state of mind to which he'd been reduced. Earlier, waiting at the post office window, watching from the saddle as the postmaster vainly dug through a pile of newspapers and letters, he'd heard a train approaching the platform behind him, and that sound, together with the engine's steam, made him think of Kursk Station and Moscow in general: he was stunned by the happiness those memories entailed. Later, as he rode through the village, he was startled to discover something of Katya in the swaying hips of every petite young woman who walked before him. In the fields he met three horses pulling a *tarantass*, and as it shot by, Mitya glimpsed two hats inside the carriage, one of which was worn by a young girl: this nearly made him scream out Katya's name. The white flowers blooming along the roads suddenly merged with her white gloves in his mind; the dark blue mullein took on the color of her veil. . . .

The sun was setting when he started down the avenue at Shakhovskoe; the sweet, dry smell of the firs and the luxuriant scent of jasmine produced such a sharp sensation of summer, so strongly brought to mind the antiquated life of that rich and wonderful estate, that when he glanced through the red and gold light of the evening sun that had filled the avenue, and looked toward the house that stood in the deepening shadows beyond those rows of black firs, Mitya suddenly found Katya there, saw her descending from the balcony toward the garden with all her female charm in force, her image as distinct as the jasmine and the house itself. He had long ago lost any recollection of how she actually appeared in life, and now she came to him almost every day in some new and more remarkable transfiguration. Her image that evening possessed such power, exuded such an air of utter triumph, that Mitya found it even more terrifying than that moment at midday when the cuckoo's song had begun to pulse above him.

XIX

He stopped riding to the post office, forced himself through a drastic, desperate act of self-will to end those daily trips. He stopped himself from writing too. After all, everything had been written: frenzied avowals of love that had no equals on this earth; degrading pleas for her affection—or at least her "friendship"; shameless hints that he was ill—that he was writing while he lay in bed—in the hopes this might elicit some small expression of pity, some slight attention; even threatening suggestions that it was time to make life simpler for Katya and his "more fortunate" rivals by ending his existence on earth. No longer writing, no longer seeking a response from her, he used his strength to eradicate all vestiges of expectation, to force himself to wait for nothing (while secretly hoping that a letter would arrive at that moment when he'd somehow reached a state of true indifference or had managed to deceive fate by pretending so convincingly that he no longer cared). He did everything he could to keep Katya from his mind, searched everywhere for some salvation from her terrifying presence. And to that end he started once again to read whatever he happened to pick up, began to go on errands with the steward to the neighboring villages, ceaselessly repeating to himself, "It's all the same—whatever happens, happens."

And so it was that they were returning one day from a nearby farm. The cart horse was cantering hard, as usual. They were sitting high on the upper bench—the steward, who held the horse's reins, was perched in front while Mitya sat behind him. Both men bounced violently in their seats from the blows of potholes in the road, particularly Mitya, who clutched the bench's padding as he rode, studying the back of the steward's red neck and the fields that jumped before his eyes. As they approached the house, the steward let go of the reins; the horse slowed to a walk, and he began to roll a cigarette.

"Well now, *barchuk*," he said, grinning down at his tobacco pouch. "You were angry with me a little while ago. But really, didn't I tell you the truth? A book's a fine thing. Why not read when you want a little rest? But your books won't go away without you. You have to know the proper time for things."

Mitya blushed and surprised himself by answering with contrived simplicity and an awkward smile: "There's nothing else to do, really. . . . And no one's caught my eye. . . ."

"What do you mean?" said the steward. "With so many girls? So many women?"

"Girls just like to play games," Mitya answered, trying to speak in the same tone as the steward. "You can't hope for anything from them."

"They'll do more than play games. You just don't know how to approach them," the steward said admonishingly. "And you can't be stingy. A dry spoon scrapes the mouth."

"I wouldn't be stingy at all if there were some real chance of something," Mitya suddenly answered shamelessly.

"If you can be a little generous, then everything will work out fine," the steward said, lighting a cigarette. He still sounded slightly offended. "You don't even have to give me a whole ruble. It's not a present from you that matters to me. I want to do something nice for you. Every time I look around, I see the *barchuk's* feeling gloomy. No, I think to myself, this can't be! We can't just leave this as it is! I always take my masters into account. This is already my second year living here with you—and I've never heard a bad word, thank God, not a single bad word from you or your mother. What do the others say, for example, about the owner's cattle? If they're fed, fine, if not, to hell with it. But not me. I'm not like that. The cattle's dearest of all for me. And I say to the boys: Do what you want with me, but the cattle must be fed!"

Mitya had begun to wonder if the steward was drunk, but he suddenly dropped the intimate, slightly injured tone he'd adopted and shot an inquisitive look over his shoulder. "What could be better than Alyonka?" he asked. "She's a saucy girl! Young. Husband's in the mines. . . . Only, you'll have to stick some kind of little present in her hand. . . . Spend, let's say, five rubles on the whole business. . . . One ruble on entertaining her and two in her hand. And something for a little tobacco for me. . . ."

"That won't hold things up," Mitya answered, again against his will. "Only, which Alyonka do you mean?"

"You know—the forestkeeper's Alyonka," said the steward. "Don't you know her? She's married to the forestkeeper's son. It seems to me you saw her in church last Sunday. . . . Right then I thought—she's just what our *barchuk* needs! Only married two years. Keeps herself clean. . . ."

"Well then," Mitya answered, smiling, "set it up."

"I'll do my best," said the steward, picking up the reins. "I'll sound her out the next few days. And in the meantime you should keep awake. Tomorrow she'll be working with the other girls on the garden wall—on the embankment. You come too. . . . That book of yours won't go anywhere at all. . . . Besides, you can always read your fill in Moscow. . . ."

He flicked the reins; the *drozhky* began to jump and shudder again. Mitya held firmly to the seat padding, and, trying to avoid the steward's fat, red neck, looked past the trees of his garden and the willows in the village, looked toward the valleys lying far beyond the houses nestled in the sloping river bed. Something absurd and wildly unexpected was already halfway to completion, and it now produced a chill in him, a cold languor that slowly spread through his body. Already the bell tower that he'd known since childhood seemed to have changed; already there was something different about the way it rose before him now, its cross glinting in the evening sun above the garden trees.

XX

Mitya was so thin that the girls on the estate called him "the Borzoi." He belonged to that breed of people who always seem to hold their large, black eyes wide open, and who can grow only a few curly hairs instead of a full beard or moustache, even as adults. Nevertheless Mitya shaved on the morning after his conversation with the steward and put on a yellow silk shirt, which cast a strange and pleasant light on his exhausted yet somehow animated face.

Sometime after ten he started walking slowly toward the garden, trying to look aimless and bored.

He came out onto the main porch. It faced north, where an overcast sky the color of slate hung above the roof of the carriage house, the cattle barn, and that part of the garden where the bell tower showed behind the trees. Everything was dull. The air was heavy and damp; it smelled from the chimney of the servants' quarters. Mitya went around the house and started down the avenue of lindens, looking at the sky and the tops of the trees. A hot, weak wind rose from the southeast, where a clotted mass of rain clouds hung above the garden. The birds were not singing; even the nightingales were silent. Countless bees sailed noiselessly across the garden, carrying their nectar home.

The girls were working near the grove of firs again, repairing a low embankment that ran along the garden's edge. They were closing up gaps the cattle had trodden into the wall, using dirt and fresh, pleasant-smelling manure that workers delivered periodically from the livestock barn, driving it across the avenue, which was now thickly strewn with the damp and shining droppings. There were six girls there. Sonka was not among them; despite all, her father had finally committed her to be married, and she was at home, preparing something for the wedding. The group consisted of three weak and feeble-looking girls, the chubby and appealing Anyutka, Glashka—who seemed to grow ever more severe and masculine—and Alyonka. Mitya picked her out immediately among the trees and understood exactly who she was, though he'd never seen her before. And some essential similarity between her and Katya—some likeness that perhaps he alone could see—struck him with such force that he was stunned, like the victim of a lightning bolt. He stopped in his tracks, went dumb, then walked decisively toward her, never lowering his eyes.

She too was small and full of life. Despite the grimy work she'd come to do, she was dressed in a good cotton blouse (white, with red polka dots), and a matching skirt, a black patent-leather belt, a pink silk headscarf, and red wool tights. Some feature of Katya seemed particularly pronounced in the black felt boots she wore (or, perhaps it was her small, delicate feet), for they combined something childlike with the feminine. Her head was small, and both the setting and the shine of her dark eyes were almost identical to Katya's. When Mitya arrived, she alone was not working. As if sensing her somewhat privileged position among the others, she stood on the broad embankment with one foot resting on her pitchfork and talked with the steward, who was reclining under an apple tree on his coat with its tattered lining, smoking and leaning back on one arm. As Mitya approached them, the steward deferentially moved onto the grass in order to make room for him on the coat.

"Please, sit down, Mitry Palych," he said in a polite and friendly voice. "Have a cigarette."

Mitya glanced furtively at Alyonka and noticed the pleasant light that her pink headscarf cast on her face. Then he sat down, lowered his eyes, and lit a cigarette (he'd quit several times during the winter and summer, and now found himself starting once again). Alyonka offered him no greeting—it was as if she hadn't noticed his arrival. The steward continued telling her something that Mitya didn't fully understand, not knowing where the conversation had begun. Alyonka laughed, but she did so in a way that made her laughter seem cut off, utterly divorced from both her mind and heart. The steward's tone was insultingly familiar, and he dropped obscene little innuendos into almost every phrase he spoke. She answered him with easy, sharp derision, mocking his designs on some young woman and showing him to be both a crass and stupid lecher and a gutless coward frightened by his wife.

"Ah well, I can't yelp as loud as you," the steward said, interrupting their exchange as if he'd grown tired of the pointless argument. "You'd do better to come sit here with us. The *barin* wants a word with you."

Alyonka looked aside, tucked a few curls of her dark hair back inside her headscarf, and didn't move.

"Come here, I said, you fool!" the steward insisted.

Alyonka paused to think for another moment, then gracefully jumped down from the embankment and ran toward Mitya. A few steps from where he lay on the steward's coat, she squatted on her heels and looked into his dark, wide-open eyes with playful curiosity.

"Is it true you live without girls, *barchuk*?" she asked. "Like a deacon or something?"

"How would you know if he lives without them?" asked the steward.

"I just know. I heard about it," Alyonka answered. "But the *barchuk's* not allowed. . . . He has someone in Moscow," she said, suddenly directing a flirtatious glance at Mitya.

"There's no one suitable for the gentleman here, so he does without," the steward answered. "You don't know a thing about their ways."

"What do you mean not suitable? With so many girls?" Alyonka answered laughing. "There's Anyutka—what could be better? Anyutka, come here. We need to talk!" she shouted, her voice ringing out.

Anyutka's back was wide and soft, and her arms were short. She turned—her face was appealing, her smile kind and pleasant—and shouted something back in a melodic voice, then set to work with even greater energy.

"They say for you to come here," Alyonka repeated, even more resoundingly.

"You don't need me there. I don't know the least about those things," Anyutka sang out joyfully.

"We don't want Anyutka. We need someone cleaner. With more breeding," the steward said in a cultivated tone of voice. "We know who we need." He looked deliberately at Alyonka, who grew flustered, lightly blushed.

"No, no, no," she answered, concealing her embarrassment with a smile. "You won't find better than Anyutka. And if you don't like her, there's Nastka. She keeps clean too. She used to live in town. . . ."

"Enough, already. Close your mouth," said the steward with sudden sharpness. "Stop nattering and go back to work. Enough already. The mistress yells at me as it is, says you all just misbehave with me."

Again with surprising lightness, Alyonka jumped to her feet and picked up her pitchfork. But at that moment a worker who'd just emptied the last wagonload of manure shouted "Lunch," flicked his reins, and went rattling down the avenue in his empty cart.

"Lunch, time for lunch," the girls called out in varied tones as they dropped their shovels and pitchforks, leapt over the embankment or skipped down from its top, their bare legs and different-colored tights flashing as they hurried toward the edge of the fir grove where their bundles lay.

The steward shot a sidelong look at Mitya and winked, as if to say, "We're on our way."

"Well, if it's time for lunch, it's time for lunch," he said in an authoritative voice as he sat up.

The girls stood out brightly against the dark backdrop of the fir grove as they spread out on the grass in random groups. They untied their bundles and took out loaves of unleavened bread, set them carefully on the hems of their skirts, between their outstretched legs—and then began to chew, washing down their bread with milk or *kvass* they swigged from bottles while talking raucously, bursting into laughter with every word and glancing constantly at Mitya with curious, inviting eyes. Alyonka leaned toward Anyutka and whispered something in her ear. Unable to hold back a charming smile, Anyutka firmly pushed her away (Alyonka toppled over with her head bent toward her knees, choking on her laughter) and began to shout with mock indignation, her pleasant voice carrying through the grove.

"You fool! What's so funny? Why do you keep giggling?"

"Let's leave this sinful scene, Mitry Palych," said the steward. "The devil's in them all!"

XXI

The next day was Sunday, so no one worked in the garden.

A heavy rain had fallen the night before, streaming loudly over the roof while again and again the garden filled with a pale light that spread far into its depths and made it look like something from a story told to a child. By morning, however, the weather had cleared, and once again everything seemed simple and benign when Mitya woke to the cheerful, sun-filled pealing of the church bells in the tower.

He washed and dressed unhurriedly, drank a cup of tea, then left for church. "Your mother already left. . . . Anyone would think that you're a Tatar," Parasha said with gentle chiding.

There were two ways to reach the church. One could walk along the pasture, pass through the estate's main gate, and then turn right; or, alternatively, one could follow the main avenue away from the house, take the road between the garden and the threshing barn, and then turn left. Mitya set off through the garden.

Summer was in full force. He walked directly in the sun, which fell hard between the trees of the avenue and shone with a crisp light on the fields and the threshing barn. The pealing of the church bells streamed gently, peacefully into that brilliant light, co-alesced with all the details of that morning in the country—with the simple fact that Mitya had just washed and combed his glistening black hair, had just put on his student's hat—and suddenly everything seemed so good that Mitya, having passed another sleepless night in the grip of his wildly ranging and erratic thoughts, was suddenly seized by hope, momentarily believed that his torture might be ended, that he might one day be released, saved from further agony. The bells continued ringing, calling playfully, and the threshing barn gleamed hotly in the sun before him. A woodpecker paused on one of the lindens, raised its crested head, then scampered up the knotted bark until it reached the tree's pale green, sunny top. Black and red bumblebees climbed into the flowers in the glades, inserting their velvet bodies with solicitude into the sunshot blooms while everywhere in the garden birds poured out their sweet, untroubled songs. . . . It was all as it had been many, many times before in childhood, in adolescence. And those carefree, captivating years returned to him with such lucidity that he was suddenly convinced that God would pity him, that even without Katya he might find a way to live his life on earth.

"I really should go to see the Meshcherskys," he thought to himself.

But then he raised his eyes and saw Alyonka passing by the gate some twenty feet before him. Her hair was again covered by a headscarf of pink silk. She wore a light blue, stylish dress with frill, and new half-boots, their heels lined with steel strips. Her haunches swayed seductively as she hurried past, not seeing Mitya, who bolted from the avenue and hid behind a tree. He waited until she'd passed from sight, then started back, hurrying toward the house while his heart pounded. Suddenly he understood that he had left for church with a hidden motive: to see Alyonka there. And it was wrong to look for her in church. Wrong.

XXII

During lunch a courier from the station brought a telegram: Anya and Kostya sent word that they'd arrive tomorrow evening. Mitya was utterly indifferent to this news.

After lunch he went out to the balcony, lay on his back on a wicker couch, closed his eyes. He could feel the hot sun that reached the balcony's edge, could hear the summer drone of flies. His heart seemed to tremble. His head was filled with questions that he couldn't answer. How will these plans with Alyonka be made? When will it be settled once and for all? Why didn't the steward ask her yesterday if she agrees—and if she does, when and where? And together with these thoughts, another line of questions troubled him: Should he make another trip to the post office despite his resolution to end those excursions? Why not go there one last time? Would he wind up making a fresh mockery of his pride for no real reason? Would he just be torturing himself once more with pathetic hopes? But how could the trip really deepen his misery? After all, it's really just a reason to get out of the house. Isn't it completely obvious that everything in Moscow's finished for him now? What's he supposed to do?

"*Barchuk*," a quiet voice sounded sharply near the balcony. "*Barchuk*, are you asleep?"

He opened his eyes: the steward was standing in front of him, festively dressed in a new cotton shirt and a new cap. He looked self-satisfied, slightly sleepy, and half drunk.

"*Barchuk*, let's go quickly to the forest," he whispered. "I told your mother that I need to see Trifon to talk about bees. Let's go before she wakes up from her nap, rethinks it all, says no. We'll get a little something for Trifon along the way. He'll have a bit to drink, get a little tipsy, and you'll chat with him while I find a way to slip Alyonka a few little words. Let's go quickly, now. I'm already harnessed. . . ."

Mitya jumped up and ran through the servants' hall, grabbed his cap, and headed quickly to the carriage house, where a spirited young stallion was harnessed to a *drozhky*.

XXIII

The stallion went from standing still to flying like the wind: they barreled through the gate at a full gallop, stopped at a shop across from the church to buy a bottle of vodka and a pound of *salo*, then set off flying once again.

As they drove out of the village, a hut flashed by where Anyutka stood, dressed up and looking lost, as if she couldn't think of anywhere to go. The steward shouted something crude and unpleasant that he intended as a joke, then lashed the horse's rump, snapping his reins with senseless, cruel, and drunken showmanship. The stallion ran even harder.

Mitya held on with all his strength as he bounced wildly in his seat. The sun's warmth felt pleasant on the back of his head; a hot wind blew into his face from the fields. It smelled of the flowering rye, axle grease, dust from the road. Small currents of wind rippled through the rye, which flashed its grey and silver lining like some miraculous fur while countless larks shot up from its waves, sailed slantwise in the breeze and sang, then dove back down. The forest was a soft dark blue in the distance.

Fifteen minutes later they were already in those woods, their wheels knocking over roots and stumps as they sailed down the shady road, made cheerful now by brilliant spots of sunlight and countless flowers in the tall grass on the sidings. Still wearing her blue dress and short boots, Alyonka sat embroidering in a little grove of young oaks, her legs stretched straight and evenly before her. The steward brandished his whip at her as they flew by, then deftly reined in his horse at the front door. Mitya was astounded by the fresh, bitter scent of the forest and the young oaks—and deafened by the dogs that quickly surrounded the *drozhky*, filled the woods with their barking. They stood there yelping furiously in almost every tone imaginable, but their shaggy faces were friendly, and their tails were wagging.

Mitya and the steward climbed down from the *drozhky* and tied the stallion to a withered tree, evidently struck by lightning, that stood before the windows. Then they passed through a small, dark anteroom and entered the hut.

It was clean and comfortable inside, crowded and hot from the sun, which slanted through the forest and shone in both windows, and from the stove, which had been lit that morning to bake bread. Alyonka's mother-in-law, a clean and pleasant-looking woman named Fedosya, was sitting at the table, her back to one of the small windows, which was filled with sunlight and gnats. Seeing the *barchuk*, she stood and made a low bow. Mitya and the steward greeted her, sat down, and began to smoke.

"And where is Trifon?" asked the steward.

"He's resting in the shed," Fedosya said. "I'll go and call him."

"Things are moving now!" the steward whispered, winking with both eyes the moment she left.

But Mitya saw no movement at all. So far the visit had produced nothing but excruciating awkwardness, for it seemed Fedosya understood precisely why they'd come. For the third straight day a horrifying thought flitted through his mind: *What am I doing? I'm going insane!* He felt as if he were a sleepwalker who'd fallen under the control of some external force that now led him with increasing speed toward a terrible but irresistible abyss. All the same, he still tried to appear forthright and relaxed as he sat and smoked, looked around the hut. He was particularly ashamed to think that Trifon would soon come into the room: he was said to be both smart and ill-tempered, a calculating *mouzhik* who'd see the reasons for this visit right away, understand it still more clearly than Fedosya. But another thought accompanied this one: Where does she sleep? On that plank bed? Or in the shed? The shed, of course, he thought. The windows have no frames, no glass. All night the drowsy whispering of the forest. And she lies there, sleeping. . . .

XXIV

Trifon made a low bow to Mitya as he entered the room but did not speak or look him in the eye. He sat down on a bench before the table and began to talk with the steward. His tone was dry, unwelcoming: What had happened? Why had they come? The steward hurriedly explained that the mistress had sent him to ask that Trifon come to examine their beehives. The estate's beekeeper, he said, was a deaf old fool, whereas Trifon's knowledge and understanding of bees was unequalled in the entire region. Here he quickly pulled the bottle of vodka from one pocket of his pants, the pound of *salo*—its wrapping of grey paper already soaked through with grease—from the other. Trifon looked askance at him with cold derision but rose nevertheless to get a teacup from the shelf. The steward poured for Mitya first, then Trifon, followed by Fedosya—who drained her cupful slowly, as if savoring the taste—and finally himself. As soon as he had drunk, he started pouring seconds, chewing on a piece of bread, his nostrils flaring.

Trifon showed signs of being drunk quite quickly, but he remained unfriendly, speaking with thinly veiled derision to the steward, who had fallen into a complete stupor after his second drink. Although their conversation appeared reasonably amicable on the surface, both men's eyes displayed hostility and distrust. Fedosya sat without speaking, looking at them politely but obviously not happy they were there. Alyonka did not appear. Having given up all hope that she might come into the house, and seeing clearly now that this had been an absurd plan—how would the steward "slip her a few little words" if she wasn't even there?—Mitya rose and said sternly that it was time to go.

"In a minute. We've got a little time," the steward replied sullenly. "I need to say a little word or two to you in private."

"You can tell me on the way home," Mitya said, his voice restrained, but even sterner. "We're going."

But the steward slapped his palm on the table. "I told you—I can't say this on the way home. Come outside with me for a minute," he said with besotted stealth. He rose heavily from the table and threw open the door to the little front room. Mitya followed him.

"Well, what is it?"

"Quiet," the steward whispered conspiratorially, swaying as he closed the door behind him.

"Be quiet about what?"

"Be quiet."

"I can't understand you."

"Be quiet. She's ours. On my word!"

Mitya pushed past him and went outside. He paused on the front step, not knowing what to do. Wait a little longer? Drive home alone? Walk?

Ten feet from him stood the thick green forest, already filled with an evening shade that made it seem cleaner, fresher, even lovelier than before. The sun had already slipped behind the tops of the trees; its unclouded light fell through the branches in beams of reddish gold. Suddenly a female voice rang out in the forest's depths, echoing among the trees beyond the ravine. It carried with it all the alluring charm that a voice acquires only in a forest when the sun is setting.

"Aaa-ooo"—the voice produced another drawn-out call, its owner evidently playing with the forest echo. "Aaa-ooo."

Mitya bolted from the step, ran through the tall grass and the flowers into the forest, which sloped toward a rocky ravine. Alyonka stood at its bottom, chewing on a cowslip stem. She looked up with a startled expression as Mitya ran to the ravine's edge and stopped.

"What are you doing here?" he asked quietly.

"Looking for Maruska and our cow," she answered, lowering her voice as well. "What's it to you?"

"Well, will you come or not?"

"Why should I just for free?" she said.

"Who said it was for free?" asked Mitya, almost whispering. "Don't worry about that."

"When?" Alyonka asked.

"Tomorrow. . . . Can you come tomorrow?"

Alyonka paused to think. "I'm going to my mother's to shear her sheep," she said, looking carefully around the forest on the slope behind Mitya. "I'll come after that. In the evening, when it gets dark. But where? The threshing barn's no good—someone might come in. We could go to the hunter's hut, if you want. The one in your garden, in the dip. Only don't play games with me. . . . I'm not doing it for free. This isn't Moscow, after all," she said, glancing up at him with laughter in her eyes, "I hear women pay to get it there. . . ."

XXV

The trip home was disgraceful.

Trifon had not remained in debt for long. He opened a second bottle, and the steward drank himself into such a state that when they finally went to leave, he fell against the *drozhky* and the startled horse almost ran away without them. But Mitya said nothing, watched the steward indifferently, waited patiently for him to climb into his seat. Once again the steward drove with senseless fury. Mitya remained silent, holding firmly to the seat, looking at the evening sky, at the fields that jumped before him. The larks were finishing their short songs above the rye as the dusk deepened in the west; to the east it had already taken on the dark blue shade of night, flickering occasionally with those peaceful sheets of summer lightning that presage nothing but fair weather. Mitya understood all the beauty of the evening that surrounded him, but it was foreign now, completely alien. His mind and soul were occupied by one idea: tomorrow night!

At home he was greeted by the news that Anya and Kostya would arrive tomorrow on the evening train. He was horrified: they'll arrive and go running to the garden, blunder into the hunter's hut in the hollow! But then he remembered that they would not arrive from the station before ten that night, and then they would eat, have tea. . . .

"Are you going to meet them at the station?" Olga Petrovna asked.

He could feel himself blanching. "No, I don't think so. I don't really feel like it for some reason. And there's no room for me."

"Well, you could go on horseback."

"Yes, of course. I don't know . . . I mean, what for, really?. . . I don't feel like it right now."

Olga Petrovna stared at him. "Are you all right?"

"Absolutely," Mitya answered almost rudely. "I just need to sleep."

Without another word he went into his room, lay down on the couch in the dark, and fell asleep without undressing.

During the night he heard the slow, muted strains of distant music and saw himself suspended over a huge, dimly lit abyss. It grew steadily brighter, more and more brilliant with gold, more and more crowded with people. Its bottom continued to recede from view until it seemed there was no end to the abyss, and the music grew completely clear, its every note distinct: with sorrow and a tenderness too delicate for words, the melody and singing came to him: "There was a king of Thule. . . ." He quavered with emotion, rolled over, fell back to sleep.

XXVI

The day seemed endless.

Lifeless as a mannequin, Mitya left his room for tea and lunch, then lay back down, picked up a book by Pisemsky that had been lying on his desk for weeks, and read without comprehending a single word. Sometimes he just stared at length at the ceiling, listening to the even, satinlike sounds of the garden filled with sun beyond his window. . . . He rose once and went to the library to change his book, but with its peaceful views—one window opening on his cherished maple, the others taking in the brilliant western sky— that room, which once felt charmingly old-fashioned, now seemed so much a part of Katya, and reminded him so sharply of those spring days (now as distant as the Earth's creation) when he would sit among its shelves and read old journals filled with poetry, that he abruptly turned away. To hell with it, he thought with irritation. To hell with love's poetic little tragedies!

With indignation he recalled his sincere intentions to shoot himself if no letter came from Katya within a week, then again took up his book by Pisemsky. But he understood no more than he had before, and from time to time a trembling began in the pit of his

[61]

stomach, then spread through his entire body as he stared at the book and thought about Alyonka. The closer evening came, the more frequently those fits of shuddering passed through him. Footsteps, voices in the house, people talking in the courtyard, where a *tarantass* had already been harnessed for the trip to the station—these sounds came to him the way they do when you are sick in bed and ordinary life continues all around you—utterly indifferent to your condition and therefore alien, almost hostile. At last Parasha shouted somewhere, "The horses are ready, Madame!"—and he heard the dry prattling of little harness bells, then the tread of hooves, the rustling of the *tarantass* as it rolled toward the front porch. "For God's sake, when will it end!" Mitya muttered to himself with impatience. But he didn't move, just listened anxiously as Olga Petrovna called out final instructions in the servants' hall and the harness bells began to prattle once again. As the *tarantass* rolled downhill, their noise blended with the larger racket of the carriage wheels, then died away entirely. . . .

Mitya stood up quickly and went into the hall, which was empty and full of light from the clear, yellowish dusk. The entire house was empty; something in that emptiness felt strange and sinister. With the odd sensation that he was leaving for a long time, Mitya looked down the line of silent rooms adjoining one another—the den, the drawing room, and the library, where through one window he could see the dark blue light of the evening sky and the maple's green, magnificent top, above which hung the pink star of Antares. Then he glanced into the servants' hall to make sure Parasha wasn't there. Convinced that it too was empty, he snatched his hat from the coatrack, ran back into his room, and climbed out the window, stretching his long legs down to the flower bed. Once down, he froze for a moment, then ran hunched over through the garden and plunged into an overgrown, silent avenue, thickly hedged by lilac and acacia.

XXVII

Since there was no dew, the garden's scents could not have been especially strong. But even though he acted that evening like a man who'd lost all conscious contact with the world around him, Mitya couldn't think of any time in his life—other than perhaps his childhood—when he'd encountered such diverse and heady smells as he did now. Everything was pungent: the bushes of acacia, the leaves of lilac and black currant, the wormwood and the burdock, the flowers and the dirt and the grass. . . .

He took several quick steps with a new and terrifying thought: What if she doesn't come? Suddenly it seemed that his entire life depended on her meeting him. Among the scent of blooming shrubs and flowers, he caught the smell of smoke from the village and stopped again, looking back. A beetle hummed and slowly drifted through the air beside him; the twilight and the evening's peaceful calm seemed to spread out from its tiny wings as it rose. The sky was still light, its western half firmly occupied by the level, slow-burning rays of the first summer sunset. High above the house, visible in snatches through the trees, a sliver of the nascent moon hung like the severe, sharp blade of a scythe in the sky's blue, transparent void. Mitya glanced at it, quickly crossed himself with shallow strokes below the center of his chest, and stepped into the bushes of acacia: the avenue he'd started following would lead him down into the hollow, but he had to veer off to the left now to reach the hunter's hut. As soon as he was out of the acacia, Mitya began to run through the trees, pushing past or crouching to avoid their splayed, low branches. He reached the agreed-upon meeting place in no more than a minute.

He was afraid when he stepped into the hut, its darkness smelling heavily of dry and musty straw. He peered into the gloom and almost joyfully assured himself that he was still alone. But the fateful moment was drawing near; he stayed beside the hut, straining for a sign that someone was approaching, all his senses focused on the woods. An intense physical excitement had left him for no more than a few minutes during the entire day. Now it seemed to reach its apex. But just as it had been all day, this sensation remained oddly disconnected, isolated: it absorbed his body but left his soul unmoved. Still, the beating of his heart was terrible, and the silence that surrounded him was so astonishingly complete that he heard nothing but that violent pounding in his chest. Colorless moths hovered soundlessly among the branches of the apple trees, fluttering their soft, tireless wings among the intricate and varied patterns of the grey foliage silhouetted against the evening sky. And because of them, the silence seemed to deepen, as if those moths were practicing some kind of magic, as if they'd cast a spell. Startled by the sound of something crackling behind him, Mitya turned abruptly and looked through the trees toward the garden wall: something black seemed to be rolling toward him beneath the branches. Before he'd had a chance to understand what it was, the black shape approached him, rose up in a sweeping motion, and revealed itself to be Alyonka. She'd covered her head with her skirt, and now threw off its short, black hem of homemade wool, revealing her face, a bright and frightened smile. She was barefoot, wearing just a simple, unbleached blouse she'd tucked into the skirt, taut across her girlish breasts. The wide cut of its collar revealed her neck and part of her shoulders; the sleeves were rolled up past her elbows, exposing her full arms. Everything about her—from her small head and the yellow silk kerchief that covered it to her petite bare feet, feminine and child-like—everything was so good, so graceful and alluring that Mitya gasped to himself. She'd always worn somewhat stylish clothes whenever he encountered her before; the simple charm of her appearance now was startling.

"Don't take all night, okay?" she said in a cheerful, furtive whisper, and plunged into the musty twilight of the hut.

There she stopped, and Mitya, clenching his teeth to stop their chattering inside his head, quickly stuck his hand into his pocket—his legs were so tense they felt like something made of iron—then thrust a crumpled five-ruble note into her palm. She quickly hid it in her blouse and sat down on the ground. Mitya sat beside her and put his arms around her neck, not knowing what to do. Should he kiss her now, or not? The smell of her kerchief and her hair, the slight scent of onions mixed with smoke and all the other smells of a peasant hut that seemed to come from her—it was enough to make him giddy with desire. And Mitya felt this, recorded it with all his senses. But at the same time nothing had changed: he felt a physical desire of terrifying potency, but it bore no link to the longings of the soul, to bliss or ecstasy; it couldn't bring that joyful lassitude that washes over one's entire being. She leaned back, stretched out on the ground. He lay down as well, pressed against her side, stretched his hand toward her. She caught it, pulled it down with an awkward, nervous laugh.

"None of that's allowed," she said, her voice half serious, half joking.

She drew his hand away and held it firmly in her small grip, aimed her stare at the triangular window of the hut, the branches of the apple trees outside, the darkening blue of the sky beyond those limbs, and the fixed, red point of Antares, which still hung there, alone. What did those eyes express? What was he supposed to do? Kiss her neck, her lips?

"Don't take all night, okay?" she said abruptly, reaching for her short black skirt. . . .

When they rose—when Mitya rose completely stunned by the depth of his disillusionment—she straightened her hair and retied her kerchief, speaking in an animated whisper, as if she'd now become an intimate, as if she were his lover.

"They say you went to Subbotino. The priest there's supposed to be selling pigs for cheap," she said. "Did you hear about that?"

XXVIII

The rain began on Wednesday and continued through the week without a pause; on Saturday it grew into a torrent, pouring from the cheerless sky in heavy gusts.

And all day Mitya walked in the garden. All day he wept so terribly that he himself was sometimes startled by the violence and abundance of his tears.

Parasha looked for him, shouted his name in the avenue of lindens and the courtyard; she called him to lunch and to tea—he didn't answer.

It was cold. The rain and damp bore into everything. Black clouds clotted the sky: against their dark mass the greenery of the garden stood out brightly, looked especially full and fresh. The wind would sometimes race through the trees and bring down another shower, a stream of drops shaken from the leaves. But Mitya saw nothing, took no account of anything around him. His once white hat was so completely sopped that it had turned dark grey and lost its shape; his student's coat was black; his boots were spattered with mud up to his knees. It was terrible to see him—his clothing drenched, soaked through; his face devoid of blood and color; his half-mad eyes worn out and swollen from his weeping.

He smoked one cigarette after another as he strode through the mud in the avenue or at random moments set off where there was no path, wading through the high, wet grass among the pear and apple trees, stumbling among their crooked, gnarled branches, flecked with grey-green lichens sodden from the rain. He sat on benches that were black and swollen, walked into the hollow in the garden, went into the hunter's hut, lay down in the wet straw precisely where he'd lain not long ago with Alyonka. His big hands had turned blue from the cold and the raw damp; his lips were purpling; the deathly pallor of his face and sunken cheeks now took on a violet tinge. Lying on his back with one foot resting on the other and

his hands behind his head, Mitya stared uncomprehendingly at the
blackened thatch of the roof, which dripped large beads of water
the color of rust. Then his eyebrows began to twitch, his jaw
clamped shut. He leapt convulsively to his feet and pulled a letter
from his pocket—a letter he'd received late last evening, delivered
by a land surveyor who'd come to the estate for several days on business. Mitya had already read the smudged and tattered letter a hundred times, but now he greedily consumed it once again:

> *Dear Mitya,*
> *Don't think ill of me! Forget everything, forget all of it! I am rot-*
> *ten, fallen, foul.*
> *I'm not worthy of you in the least. But I madly love my art. And*
> *now I've decided.*
> *The die is cast: I'm leaving—you know with whom. . . . You're so*
> *sensitive and smart, I know you'll understand me. I beg you not to tor-*
> *ture yourself, or me. You mustn't write—it's useless. . . .*

When he reached that sentence, Mitya balled the letter up
and buried his face in the wet straw, violently clenching his teeth
and choking on sobs, for there she had addressed him inadvertently
with the informal form of "you" in Russian—*ty*. And with all the intimacy it invoked, that accidental *ty* was more than he could bear: it
reminded him of everything he'd lost and at the same time estab-
lished all their closeness once again. Reading it, a lacerating tenderness welled up inside his heart. It was beyond all human strength!
And together with that *ty* came a strict assertion that even writing
was no use. But yes—he knew that now. Useless! Absolutely useless!
And everything was finished, finished for eternity!

The intensity of the crashing rain seemed to grow tenfold toward evening, and this, combined with unexpected claps of thunder, finally drove him home. Soaked from head to foot, his teeth
chattering wildly from the bitter chill and the violent shuddering of

his entire body, Mitya peered out from the trees. Convinced that he would not be seen, he ran up to the window of his room, raised it, and climbed inside. He locked the door and threw himself on the bed.

It began to grow dark quickly. He heard the rain everywhere — on the roof, around the house, in the garden. But it made two distinct and separate sets of sounds. One came from the garden, the other from the house, where water splashed and murmured ceaselessly as it streamed from gutters into puddles. For Mitya, who had momentarily gone blank and rigid, this phenomenon produced an inexplicable alarm and virtual narcosis: while a sudden heat raged inside his head, blazed within his mouth and nostrils as he breathed, those dual sounds of the falling rain brought forth some other world, some other moment just before the evening's onset in some other house — one filled with terrible presentiments.

He knew he was in his room, where it was almost dark from the rain and the approaching night; he knew he could hear the voices of his mother, Anya, Kostya, and the land surveyor as they had tea nearby in the hall. But at the same time he was moving through some unfamiliar house, following a young nursemaid as she walked away from him. A mysterious and ever-growing fear held him in its grip, but it was mixed with desire, a premonition that someone would soon draw close to someone else, that they would share an intimacy that was unnatural and repulsive — an intimacy in which he too was bound, somehow, to participate. These feelings were triggered in him by a child with a large white face whom the nursemaid carried and rocked in her arms, leaning back to support the extra weight as she walked. Believing that she might be Alyonka, Mitya hurried to pass the nursemaid in order to see her face, but suddenly he found himself in a gloomy classroom with chalk smeared on the windows. She who stood in the front of the room before a chest of drawers and a mirror could not see him — he had suddenly become invisible. She wore a yellow silk slip that clung tightly to her rounded hips, high-heeled shoes, and fine, black fish-net stockings that revealed her flesh: She was sweetly bashful and ashamed; she knew what was about to happen. She had already had time to hide the baby in one of the dresser drawers. She tossed her braid over one shoulder and began to redo it, hurrying as she glanced sidelong at the door or looked directly in the mirror, where her small, slightly powdered face, her bare shoulders, her milky blue breasts and pink nipples were reflected.

The door flew open, and a gentleman dressed in a tuxedo looked around the room with horrifying joviality. He had short, black, curly hair and a clean-shaven face completely drained of color. Once inside the room, he took out a thin, gold cigarette case and casually began to smoke. She finished with her braid and looked at him timidly, evidently understanding his intentions, then swung her braid behind her shoulder, raised her bare arms. . . . He held her condescendingly around the waist as she clung to his neck, revealing her dark underarms. She pressed herself to him. She nestled her face against his chest.

XXIX

Mitya came to himself in a sweat with the shockingly clear realization that he was destroyed, that nothing in the underworld or in the grave could be as hopeless, as monstrously gloomy as the world that now surrounded him. It was dark in his room; the rain tapped and splashed outside his window, and that sound, those glinting drops (even the sound alone) were more than his body, trembling with fever, could endure. But even more horrific and unbearable was that perversion, that hideously unnatural act of human copulation, which it seemed he'd shared with that clean-shaven gentleman. He could hear voices, laughter in the hall. And those sounds also seemed to him both terrible and perverse, for they were full of life's vulgarity; they were absolutely alien to him, merciless, indifferent.

[69]

"Katya," he said, sitting up, swinging his legs to the floor. "Katya, what is happening?" he said out loud, absolutely certain that she could hear him, that she was there but didn't speak, didn't call to him because she too was completely despondent, grasping the utter, irrevocable horror of everything she'd done. "Ah, it's all the same, Katya," he whispered bitterly, tenderly—wanting to say that he'd forgive her for everything she'd done if she would only once more rush toward him so that they could save themselves, save their love in this beautiful spring world, which had so recently resembled paradise. But as soon as he had whispered, "Ah, it's all the same, Katya," he understood that no, it wasn't all the same: there was no salvation, no going back to that marvelous vision once granted him in Shakhovskoe, on a balcony overgrown with jasmine. There was no return, and there never could be. Realizing this, he began quietly to weep from the tearing pain inside his chest.

And that pain grew so strong, so unbearable, that he did not consider what would come of it, did not contemplate his actions, but rather, wished for just one thing—to save himself for a moment from that agony, not to fall back into the awful world where he had spent the day, where he had plunged into the most horrific and repulsive of all dreams possible on earth—as he groped for the night-stand drawer and pulled it open, as he felt the cold and heavy mass of the revolver and deeply, gladly sighed, then opened his mouth and pulled the trigger hard, pulled it with delight.

[Maritime Alps, 1924]

Cleansing Monday

WHEN THE grey winter day was darkening; when the street lamps were freshly lit and their gas flames burned with a cold radiance while warm light filled the storefronts and the shops; when the day's demands finally let go and Moscow's evening life began to stir; when the cabbies drove with extra energy and bustle, and their horse-drawn sleds began to fill the streets; when the vague, dark figures of pedestrians moved with new vitality along the snowy walks; when the roar of packed trams plunging down the tracks grew stronger, and green stars were visible, already, as they fell hissing from the cables in the heavy dusk—always at that hour my driver whirled me through the streets, always at that hour I was sailing in a sled, pulled fast by a strong and spirited trotter from Krasnye Vorota to the Cathedral of Christ the Savior, which stood directly opposite the building where she lived. And every evening I took her to dinner at the Hermitage, the Prague, or the Metropol, then to the theatre or a concert, and finally to the Strelnya or the Yar. I didn't know where all of this would lead, and I didn't want to think about it, for I could come to no conclusion, and there was little point in trying—just as there was little point in asking her about the future: she'd ruled out all such conversations. She was enigmatic, at times inscrutable to me. Our intimacy was incomplete, and our relationship resisted definition: thus I was wracked by hope, suspended in a state of constant, painful expectation. And still, every hour spent near her brought me a joy beyond all words.

For some reason she was studying at the university. She rarely went to classes—but she went. When I asked her why, she shrugged and said: "Why do we do anything on this earth? Do we really understand anything about our actions?. . . And anyway—history interests me." She lived alone. Her widowed father, a cultured man from a distinguished merchant class, lived a quiet life in Tver, where, like all merchants, he collected something. Primarily for the view it afforded of Moscow, she rented a fifth-floor corner apartment in a building that faced the Cathedral of Christ the Savior; it consisted of only two rooms, but they were spacious and well furnished. The first was largely occupied by a wide ottoman; it also contained an expensive piano, on which she constantly practiced the beginning of the Moonlight Sonata—playing again and again those slow, enchanting, dreamlike notes, and nothing else. Elegant flowers stood in cut-glass vases on the piano and her dressing table; fresh bouquets were delivered to her every Saturday by my order, and when I arrived in the evening to find her lying on the couch, above which hung, for some reason, a portrait of Tolstoy in his bare feet, she would slowly extend her hand for me to kiss, and say distractedly, "Thank you for the flowers. . . ." I brought her boxes of chocolates, new books by Hofmannsthal, Schnitzler, Tetmajer, and Przybyszewski—and always I received the same "thank you," the same warm, extended hand, an occasional order to sit beside her on the couch without removing my coat. "I don't know why," she'd say pensively, looking at my beaver-fur collar, "but it seems there's nothing better than the smell of winter air that you bring into this room from the street." It seemed she needed none of this—not the flowers or the books, not the lunches or the theatre tickets or the dinners outside town—and yet she strongly preferred certain flowers to others, read every book I brought her, consumed each box of chocolates in no more than a day. At lunch and dinner she ate as much as I, having a particular affection for burbot pasties with eelpout stew and pink hazel grouse in heavily fried sour cream. Sometimes she would say, "A whole lifetime of lunches and dinners—I don't understand it. Why don't people get tired of this?" And yet she ate her own lunches and dinners with all the zest and understanding of a seasoned Muscovite. Her only glaring weakness was for clothes—expensive furs, velvet, silks.

We were both rich, healthy, and young—and so attractive that people often turned their heads to look at us in restaurants and concert halls. Although born in the Penza province, I for some reason possessed the flamboyant good looks of a southerner. Indeed, an acclaimed actor—a monstrously fat man who was famous for his wit and gluttony—once told me I was "obscenely handsome." "Only the devil knows what you are—some kind of Sicilian or something," he added in his drowsy voice. And it was true—there was something southern about my character, something prone to easy smiles and good-natured jokes. She possessed a kind of Indian or Persian beauty—a complexion like dark amber, hair so black and full it seemed almost sinister in its magnificence. Her eyebrows gleamed softly like sable; the rich blackness of velvet and coal filled her eyes. One had to overcome a small spell to look away from her mouth, her rich red lips, and the dark, delicate down above them. When we went out, she usually wore a garnet velvet dress and matching shoes with golden clasps, but she attended lectures dressed as modestly as any student, and afterward ate lunch for thirty kopecks in a vegetarian cafeteria on the Arbat. She was as taciturn and introspective as I was voluble and blithe—forever disappearing into her own thoughts, carefully exploring something deep inside her mind. As she lay reading on the couch, she'd often lower her book and stare meditatively into the distance: I observed her doing this several times when I stopped to see her in the afternoons, for each month she refused to leave her rooms for three or four entire days, and during these periods I was forced to sit beside her in an armchair, reading silently.

"You are awfully talkative, you know. And you fidget constantly," she'd say. "Just let me finish this chapter."

"If I weren't so talkative and fidgety, I might never have met you," I answered, reminding her of our first conversation. Sometime in December I'd wound up sitting next to her at a lecture by Andrey Bely, which he delivered in song as he ran and danced around the stage. I shifted in my seat and laughed so hard that she looked at me in surprise for some time, then also broke into laughter—and I immediately began to chat lightheartedly with her.

"True enough," she said. "But please be quiet for a little longer. Read a little more. Have a cigarette. . . ."

"I can't be quiet! You don't understand how intensely I love you—you have no idea! And you clearly don't love me. . . ."

"I do understand. And as for my love, you know perfectly well that I have no one on earth other than you and my father. You're my first and last—isn't that enough? But let's stop talking about this. Reading with you is clearly impossible, so let's have some tea."

I would get up then and put water on to boil in the electric teapot that stood on a small table beside the couch, take cups and saucers from the walnut cabinet in the corner—and all the while say whatever came into my head:

"Did you finish reading *The Fire Angel?*"

"I skimmed through it to the end. It's so pretentious I'm ashamed to read it."

"Why did you leave Chaliapin's concert so abruptly yesterday?"

"It was such a display—too much for me. And I've never been a great fan of all that dreck about 'Fair Haired Rus.'"

"You don't like anything."

"Not much."

"A strange love," I would think to myself, as I stood waiting for the water to boil and looked out the windows. The scent of flowers filled the room, a scent inextricably linked to her in my mind. Beyond one window, a huge panorama of the city sprawled far beyond the Moscow River, all of it blue-grey under snow. The other window, to the left of the first, looked out onto a section of the Kremlin, across from which stood the Cathedral of Christ the Savior: its white mass seemed excessively close to the fortress wall, and all of it looked too new. The reflections of jackdaws hung like blue spots in the golden cupola as they flew in endless circles around it. . . . "Such a strange city," I said to myself, thinking of Moscow's old streets, thinking of St. Basil's Cathedral and Iver-skaya Chapel, thinking of the church known as Spas-Na-Boru, the Italian cathedrals inside the Kremlin—and then, those fortress walls before me, their guard towers and sharp points like something from Khirgizia.

Arriving at dusk, I sometimes found her on the couch wearing just a silk gown trimmed with sable fur—a gift she said her grandmother from Astrakhan had bequeathed her in her will. I'd leave the lights off and sit beside her in the half dark, kissing her arms and legs, her stunningly sleek and graceful body. . . . She resisted nothing but maintained a steadfast silence. Again and again I'd seek out her warm lips with my mouth, and she would give them to me, breathing fitfully—but never uttering a word. And when she finally sensed that I would soon lose all control, she'd push me aside and sit up, ask me to turn on the light, her voice completely calm. I'd do as she requested; she would rise and go into the bedroom while I sat on the piano stool, like someone waiting for a drug's hot flush and delirium to pass. Fifteen minutes later she'd come out dressed and ready to leave, calm and matter-of-fact, as if nothing ever happened.

"Where to today? The Metropol, perhaps?"

And again we'd talk all night about something unimportant and extraneous. Soon after our affair began, I'd spoken about marriage, and she'd said, "No—I'll be no good as a wife. I'll be no good at all. . . ."

But this did not eradicate my hopes. "We'll see," I told myself, and talked no more of marriage, hoping she would change her mind eventually. There were days when our incomplete intimacy seemed unbearable, but then, what remained for me, other than the hope held out by time? Once, sitting near her in the evening semi-dark and silence, I clutched my head in my hands. "No, this is beyond my strength," I said. "Why, why should you and I be tortured this way?"

She didn't speak.

"And really, all the same—this isn't love. This isn't love. . . ."

She answered calmly from the dark. "Maybe not. Who knows what love is?"

"I do! I know what love is—what happiness is," I exclaimed. "And I'll wait for you to recognize it too."

"Happiness . . .," she said. "Our happiness, friend, is like water in a fishing net. As you pull it in, the net seems full. But lift it out—and nothing's there."

"What's that supposed to mean?"

"Platon Karataev says that to Pierre."

I waved my hand. "Oh, please—spare me the Eastern wisdom. . . ."

And again I talked all night about something peripheral to our lives—a new production at the theatre, a new story by Andreev. . . . And again it was enough for me to know that I would sit close to her in the sleigh; that I would hold her in soft, rich furs as we rocked from side to side and the runners sailed along the snowy streets; to know that I would enter a crowded restaurant with her while an orchestra played the march from *Aida*; that I would eat and drink beside her; that I would hear her slow voice, look at her lips, remember how I kissed them an hour ago—*yes, I kissed them,* I would say to myself, looking with gratitude and joy at those lips and the soft down above them, looking at the rich red velvet of her dress and the slope of her shoulders, looking at the oval of her breasts as the light, almost spicy fragrance of her hair penetrated my senses, and I thought "Moscow, Astrakhan, India, Persia!". . . Sometimes in restaurants outside town, toward the evening's end, when the room was filled with smoke and noise—and she was tipsy, had herself begun to smoke—she'd lead me to a private room and ask to hear the gypsies sing. They'd come to us with a deliberate racket, overly familiar and relaxed. A woman with a low forehead and tar-black bangs would lead the small choir while before it stood an old man wearing a knee-length coat with galloons, a guitar on a blue ribbon over his shoulder, his dark, hairless scalp like cast iron, his blue-grey face resembling a drowning victim's. . . . She always listened with an enigmatic, languid, almost mocking smile. . . . At three or four in the morning I'd drive her home; on the steps of her house I would close my eyes from happiness and kiss the damp fur of her collar—and then, plunged into some strange mix of ecstasy and despair, I'd sail home to Krasnye Vorota. And it will be the same, I always thought, tomorrow and the day after and the day after that—the same torture and the same joy. . . . What else is there to say? It was happiness. Great happiness.

So January and February passed. So *Maslenitsa* came and went. On the Sunday of Forgiveness she told me to come to her after four in the evening. When I arrived, she was already wearing black felt boots and a hat and short coat made of dark astrakhan fur.

"All in black," I said, ecstatic as always.

A tender, quiet expression played in her eyes.

"Well, tomorrow's Cleansing Monday," she said, drawing her gloved hand from her muff to give to me. "Lord God, master of my life . . ." she said in Old Church Slavonic, reciting the first words of St. Yefrem Sirin's prayer. "Let's go to Novodevichy," she added suddenly. "I'd like to walk around the graveyard and the abbey. Will you go with me?"

I was surprised but answered hurriedly, "Yes, of course."

"What are we doing, after all?—every day another meal in some seedy tavern somewhere . . .," she added. "Yesterday morning I went to Rogozhskoe. . . ."

I was even more surprised. "The cemetery? For schismatics? Why?"

"Yes, the schismatics. It's old Russia—Rus before Peter. . . . They were burying an archbishop. Just try to imagine it: the coffin's made from the trunk of an oak, just the way they did it in ancient times; it has a gold brocade that looks like it's been hammered out. The dead man's face is covered by a white pall that's patterned with rough, black thread. . . . Everything about it's beautiful and terrifying. The deacons stand beside the coffin, holding *Ripidas* and *Trikirys*. . . ."

"How do you know all this? *Ripidas*, Trikirys!

"You just don't know me—that's why you're surprised."

"I didn't know that you're so religious. . . ."

"It's not religiousness. . . . I don't know what it is, exactly. But, for instance, sometimes in the morning—or in the evening, if you aren't dragging me off to some restaurant—I go to the cathedrals in the Kremlin. You never suspected that, I'm sure. . . . But listen to the rest—about the funeral: you just can't imagine the deacons there. . . . It's like you're looking at those monks who drove the Tatars out five hundred years ago—it's as if Peresvet and Oslyabya themselves were standing in front of you! There were two, separate choirs, and all the singers were like Peresvet as well—tall and powerful, wearing long black caftans. They sang in answer to one another—first one choir, then the other. They sang in unison, but they weren't following the kind of musical notes you see today; they were singing by *kryuk*—those ancient notes without lines. . . . The grave was covered with fresh, bright branches from an evergreen. . . . And outside—a heavy frost, sunlight, blinding snow. . . . No, none of this makes any sense to you. . . . Let's go. . . ."

It was a peaceful, sunny evening, with frost hanging in the trees and jackdaws perched on the blood-red walls of the convent, lingering in the silence like little nuns. The sad and delicate chimes of the clock tower played over and again as we passed through the gates and set out along the silent paths between the graves, our shoes squeaking in the snow. The sun had recently set, but the evening was still bright. And it was stunning—how the icy boughs became grey coral before the gold enamel of the sky, how the undying flames of icon lamps glimmered all around us, like furtive, wistful lights scattered among the graves. Walking behind her, I looked at the small stars her new, black boots left in the snow, and a great tenderness welled up inside me: she felt it too, and turned.

"It's true, you really do love me," she said, shaking her head in quiet amazement.

We paused at the graves of Ertel and Chekhov. She stood for a long time, looking at Chekhov's headstone, holding her muff low, her hands clasped together inside it.

"The Moscow Art Theatre and a saccharine Russian style," she said, shrugging her shoulders. "What an irritating mix."

It began to grow dark and cold. We slowly left through the gates and found Fyodor, my driver, waiting patiently nearby with the sleigh.

"Let's drive around a little more," she said. "And then go to Yegorov's for our last *blini*. We'll take it slowly, though, all right Fyodor?"

"As you wish."

"Somewhere in Ordynka there's a house where Griboyedov lived. Let's go and look for it."

And so we went for some reason to Ordynka, where we drove for a long time along alleys that looked onto private gardens and backyards. We even came to Griboyedov Alley, but not a single passerby could point us to the house in which he'd lived. What did Griboyedov mean to them? It had grown completely dark a long time ago, and the lights of the rooms that we glimpsed through the trees glowed pink behind rime-covered glass.

"There's an abbey near here too," she said. "Marfo-Mariinskaya. . . ."

I laughed. "Again to the nunnery?"

"No, I just . . ."

The first floor of Yegorov's Inn at Okhotny Ryad was as hot as a sauna and completely packed with rough-looking cabbies wearing bulky coats as they cut into big stacks of *blini* drenched in butter and sour cream. The second floor was warm as well; there, old-style merchants ate their *blini* with large-grained caviar and cold champagne. We passed into the back and sat on a black leather couch before a long table; in one corner of the room an icon lamp hung before the blackened image of *The Virgin with Three Arms*. A delicate frost had gathered in the slight down above her lip, and a soft pink flush had risen in her amber cheeks; her pupils seemed to merge completely with the black rings of her irises. I couldn't take my ecstatic eyes from her.

"Just right," she said, drawing a handkerchief from her perfumed muff. "Completely savage *mouzhiki* downstairs, while here we have *blini* with champagne and *The Virgin with Three Arms*. Three Arms! It's India! You, my dear friend from the nobility—you cannot begin to understand this city the way I do."

"I can, and I do," I said. "And now let's order an *obed silen*."

"What's that?—'*silen*'?"

"'Mighty'—a 'mighty feast.' Don't you know that? It's Old Church Slavonic: 'So spake Gyurgy . . .'"

"Oh, that's nice—'Gyurgy . . .'"

"Yes, Prince Yury Dolgoruky—Gyurgy. 'So spake Gyurgy to Prince Svyatoslav: "Come to me, brother, in Moscow," and he commanded that they prepare an *obed silen*—a mighty feast.'"

"Oh, that's lovely. . . . Where can you hear words like that now? And you can find that old Rus only in a few monasteries in the north. And in the church songs. I went to Zachatyevsky Monastery the other day. You wouldn't believe how beautifully they sing there! It's breathtaking! And it's even better at Chudov. I went there every day during Holy Week last year. Oh, it was lovely. Puddles everywhere, the air already soft—already filled with spring. There's something tender and sad that enters your soul. And you sense all the time that this is your homeland—this is its ancient past. . . . All day the cathedral doors stand open; all day ordinary people come in and out; all day the services continue. . . . Oh, I'll put on the veil one day! I'll enter a convent in the middle of nowhere—some place deep in the heart of Vologda or Vyatka! . . ."

I wanted to tell her that then I too would enter a cloister—or slit someone's throat in order to be shipped away to Sakhalin. Distracted by the sudden surge of emotion her words brought on, I forgot where we were and started to light a cigarette—but the waiter came immediately.

"I'm very sorry, sir, but there's no smoking here," he said respectfully. He wore a white shirt and white pants, belted with a bright red braid. "What would you like with your *blini*?" he asked, and launched into a complicated list with distinct diffidence: "Herb vodka? Caviar? Salmon? We have an unusually good sherry to go with the fish stew, and for the cod. . . ."

"Sherry for the cod as well," she interjected, delighting me with this lighthearted banter, which she kept up all evening. I listened to her happily, not caring what she said. "I love Russian chronicles and legends," she continued, a quiet light playing in her eyes. "In fact, I'm rereading my particular favorites until I've learned them by heart: 'There once stood on Russian soil a city known as Murom. Over it reigned a prince named Pavel, a follower of God. The devil sent a winged serpent to tempt his wife with fornication. And as a man most alluring did the serpent come to her. . . .'"

I opened my eyes wide with mock horror. "Oh, how terrible!"

She ignored me and continued: "God tested her that way. 'And when the time of her passing came, that prince and his wife beseeched God to take them on the same day. Together they agreed to lie in one grave. They deemed that two chambers be carved in one tomb. They put on the clothes of the cloistered. . . .' "

Again my idle listening turned to sharp surprise, even alarm—what was going on with her?

I took her home that night sometime after ten, an extraordinarily early hour for us. As we parted, she suddenly called out from the steps to her house:

"Wait, wait. Don't come before ten tomorrow. There's an actors' party at the Art Theatre."

I was already sitting in the sleigh again. "And so? You mean—you want to go to a *kapustnik?*"

"Yes."

"But you've always said there's nothing more vulgar or more stupid than those actors getting drunk and acting like fools on stage. . . ."

"There isn't. But I want to go all the same."

I shook my head to myself: What caprice this city breeds! But I called out cheerfully in English: "All right."

At ten o'clock the next evening I took the elevator to her apartment, opened the door with my key, and paused in the darkened foyer: it was surprisingly bright in the rooms before me. Everything was lit: the chandeliers, the candelabra on the sides of the mirror, the tall lamp with the cloth shade that stood behind the ottoman. I could hear the beginning of the "Moonlight Sonata" being played on the piano—each slow, invocatory note unfolding with the mystic logic of a sleepwalker's steps, each growing stronger, almost overwhelming in its sorrow and its joy. I closed the foyer door heavily behind me: the music broke off and I heard the rustling of a dress. When I entered the room she was standing very straight and somewhat theatrically beside the piano in a black velvet dress that made her look even more slender than usual. She was radiant in all her finery, with her pitch black hair elaborately arranged, with the dark amber of her arms and shoulders and the delicate, full beginning of her breasts exposed, with the fractured light of diamond earrings playing on her lightly powdered cheeks—with the coal black velvet of her eyes, with the deep velvet-red of her mouth. Fine glossy braids hung from her temples, curling up toward her eyes like the hair of exotic, eastern beauties in those simplistic prints so popular among the masses.

"If I were a singer on stage," she said, looking at my dazed expression, "this is how I'd answer the applause—a friendly smile, a light bow to the right and to the left, then to the balcony and the floor. . . . And at the same time I'd very carefully, very discreetly be using my foot to slide the train of my dress back a safe distance—to make sure I didn't step on it. . . ."

At the *kapustnik* she smoked a great deal and steadily sipped champagne, watching intently as the players on stage shouted and sang in little outbursts while performing something supposedly Parisian, and Stanislavsky, with his white hair and black eyebrows and big frame, performed a can-can with Moskvin, who was stocky and wore a pince-nez on his big washtub face: together they pretended to struggle desperately with the dance, eliciting loud, raucous laughter from the audience as they fell back from the stage. Pale from drink, Kachalov approached us with a wine glass in his hand. A lock of his Belarus hair fell across his forehead, which was damp with large beads of sweat.

"Queen Maiden Shamakhanskaya! Tsarina! To your health," he said in his low-pitched actor's voice, looking at her with an affected expression of gloom and greedy desire. She slowly smiled and touched glasses with him. He took her hand and almost toppled over as he lurched drunkenly toward her, then righted himself and shot a glance at me. "Who's this little beauty?" he said, clenching his teeth. "I can't stand him!"

[83]

A barrel organ began to wheeze and whistle, then broke into the driving rhythms of a polka: Sulerzhitsky came gliding through the crowd toward us, laughing and hurrying somewhere as always. He bent his short body low before her, like an obsequious little merchant at an outdoor market.

"Permit me to invite you to dance the polka," he mumbled hurriedly. Smiling, she rose and went with him, her diamond earrings, her dark arms and bare shoulders gleaming in the lights. Together they moved among the tables, where people clapped their hands or stared with rapt attention as she stepped lightly to the music's rhythm, and he threw back his head to shout like a bleating goat: "Come, come, my friend—it's time to dance the polka!"

Sometime after two she rose and put her hand over her eyes. As we dressed for the sleigh ride home, she looked at my beaver-skin hat, stroked the fur collar of my coat.

"Of course, you are a beauty. Kachalov's right," she said as she moved toward the exit, her voice equally serious and lighthearted. "'And as a man most alluring did the serpent come to her. . . .'"

During the ride home she sat without speaking, hiding her face as we drove into a bright stream of snow blowing through the moonlight. "Like some kind of luminous skull," she said later, watching the half-moon plunge in and out of the clouds above the Kremlin. When the bells in Spasskaya Tower struck three, she spoke again:

"What an ancient sound. Some kind of tin and cast iron. They rang with the same sound when it was three o'clock in the fifteenth century. In Florence the bells sound exactly the same—they always reminded me of Moscow there. . . ."

When Fyodor stopped before her house, she said lifelessly: "Let him go. . . ."

I was stunned—she never allowed me upstairs at night.

"I'll walk home, Fyodor," I said, bewildered.

Without speaking we rode the elevator to her floor, entered the silence and dark warmth of her apartment, where little hammers tapped inside the radiators. I took off her snow-slick coat, and she cast into my hands the wet down shawl she'd used to cover her hair, then walked quickly to the bedroom, her silk slip rustling. I took off my coat and hat, went into the living room, and sat down on the ottoman, my heart going still, as if I'd come to the edge of an abyss. I could hear her every step through the open doors to the bedroom, where a light was burning—could hear her dress catching on her hairpins as she slid it over her head. . . . I got up and went toward the doors. Wearing only swan's-down slippers, she stood before the pier glass with her back to me, running a tortoiseshell comb through the long, black strands of hair that fell along her face.

"And all that time he kept complaining. Kept saying that I don't think of him enough," she said, dropping the comb on the table, tossing back her hair. "No, I thought of him," she said, and turned to me. . . .

I felt her moving at dawn and opened my eyes: she was staring fixedly at me. I raised myself up from the warmth of her body and the bed. She leaned closer.

"This evening I'm leaving for Tver," she said in a quiet, even voice. "God only knows for how long. . . ." She laid her cheek against mine. I felt the dampness of her lashes as she blinked.

"I'll write everything as soon as I arrive. I'll write everything about the future. But forgive me, I need to be alone now. I'm very tired. . . ." She laid her head back on the pillow.

Timidly I kissed her hair; carefully I dressed—and quietly stepped out into the stairwell, already bathed in pale sunlight. I walked in fresh, damp snow. The storm from last night had already passed, and now everything was calm. I could see far into the distance along the streets; the scent of the new snow mixed with the smell of baking from the nearby shops. I walked as far as Iverskaya Chapel: the heat inside was heavy, almost overpowering, and the candles blazed like banked fires before the icons. I knelt in the melting snow that had been tracked inside, knelt in the crowd of beggars and old women, removed my hat. . . . Someone reached out to my shoulder and I turned: a miserable old woman was staring at me, crying out of pity.

"No, no—you must not grieve this way," she said, her face contorted by her weeping. "Such black grieving is a sin. A sin!"

The brief letter I received some two weeks later was tender but unyielding in its request that I wait for her no longer—and make no attempt to find or see her. "I won't be coming back to Moscow. For now I'll serve as a lay sister, then, perhaps, put on the veil. . . . May God give you the strength to make no answer to this letter. It's pointless to intensify this suffering, to prolong our torture. . . ."

I complied with her request. I lost myself for a long time in the most squalid bars and taverns—drinking each day, letting myself sink deeper and deeper each day. And then, slowly, bit by bit, hopelessly, indifferently, I began to recover. Almost two years had passed since that Cleansing Monday, that first day of the Great Fast.

In 1914, just before the New Year, there was another quiet, sunny evening—much like that evening I cannot forget. My driver took me to the Kremlin. There I went inside Arkhangelsky Cathedral. It was empty; I stood for a long time without praying in the twilight, stood and looked at the dull gleam of the old gold in the iconostasis, the stone slabs above the graves of Moscow tsars: it seemed that I was waiting for something in the silence—that silence which occurs only in an empty church, when you're afraid to breathe. I climbed back into my sleigh, told the driver to continue at a walk to Ordynka—and slowly I followed the same little side streets as before, passing gardens and backyards beneath lit windows, traveling an alley named for Griboyedov while I wept and wept. . . .

At Ordynka I stopped the driver near the gate to Marfo-Mariin-skaya Abbey. Black carriages stood in the courtyard; beyond them I could see the open doors of the small, brightly lit church, from which the singing of a female choir drifted mournfully into the open air. For some reason I felt an urge to go inside immediately. The groundskeeper blocked my way at the gate.

"It's closed, sir," he said in a soft, imploring voice.

"What do you mean 'closed'? The church is closed?"

"Well, you can go inside, sir, of course, but I'm begging you not to. Not now. The Grand Duchess Elzavet Fyodorovna is there, sir, with Grand Duke Mitry Palych. . . ."

I stuck a ruble in his hand; he sighed as if stricken with grief, and let me pass. But as I entered the courtyard, a procession carrying icons and holy banners came from the church, followed by the duchess, who wore long white robes and a white veil with a golden cross sewn into its front. Tall, thin-featured, she carried a large candle and walked slowly, devoutly, with lowered eyes. Behind her stretched a long row of women identically dressed in white, singing as they walked, their faces illuminated by the candles they held. I couldn't tell if they were nuns or women of the laity, and I didn't know where they were going. But for some reason I watched carefully as they passed. And suddenly, near the middle of that line, one of them raised her head in its white veil as she walked. Shielding the flame of her candle with one hand, she aimed her dark eyes into the darkness, as if staring straight at me. . . . What could she see in the darkness? How could she have felt my presence there? I turned. I went quietly back through the gate.

[*May 12, 1944*]

The Elagin Affair

I T WAS a strange and terrible affair. Inexplicable. Confounding. . . .
At first, perhaps, it seems simple—like the plot of a cheap paper-
back (everyone in town referred to it this way). But a slight shift in
perspective—and suddenly it turns elusive, recondite—resists all
easy answers. Lends itself, almost, to the writing of real literature. . . .

The defense attorney put it well in court:

"There seems to be no room for me to argue with the prosecu-
tion in this case," he said in his opening statement. "For the defendant has already admitted his guilt, and almost everyone in this hall
finds his crime and his character—like that of his supposedly un-
willing victim—far too common and too shallow to warrant careful
examination or serious debate. But such opinions are completely
wrong, for they take into account only outward appearances. There
is a great deal to argue about here. There are many, many reasons
why we ought to pause, reflect, debate. . . ."

And he continued:

"Let us suppose that my sole purpose is to gain leniency for the accused. Were this the case, there would be relatively little I could say. Our legal system offers no guidelines for a judge to follow in a case like this. Instead it grants that judge great leeway in his rulings. It assumes that his conscience, his informed opinion, and his intelligence will lead him to identify the proper legal code by which to treat the crime at hand. . . . Obviously, then, if my goal were simple leniency, I would appeal to the court's reason and its conscience; I would try to sway its opinion by focusing all attention on the defendant's most positive qualities. I would emphasize those circumstances that mitigate his guilt; I would persistently arouse feelings of benevolence toward my client until the court dismissed at least one element of the case against him—the charge of conscious, premeditated evil. But could I even then avoid an argument with the prosecutor, who has labeled my client as nothing more and nothing less that a 'predatory criminal'? Everything is subject to interpretation. All events may be shaded one way or another, all statements set in a different key, all facts presented in a different light. And what do we find in this case? We find that the prosecutor and I look differently upon its every feature. We find there's not a single detail he and I can describe or elucidate without drastic disagreement. Every minute I must say to him, 'It wasn't so,' and that phrase—'it wasn't so, it wasn't so'—is more important than anything else in this case: it is the heart of the matter before us."

It had a terrible beginning, this strange affair.

It was the nineteenth of June of last year. Early morning, sometime after five. The dining room of Hussar Captain Likharyov had grown stuffy, hot and dry in the strong summer sun that already blanketed the city, but it was still quiet, for the captain's quarters were part of a Hussar barracks in the suburbs. The captain, taking full advantage of his youth amid this quietude, was sound asleep. On a nearby table stood various bottles of liquor and cups of cold,

IVAN BUNIN

unfinished coffee. A staff captain, Count Koshits, was sleeping in
the adjoining guest room, and farther on, in the study, dozed Cornet Sevsky. All in all, a very ordinary morning. But as is so often the
case when something extraordinary occurs amid the everyday, this
quotidian scene would make even more terrible, fantastic, and surprising those events that were about to unfold in the early morning
of June 19 in the apartment of Hussar Captain Likharyov. In the
midst of the sheer morning silence, a bell suddenly rang in the
foyer, and the captain's orderly ran to open the front door, his bare
feet padding lightly, cautiously across the floor. A deliberately loud
voice rang out:

"Is he home?"

The arriving visitor came inside with the same deliberate
racket. There was a particular recklessness in the way he flung open
the dining room door, a marked audacity to the chinking of his
spurs, the scraping of his boot heels. Astounded and still half asleep,
the captain raised his head from his pillow: before him stood a colleague from the regiment, Cornet Elagin—a small, frail man with
red hair and freckles. His legs were bowed and unusually thin, and
his boots revealed a certain foppishness, which Elagin himself often
called his "most essential" weakness. He quickly removed his officer's coat and threw it on a chair.

"Here, take my stripes," he said loudly as he crossed the room
and collapsed onto a couch that stood against the wall, then put his
hands behind his head.

"Wait, hold on," muttered the captain as he watched Elagin,
his eyes wide with surprise. "Where did you come from? What's
wrong?"

"I killed Manya," said Elagin.

"Are you drunk? Who's Manya?" asked the captain.

"Mariya Iosifovna Sosnovskaya, the actress."

The captain lowered his feet to the floor. "What? You're joking, right?"

"Alas, no. Sadly, I'm not joking in the least. But then, that might be for the best."

"Who's there? What's going on?" shouted the count from the living room.

Elagin stretched out one foot and lightly kicked the door open. "Don't shout," he said. "It's me—Elagin. I shot Manya."

"What?" said the count. He fell silent for a moment, then burst into laughter. "Of course—yes, that's good. Very funny! You had me for a second," he called out happily. "We'll forgive you this time, as we needed to be woken up. Otherwise I'm sure we would have overslept—we were up until three again last night, fooling around."

"I give you my word that I killed her," Elagin said again insistently.

"You're lying, brother—lying!" shouted the captain, picking up his socks. "You had me worried for a moment. I thought that something really happened. . . . Yefrem—tea!"

Elagin thrust his hand into his pocket, pulled out a small key, and deftly tossed it over his shoulder onto the table. "Go and see for yourselves."

In court the prosecutor revisited this scene many times, speaking at length of the horror and cynicism it revealed, like many other moments in Elagin's drama. He forgot, however, that on the morning in question, only a few more moments would pass before the captain was stunned by Elagin's appearance—the "supernatural" pallor of his skin, something "inhuman," as he later put it, in the cornet's eyes.

II

Here, then, are the events as they unfolded on the morning of June 19 last year.

Half an hour after Elagin's declaration, Count Koshits and Cornet Sevsky were already standing at the entrance to Sosnovskaya's house. There was no joking anymore.

They'd made their driver race through the streets and had leapt headlong from the cab as it stopped, then tried to jam Elagin's key into the lock while frantically ringing the front bell. But the key did not fit, and everything beyond the door was silent. Losing patience, they hurried to the courtyard where they found the yardman; he ran from the servants' entrance to the kitchen, then returned and reported that, according to the maid, Sosnovskaya did not sleep at home last night, having left earlier in the evening with some sort of package in her hands. The count and the cornet were at a loss: what to do in light of such news? They paused to think; they shrugged their shoulders; and then they took a cab to the police station, insisting that the yardman come as well. From the station they called Captain Likharyov.

"Soon I'll be a raving lunatic because of this fool!" he shouted into the receiver. "He forgot to mention that you shouldn't go to Sosnovskaya's at all. There's another place—an apartment where they had their trysts. Fourteen Starogradskaya. Do you hear me?—house fourteen, Starogradskaya. It looks like some kind of Parisian call girl's house. The door to their rooms opens right onto the street."

They galloped off to Starogradskaya.

The yardman rode beside the cabby on the driver's box while a policeman joined the officers inside the carriage, sitting across from them with an air of quiet independence. The day was already hot, the streets crowded and noisy. It seemed unimaginable that on such a sunny, lively day someone could be lying dead somewhere. And it boggled the mind to think that twenty-two-year-old Sashka Elagin had done this. How could he have brought himself to murder? Why did he kill her? How? None of it made the slightest sense, and all of these questions were impossible to answer.

When they finally stopped before an old, unpleasant-looking, two-story house on Starogradskaya, the count and the cornet, in their words, "fell into complete despair." Was *that* really here? Was it really necessary that they go to see it—though, of course, it pulled inexorably; it urged one to look. . . . The policeman's mood, on the other hand, immediately improved as he assumed the role of a strict and self-assured professional. "The key, please," he said in a cold, firm voice. The officers hurried to relinquish it, deferential as the yardman would have been. The front of the house was divided by a gate, beyond which they could see a small courtyard where a sapling grew. Its green leaves seemed unnaturally bright, perhaps because of the dark grey walls of stone surrounding it. To the right of the gate stood the door about which they'd been told—that secret door onto the street, that door they had to open. The policeman frowned and inserted the key: the door swung back, and the count and the cornet saw what seemed to be a pitch black corridor. As if guided by some sixth sense, the policeman swept his hand along the wall and threw a switch: the lights came on in a narrow room, in the depths of which they found a small table between two chairs, a few plates of uneaten fruit and wildfowl. But something even gloomier appeared before them as they walked into those quarters: on the right-hand side of the corridor they discovered a small entranceway into a neighboring room. It too was dark, illuminated only by a small lamp that hung from the ceiling and cast a morbid, opalescent light beneath a huge umbrella of black silk. Every wall of that windowless and muffled room was also draped in black from top to bottom. In its farthest recess stood a wide, low, Turkish couch—and there a woman of rare beauty lay, wearing nothing but a camisole, her lips and eyes half open, her head drooping to her chest, her arms stretched along her sides and her legs slightly parted, her body white.

They stopped and froze before her.

III

The dead woman's beauty was extraordinary in the degree to which it satisfied all those demands a fashionable artist might contrive for a portrait of feminine perfection. She had all the attributes such a picture would require: a well-proportioned figure and clear, light skin; graceful legs; thick, full hair; a refined nose and delicate cheeks; a tender mouth expressing innocence and artless charm. And now, all of it was dead; all of it was turning blank and dull as stone: her beauty only made the dead woman more terrible. Her hair was perfectly arranged, as if she'd soon be going to a ball. Her head was raised by a pillow resting on the couch's arm, and her chin lightly touched her chest, giving her face and her vacant, half-closed eyes a slightly puzzled, preoccupied expression. Everything in the room was strangely lit by the opal lamp that hung from the ceiling, set far into the depths of that huge, black umbrella which spread above the corpse like some strange bird of prey with outstretched, membranous wings.

Even the policeman was shaken by this scene, but he and his companions soon began a tentative investigation of the crime scene.

The dead woman's beautiful and naked arms were extended straight along her sides. Two of Elagin's calling cards lay on her chest, which was covered only by a lacy shirt; a cavalry sword had been placed next to her legs, and now it seemed exceedingly crude beside that bare and tender feminine flesh. The count wanted to pick it up in order to remove the scabbard and check the blade for blood, but the policeman held him back.

"Oh yes, of course, of course," the count whispered. "We can't touch anything yet. But I'm surprised that I don't see any blood—indeed, I don't see any traces of the crime at all. Poisoning apparently?"

"Be patient," the policeman said reprovingly. "We will have to wait for the doctor and the investigator. But it does look like poisoning. . . ."

This was certainly the case. There was no blood to be seen anywhere—none on the floor or the couch, and none on the victim's body or her camisole. In an armchair near the couch, a pair of women's underwear and a peignoir lay on top of a light blue shirt with a pearly sheen, a skirt of very fine, dark grey material, and a woman's grey silk coat. All these items had been cast off carelessly, but none was soiled with a single drop of blood. The idea of poisoning was further confirmed by evidence discovered on a small ledge that jutted out from the wall above the couch: there, among champagne bottles and corks, candle stubs and hairpins, among scraps of paper that had been covered with words and torn to shreds—there they discovered a glass of unfinished porter and a small vial with a white label, where the menacing words "Op. Pulv." were written in black ink.

But just as the policeman, the count, and the cornet had each finished reading these Latin abbreviations, a carriage with the doctor and the investigator could be heard arriving at the house, and a few minutes later it turned out that Elagin had spoken the truth: Sosnovskaya had in fact been killed with a revolver. There were no specks of blood on the camisole, but underneath it, near the victim's heart, they uncovered a crimson spot, in the middle of which thin dark blood oozed from a circular wound with burnt edges. A wadded handkerchief had been used to cover the wound and stanch the flow of blood.

What more did the medical examination bring to light? Not much: the right lung of the deceased showed traces of tuberculosis; the gun was fired at point-blank range, and death was instantaneous, although the victim might have managed to utter a short phrase after the trigger had been pulled; there had been no struggle between the killer and his victim; she had drunk champagne and ingested a small quantity (not sufficient to cause poisoning) of opium mixed with porter; and, finally, she had engaged in sexual relations on the fateful night of her death.

But why had that man murdered her? In answer to this question, Elagin stubbornly insisted that both he and Sosnovskaya had "fallen into tragedy," that they could see no escape other than death, and that he had only been fulfilling her command when he took his victim's life. But notes written by the deceased shortly before her death flatly contradicted this statement. After all, on Sosnovskaya's chest lay two of Elagin's calling cards—and both of them bore messages written by her hand in Polish (almost illiterate Polish, it must be noted). One read:

"To General Konovnitsyn, chair of the theatre board of directors: My friend! I thank you for your noble friendship of the past several years and send you my final greetings. I ask that all proceeds from my last performances be sent to my mother."

The other:

"In killing me, this man has acted justly. Mother—my poor, unhappy mother! I will not ask for your forgiveness as I did not choose to die. Mother, we will see each other there, above. I can feel it—this is my last moment."

Before her death, Sosnovskaya wrote several other notes on Elagin's cards—they were scattered on the ledge above the couch, painstakingly torn into pieces. Later reassembled, they revealed the following messages:

"This man demands my death and his. . . . I will not leave alive."

"My final hour has come. . . . Dear God, do not leave me. . . . My last thought—my mother, the sanctity of art."

"The abyss! The abyss! This man is my fate. God save me, God help me."

And finally, most puzzling of all:

"*Quand même pour toujours.*"

All these notes—both those found lying intact on Sosnovskaya's chest and those discovered in shreds on the ledge above her—seemed to contradict Elagin's claims. But they only *seemed* to do so. For why were the two notes that lay on Sosnovskaya's chest not also torn to pieces, particularly as they bore such phrases as "I did not choose to die," words clearly fatal for Elagin? Not only did Elagin fail to destroy or remove these cards, he actually placed them in the most prominent place possible, for who else could have set them on Sosnovskaya's chest? It's certainly possible that his haste might have caused him to forget to destroy the cards. But how could his haste cause him to place those cards with all their damning statements upon his victim's chest? And was he truly in a hurry? Evidently not, for he stanched the bullet hole with a handkerchief, carefully arranged the body, and covered it with a camisole—then dressed and washed. No, here the prosecutor was correct—this act was not performed in haste.

IV

"There are two basic categories of criminal," the prosecutor told the court. "In the first we find those whom science terms as 'temporarily insane': they are ultimately criminals by accident; their evil acts are the end result of a tragic confluence of events and random irritants. The second category includes those who commit their crimes deliberately, following a malicious, premeditated plan: these are natural-born enemies of social order and society. They are predatory criminals. In which category should we place the man who sits before us now? He belongs, of course, to the second. There can be no doubt that he's a predator. He's led an idle, reckless life, and it's destroyed his sense of right and wrong, led him to commit this crime."

This tirade was quite peculiar (though it reflected the opinion of almost everyone in town), particularly because Elagin sat with his hand over his face throughout the trial, as if trying to conceal himself from the public while answering the questions put to him in a quiet but agitated voice so filled with sorrow and temerity that one's soul ached from the sound. On one point, though, the prosecutor was utterly correct: the defendant was no ordinary criminal, and he'd never come close to a state of "temporary insanity."

The prosecutor posed two questions: first, was the crime committed in a fit of passion, and, second, could it possibly be viewed as some form of accidental manslaughter? He answered both questions with absolute certainty: no.

"No," he said in answer to the first, "there could be no talk about a fit of passion, first and foremost for the simple reason that such fits last for only a few minutes—never hours. And what could have triggered such a fit in Elagin?"

To answer the second question the prosecutor posed several smaller questions to himself, each of which he immediately rejected, sometimes in a mocking tone:

"Did Elagin drink more than usual on that fateful day? No, he drank a great deal every day, and this particular day was no exception.

"Was the defendant then, and is he now, in good health? I subscribe to the opinion of those doctors who examined him: the defendant is perfectly healthy but completely unable to exercise even a modicum of self-restraint.

"Allowing that the defendant truly loved the victim, could it be that the impossibility of marriage produced in him a state of temporary insanity? No, for we know precisely that the defendant never concerned himself with marriage and never took the slightest step toward arranging such a union."

And further:

"Could not Sosnovskaya's plan to go abroad have brought him to a state of madness? No, for he'd learned long ago of her planned departure.

"Then perhaps the fear that her departure would bring an end to their relationship? Again no, for they had talked of a permanent separation many times before that night. What then could have made him lose his senses? The conversations about death? The strange milieu of the room—its, how shall I put it, hallucinatory effects? The overall oppressive atmosphere that filled that room and pervaded the entire, morbid night? But talk about death could not have been new for Elagin—he had such conversations with his lover constantly, and they, of course, had long ago grown dull for him. And it's quite comical to speak of hallucinations. For they must have passed quite quickly, given way to far more prosaic matters—dinner, the leftovers on the table, bottles, and, forgive me, chamber pots. . . .

"Elagin ate, drank, satisfied his bodily demands, went into the next room for a glass of wine, a knife to sharpen a pencil. . . ."

And the prosecutor concluded:

"We need not deliberate long in order to determine whether the murder Elagin committed was in fact the fulfillment of his victim's wishes. For, in order to decide that question, we must only weigh Elagin's groundless assertions that Sosnovskaya asked him to kill her against the note that Sosnovskaya herself wrote—a note containing words that are disastrous for Elagin: 'I did not choose to die.'"

V

One could take issue with many of the details of the prosecutor's speech. "The defendant is completely healthy." But where lies the border between illness and health, normality and abnormality? "The defendant never concerned himself with marriage, and never took the slightest step toward arranging such a union." But clearly he never took such a step because he was so utterly convinced of its futility. And further, is it really true that love and marriage are so closely linked? Would Elagin have found peace in marriage with Sosnovskaya? Would all the tragedy inherent to their love have ended if they'd married? And isn't it well known that a tendency to avoid marriage runs through every strong, uncommon kind of love?

But all this, I repeat, is a matter of details. The prosecutor was essentially correct: there was no fit of passion.

He continued: "Expert medical opinion has concluded that Elagin was 'in all likelihood' calm rather than agitated or insane at the time of the crime. I would maintain that he was not merely calm but surprisingly so. This becomes quite obvious when one considers the carefully cleaned room where the crime was committed, and where Elagin remained long after Sosnovskaya's murder. And then there is the testimony of the witness Yaroshenko, who saw how calmly Elagin left the apartment, how carefully, how unhurriedly he locked it with his key. And finally let us remember Elagin's behavior during his visit to Captain Likharyov's quarters. His response, for example, to Cornet Sevsky, who urged him to 'come to his senses' and remember if perhaps Sosnovskaya had shot herself. 'No, brother,' Elagin said to him. 'I remember everything *perfectly*'—and then he proceeded to describe in detail how he himself fired the shot. The witness Budberg stated that Elagin 'gave him a disturbing shock' by 'calmly drinking tea after his confession.' The witness Fokht was even more astounded. 'Sir Staff Captain,' Elagin said to him sarcastically, 'I hope you'll let me skip our drills today.' 'It was so shocking,' said Fokht, 'that Cornet Sevsky could not contain himself and began to weep.'

"True, there was a moment when Elagin also wept. The captain had gone to the regiment commander to receive orders concerning the defendant's fate. When he returned, the captain glanced at Fokht, and seeing their expressions Elagin understood that he was no longer an officer. Then he wept," the prosecutor concluded, "only then!"

Of course this statement too is quite strange, for who is not familiar with the way a random detail can shake a person out of semiconsciousness, plunge him from a stupor into grief? Something wholly insignificant and accidental falls into your field of vision, and suddenly you realize all the happiness of your previous life, all the hopelessness and horror of your present situation. And in Elagin's case it was no small fact that brought this realization: for ten generations his family had served. He was practically born an officer. And now, *voilà*—it's over. Moreover this loss occurred because the one person whom he truly loved more than his own life no longer existed. And he himself had committed this monstrous act!

But this too is a matter of mere details. The central fact remains: there was no period of "temporary insanity." What then led to the murder? The prosecutor himself recognized that "in order to make sense of this dark business, we must first examine Sosnovskaya and Elagin as individuals, then attempt to clarify their relationship." He proceeded to declare with great conviction that "these individuals were intimate despite the fact that they had not the slightest thing in common."

Is that true? Here lies the real heart of the matter.

VI

In describing Elagin I would first mention his age—twenty-two, a frightening and fateful age that determines one's entire future. Usually at this time one experiences what science calls "sexual fruition," and which in life is known as "first love." This first love is often viewed as poetic but insignificant. It's known to foster tragedies and upheaval, but no one ever thinks that such distress is linked to something deeper, something more complex than the anxiety and pain we call devotion to another. But in fact people at these moments live through something they cannot understand. A terrible blooming. A savage opening and laying bare, a solemn reckoning of all that lies between the sexes. If I were the defense attorney, I would ask the judge to note Elagin's age with precisely that point in mind, and I would urge him to recognize that the young man sitting before him was a striking illustration of the dynamic I'd described. "A young Hussar gone mad from fast living," the prosecutor said, repeating a widely held view of Elagin. To support this claim he cited the testimony of an actor named Lisovsky, who described how Elagin came to the theatre as the cast was assembling for rehearsal, and Sosnovskaya, seeing Elagin, quickly stepped behind Lisovsky with the hurried words "Help me hide from him!" "I stood there so she could keep out of sight," Lisovsky testified, "and that little hussar, who was full of wine, he just stops and spreads his legs apart, stands there like a man who's stunned or half crazy, dumbfounded: 'Where'd Sosnovskaya go?!'"

It's true of course, he was out of his mind. But what brought him to this state? Was it really idle, reckless living?

Elagin came from a wealthy, high-born family. He lost his mother (who lived, it should be noted, in a state of almost constant exaltation) while still very young, and the fear that pervaded all his youth and adolescence had long ago estranged him from his father, a severe, strict man. The prosecutor described not only Elagin's moral character but also his physical appearance with cruel abandon:

"Our hero might have cut an impressive figure when he had a uniform to wear. But look at him now, with no adornments to dress him up. He certainly does not bring Othello to mind, sitting here in a black frock coat. Indeed, we have before us just a short young man with sloped shoulders, a sparse moustache, and an utterly vacant expression on his face. We have before us a man whose physical appearance is marked by atrophy and listlessness, a weakling who is paralyzed by fear in one set of circumstances—when, for instance, he must interact with his father—and filled with bravado in another, when, freed from his father's gaze, he loses all sense of restraint, counts on never being caught or punished."

What can one say to this? There is some truth of course in the prosecutor's crude characterization of Elagin. But listening to it, I wondered at the fact that one could speak with such offhandedness about those terribly complex and tragic forces of heredity that so sharply mark some people's lives and personalities. And as I listened further, I realized that the truth contained in the prosecutor's words was actually quite small. Yes, Elagin did grow up in trepidation of his father. But when it's experienced before one's parents, such trepidation should never be confused with cowardice, especially if the man suffering this fear is one who feels acutely all the weight of those hereditary ties that bind him to his father, his grandfather, and all his other ancestors. To be sure, Elagin lacked the classic physical appearance of a hussar, but it is in this deficiency that I find evidence of his extraordinary character. And so I would say to the prosecutor, "Look more carefully at this red-haired man with skinny legs and sloped shoulders, look more carefully and you'll be startled to discover the seriousness of this freckled face, the depth of these small, green eyes that so carefully avoid our own. And then, consider once again his atrophied physique, his weakness: on the day of the murder he drilled with his regiment from early morning. At breakfast he drank six shots of vodka, a bottle of champagne, and two cognacs—and he stayed almost completely sober!"

VII

The testimony of Elagin's fellow officers contrasted sharply with the general public's poor opinion of the defendant. Indeed, these officers portrayed Elagin in only the most positive light. Here for example is the squadron commander's opinion:

"Elagin gained the respect of his fellow officers soon after joining the regiment, and he was always extremely kind, considerate, and fair with the lower ranks. His character in my opinion had only one peculiarity—a certain unevenness that never expressed itself in any unpleasant way but often caused his moods to shift sharply and abruptly from happiness to melancholy, from loquaciousness to silence, from great self-confidence to despair about his worth and fate."

And then there is the view of Captain Likharyov:

"Elagin was always a kind and good fellow officer, but he had some eccentricities. At one moment he might be modest and withdrawn, and then, suddenly, a kind of bravado would seize him. After confessing his crime, Elagin stayed in my quarters while Sevsky and Koshits went to check on Sosnovskaya. While we waited, he either wept inconsolably or laughed with bitter raucousness. When they led him away to detainment, Elagin looked at us with a savage smile and asked what tailor he should go to for civilian clothes."

Then there is the testimony of Count Koshits:

"Elagin's disposition was generally happy and affectionate. He was a sensitive young man, high strung and impressionable, even prone to fits of exaltation. Music and the theatre had a particularly strong effect on him, often moving him to tears. He himself had an unusual talent for music. He could play almost any instrument. . . ."

All the other witnesses said relatively the same things:

"A man who was consumed by his passions while at the same time always searching for some other, still more meaningful, unique experience."

"On drinking bouts with his comrades, he was usually cheerful and upbeat, a little tedious at times, but always amiable. He drank more champagne than anyone in the regiment and shared it with whoever was at hand. . . . He did everything he could to conceal his feelings for Sosnovskaya, but once his relationship with her began, Elagin changed markedly, often appearing sad and preoccupied. On several occasions he spoke of his resolve to end his life in suicide."

Such was the testimony of those who lived most closely to Elagin. Where then, I wondered as I sat in the courthouse, has the prosecutor found so much black paint for his portrait? Does he have other witnesses to call? But no, there were no other witnesses. One had to conclude, therefore, that all the prosecutor's sinister impressions stemmed from his understanding of "golden youth" in general and his reading of a letter that Elagin wrote to a friend in Kishinyov. It was the only letter in the court's possession, and in it Elagin spoke of his life with casual disregard:

"I have come, brother, to a state of complete indifference: everything, absolutely everything's the same. All's fine today—so give your thanks to God. And what will tomorrow bring? Forget about it while you can. After all, we're always wiser in the morning than at night. I've earned myself a stellar reputation here—first-class drunk and village fool. Almost everyone in town has heard of me."

The prosecutor linked this critical self-assessment to his own, more elegantly phrased argument that "in pursuit of animal pleasures, Elagin took from Sosnovskaya everything she possessed, then abandoned her to society's opprobrium. Not only did he take her life, he even robbed her of her final honor—the right to a Christian burial." But does Elagin's letter truly lead to this conclusion? It does not. The prosecutor quoted only a few lines from a longer text. This is how it reads in full:

"Dear Sergey, I received your letter and am finally writing back. I know it's late, but what can I say at this point? As you read this note, you're bound to think, 'What penmanship—it looks as if a fly fell into the inkwell, then crawled around the paper!' Well, you know what they say: if handwriting isn't a perfect mirror of the inner self, it's certainly a clear expression of the author's character. I'm just as lazy as I used to be—in fact, if you really want the truth, I'm even worse. After all, two years of independent living and *something* else must have put their stamp on me. Brother, there are certain things that even Solomon the Wise could not express! And so, please don't be surprised if one fine day you learn that I've done myself in. I have come, brother, to a state of complete indifference: everything, absolutely everything's the same. All's fine today—so give your thanks to God. And what will tomorrow bring? Forget about it while you can. After all, we're always wiser in the morning than at night. I've earned myself a stellar reputation here—first-class drunk and village fool. Almost everyone in town has heard of me. And along with that—can you believe it?—my soul seems to be filled with such agony and strength, it seems to strain and pull so hard toward the good and the sublime—toward the devil knows what!—that I fear my chest will burst. You will say that this is simply youth. If so, then why do my comrades feel nothing similar? I've grown irritable and ill-at-ease. Sometimes at night, in a freezing winter blizzard, I'll get out of bed and ride hard through the town, fly along the streets, astounding even the night patrolman who's so used to taking everything in stride. Keep in mind, I do this when I'm sober, when I haven't had a drink. It's as if I heard some fleeting, delicate refrain somewhere, and now all I want to do is hear it long enough to learn the notes. But those notes have disappeared. No matter what I do, they're gone! I'll confess one fact to you: I've fallen in love with a woman who is absolutely, utterly unlike all the other girls who fill this town. . . . But enough about that. Write to me again, please. You know the address. Remember how you said it? 'Cornet Elagin, Russia.'"

It's astounding—how could anyone who read this letter claim that Elagin and Sosnovskaya were lovers without "the slightest thing in common"!

VIII

A pure-blooded Pole, Sosnovskaya was twenty-eight—older than Elagin. Her father had worked as a petty bureaucrat until taking his own life when she was only three. Her mother lived as a widow for many years, then married another petty bureaucrat who once more left her a widow.

As you can see, Sosnovskaya's background was quite conventional. What, then, produced in her those strange spiritual qualities that made her so unusual? What gave her that passion for the stage that appeared so early in her life? I am quite sure it was neither the home where she was raised nor the private boarding school where she was educated. They say, however, that she studied well and read a great deal in her free time. In the course of that reading, Sosnovskaya periodically wrote down maxims and ideas that she found appealing—always, of course, connecting them somehow to her own life, as almost every reader does when moved to save an excerpt from a book. These notes, together with her own observations, might be called a diary if such a formal title can be applied to those scraps of paper that sometimes lay untouched for months and where, in addition to her scattered dreams and thoughts about the world, she recorded bills for laundry and new dresses. What, exactly, did she write?

"To remain unborn—the greatest happiness. The second—a quick return to oblivion." What a charming thought!

"How dull the world seems. Fatally dull. My soul strains to rise above the ordinary."

" 'People understand only that suffering from which they die'—de Musset."

"No, I'll never marry. Everyone says this—but I swear to it before God. I swear to it on my life."

"If not love, then death. But where in the universe can I find such a person—someone I can love? There is no one! But how does one die while loving life the way I do—like a woman raving in delirium?"

"There's nothing on earth or in heaven more terrible, more alluring, more mysterious than love."

"Mama, for example, says that I should marry for money. Me—for money! How unearthly it is, this word 'love.' What hell it holds, what charm—although I've never loved."

"The world looks at me with predatory eyes—like those animals at the menagerie when I was a girl. . . . Millions of those eyes."

" 'It's not worthwhile to be a man. Nor an angel. For the angels cried out in protest and rebelled against God. To be God or to be nothing—this alone has value.'—Krasinski."

" 'Who can claim to penetrate so far that he has tapped into her soul when everything she does in life is meant to bury those deep veins?'—de Musset."

As soon as she finished her studies, Sosnovskaya told her mother that she'd decided to devote herself to art. An upright

Catholic, her mother, of course, wished to hear nothing of Sosnovskaya's plans to become an actress. But her daughter was not one to abide the will of others, and she'd already begun to convince her mother that her life—the life of Mariya Sosnovskaya—could never be inglorious and ordinary.

At eighteen she left for Lvov, and there she realized her dreams, reaching the stage with little difficulty and quickly making her mark in the local theatres. Her following among stage professionals and the general public grew so substantial that at the end of her third year on the circuit she received an invitation to our city. Even in Lvov, however, the observations she recorded were much the same as those she wrote in school:

"'Everyone is talking about her. On her account they laugh or cry. But who among them knows her?'—de Musset."

"If not for mother, I would kill myself. It's my constant wish."

"I don't know what happens to me when I go somewhere outside the city. When I see the sky, so beautiful and limitless, I want to shout, sing, declaim, weep . . . love and die. . . ."

"I will compose a beautiful death for myself. I'll rent a small room and have it shrouded in black. Music will play from some other room while I lie in a simple white dress, surrounded by countless flowers, whose heavy scents will suffocate me. How wonderful it will be!"

And further:

"Everyone, everyone demands my body, never my soul. . . ."

"If I were rich, I'd travel the world, sampling love wherever I went. . . ."

"'Does a man know what he wants? Can he be sure he knows his thoughts?'—Krasinski."

And finally:

"Villain!"

Who was this villain whose transgressions are not hard to imagine? We know only that he appeared in her life—and that this appearance was inevitable. "Already in Lvov," testified the witness Zauze, a colleague from the theatre, "she didn't dress so much as she undressed for the stage. At home she received admirers and acquaintances while wearing a transparent peignoir without stockings. The beauty of her bare legs plunged them all into a kind of dazed ecstasy—especially the newcomers. And she would say, 'Don't be surprised—they're all mine, nothing artificial here,' as she raised her gown above her knees. At the same time she never stopped insisting—sometimes tearfully—that no one was worthy of her love, and that her only hope was death."

And so appeared the so-called villain, whom she accompanied to Constantinople, Venice, and Paris, and later visited in Krakow and Berlin. He was some kind of Galician landowner with extraordinary sums of money. The witness Volsky, who'd known Sosnovskaya since childhood, gave this testimony in reference to him:

"I always considered Sosnovskaya a woman of very little virtue. She didn't know how to conduct herself either on or off the stage. She loved only money—money and men. She was still a girl, almost, when she sold herself to that old boar from Galicia. The cynicism was quite astounding."

Sosnovskaya talked precisely about this boar to Elagin during their last conversation before her death. No longer guarding her words, she complained openly about him:

"I grew up completely alone—no one ever looked after me. In my own family—in the entire world!—I was always a stranger. . . . A woman—may all of her descendants go to hell—corrupted me when I was still a trusting, innocent girl. . . . In Lvov I sincerely loved a man—loved him like a father—and he turned out to be a villain, such a villain that I can't remember him without horror! He got me used to wine and hash, took me to Constantinople. He had a whole harem there! He'd lie there in his harem, looking at his naked slaves. And then he'd make me undress. A sick, vile man. . . ."

IX

Sosnovskaya became the talk of our town.

"While still in Lvov," said the witness Meshkov, "she proposed to many men that they agree to die in exchange for one night with her, while at the same time insisting that she sought a heart capable of real love. She searched for that heart very stubbornly while saying all along: 'My goal's to live—to live and use life. After all, a connoisseur must sample many different wines without getting drunk on one in particular. So too should a woman behave with men.' And she was true to her word," Meshkov continued. "I can't possibly say if she sampled all the wines, but she certainly surrounded herself with a huge quantity of them. Of course, she might have done this just in order to create a stir and gather *claqueurs* for her shows. 'Money,' she'd say, 'doesn't interest me. I'm tightfisted, sometimes stingy as a banker's wife—but somehow I don't really think about money. It's fame that counts. Everything else will follow.' I think she constantly brought up death for the same reason—to keep everyone talking about her. . . ."

Everything that had begun in Lvov continued in our town. And Sosnovskaya's notes remained much the same:

"My God, what loneliness! What misery! An earthquake, an eclipse—some relief!"

"One evening I was at the graveyard. And it was lovely there! It seemed that . . . No, I can't describe the feeling. I wanted to stay there all night, declaiming over the graves until I died of exhaustion. My performance the next day was better than anything I've done before. . . ."

And again:

"I was at the graveyard at ten o'clock last night. What a somber sight! Shafts of moonlight fell across the headstones and the crosses. It seemed I was surrounded by thousands of the dead. And I was happy, filled with joy. It was wonderful there. . . ."

Soon after meeting Elagin and learning from him that a cavalry sergeant had recently died in the regiment, she demanded that the cornet drive her to the chapel where the deceased lay. Later she wrote that the chapel and the body in the moonlight had made on her a "shockingly ecstatic impression."

The thirst for fame, for human attention, brought her to a kind of frenzy during this time. She was certainly attractive. Although her beauty was not particularly original, it possessed something uniquely its own—a rare charm that stemmed from a combination of childlike innocence and predatory cunning, a mix of constant play and absolute sincerity. You can see this in her portraits: look closely at her expression—that expression so uniquely hers—as she looks up at you with her head slightly lowered, her eyes raised to meet yours, her lips ever so slightly parted. It's both a winsome, melancholy look and an almost lurid invitation—as if she has consented to perform some secret, shocking act. She knew how to use her beauty. On stage she won admirers not only with a skillful demonstration of her charms—the sound of her voice, the taut energy of her gestures, her laughter and her tears—but also with a readiness to take on roles that usually required the baring of her flesh. At home she wore seductive Greek and Eastern clothes even as she entertained her numerous guests. Among her rooms, one was set aside, as she said, for suicide: it contained daggers and revolvers, swords with blades shaped like sickles and corkscrews, glass jars containing every possible poison. Death was her favorite topic of conversation and, moreover, while discussing the various ways to rid oneself of life, she was known at times to suddenly seize a loaded pistol from the wall, pull the trigger back, and raise it to her temple, saying, "Kiss me or I'll shoot"—or, on other occasions, to take a capsule filled with strychnine into her mouth and announce that she would swallow it if her visitor did not immediately fall to his knees and begin kissing her bare feet. The guest inevitably blanched with fear, left for home feeling doubly charmed, and soon spread all over town precisely the enticing stories she wanted to be heard.

"In general, she was never just herself," testified the witness Zalessky, who for many years was close to Sosnovskaya. "It was her constant occupation to play with people, to tease them. She was a master in the art of driving someone to the brink of madness with a tender, enigmatic glance, a suggestive smile, the sad sighs of a defenseless child. And she practiced this art with Elagin—bringing him to a white-hot pitch, then dousing him with cold water. Did she want to die? She loved life with a physical passion—and she feared death with a rare intensity. All in all, her personality was actually quite happy and lighthearted; she appreciated life and often showed it. I remember, for example, how Elagin once gave her a polar bearskin rug. She had many visitors at the time, but that bearskin made her so ecstatic that she forgot them all immediately. She spread it on the floor and, paying no attention to the other people in the room, started doing somersaults across the rug, started doing tricks that any acrobat would envy. . . . She was a captivating woman!"

But the same Zalessky also testified that the victim suffered attacks of depression and despair. Dr. Seroshevsky, who had known Sosnovskaya for ten years and was still treating her when she left for Lvov (her consumption began at that time), also testified that near the end of his acquaintance with her, the victim was plagued with such severe hallucinations, memory loss, and general nervous disorder that he feared for her mental faculties. Dr. Schumacher (from whom Sosnovskaya borrowed two volumes of Schopenhauer, which she "read very carefully and, most surprisingly of all, understood perfectly") subsequently treated her for the same nervous disorder and was repeatedly assured by his patient that she would not die a natural death. Finally, Dr. Nedzelsky gave this testimony:

"She was a strange woman. When entertaining guests she was usually very happy and flirtatious. But sometimes it would happen that, for no apparent reason, she'd suddenly go silent, roll her eyes, and lower her head to the tabletop. . . . Or she'd start to throw things, smash glasses on the floor. At such moments one had to de-mand quickly that she continue this activity—'Go on, go on, smash another one!'—and she would stop immediately."

It was with this "strange and charming woman" that the young cornet, Aleksandr Mikhailovich Elagin, would soon become ac-quainted.

X

How did that meeting occur? What drew them together? What were their feelings for each other? What was their relationship? Ela-gin spoke only twice about these matters: once—briefly and dis-jointedly—a few hours after the murder, and a second time during his interrogation three weeks later.

"Yes," he said, "I'm guilty in the taking of Sosnovskaya's life— but I did so *by her will.*

"I met her a year and a half ago through Lieutenant Budberg— we ran into her at the box office in the theatre. I loved her passionately and believed she shared my feelings. But I was not always sure of this. At times it seemed that she loved me even more than I did her, and at other times just the opposite. She was constantly surrounded by ad-mirers, with whom she flirted, and I was tormented by intense feelings of jealousy. But ultimately it was not this that led to our tragic situa-tion; it was something else—something I can't express. . . . Regardless of all else, I swear I didn't kill her out of jealousy.

"As I said, I became acquainted with her in February of last year at the theatre, near the box office. I soon began visiting her at home, but even by late October I had called on her no more than twice a month, and always during the day. In October I confessed my love for her, and she allowed me to kiss her. A week later we went with an acquaintance of mine, Voloshin, to a restaurant out-side town. The two of us returned alone. Slightly tipsy, she grew playful and affectionate in the cab—but I felt so timid in her presence that I didn't even dare to kiss her hand. Later she asked to borrow a volume of Pushkin's poems; while reading *Egyptian Nights* she asked: "Would you give up your life for one night with your lover?" I did not hesitate to tell her that I would, and hearing this, she smiled enigmatically. I was already deeply in love with her, and I saw clearly—felt clearly—that this love would prove fateful for me. As we became more intimate, I grew bolder and began to speak more freely of my love for her. I also told her of my presentiment that I'd perish . . . if only for the reason that my father would never allow me to marry her, and that she—an actress whom Polish society would never forgive for an open, illicit affair with a Russian officer—could not possibly live with me outside of marriage. She too lamented her fate and her ill-fitted soul. And although she never answered my unspoken questions about her feelings for me, the intimacy of these discussions gave me hope that she shared my love.

"And then, in January of this year, I began to visit her every day at home. I sent her bouquets at the theatre, sent her flowers at home, bought her gifts. . . . I gave her two mandolins, a polar bearskin rug, a ring, and a jeweled bracelet. And I decided to give her a brooch in the shape of a skull, for she adored all emblems of death and often told me that she'd like to own precisely such a brooch, engraved with the words, '*Quand même pour toujours!*'

"On March 26 I received from her an invitation to dinner. After dinner she gave herself for the first time to me. . . . We were in the 'Japanese room,' as she called it, and all our future encounters took place there, after the maid had been dismissed. Then she gave me a key to her bedroom, the outer door of which opened directly onto the stairwell. . . . To commemorate March 26, we ordered wedding bands and, in keeping with her wishes, had the date of our first intimacy engraved inside them.

"During one of our trips outside the city we visited a small village where a cross stood before the local Catholic church. I swore my eternal love to her before that cross, swore that before God she was my wife, to whom I would be true until the grave. . . . She stood there sadly, silently, lost in contemplation. And then she said simply, firmly: 'And I love you. *Quand même pour toujours!'*

"In early May when I was dining at her house, she produced a vial of powdered opium and said, 'How easy it is to die! Just drop a little in your glass—and it's done.' Then she poured the powder into her champagne and raised the glass to her mouth. I tore it from her hand, flung the wine into the fireplace, and smashed the glass against my spur. She said to me the next day, 'Instead of tragedy, we wound up playing in a farce yesterday. But what can be done?' she added. 'I lack resolve—and you're incapable. What a disgrace!'

"After that we saw each other less. She said she could no longer receive me in the evenings. Why? I was in hell; I nearly lost my mind. But she had changed toward me—grown cold and mocking. Sometimes she treated me as if we hardly knew each other, and she constantly derided what she called my lack of character. . . . And then, suddenly, everything changed again. She began driving to my quarters in order to go for walks, began to flirt with me— perhaps because I'd finally forced myself to act with cold restraint whenever she was near. Finally she told me to rent a separate apartment for our rendezvous. But it had to meet her specifications: an apartment in some gloomy old house on an empty and deserted street, with dark rooms decorated precisely as she ordered. . . . You've seen those rooms—you know how she wanted them.

"And so, on June 16, at 4 P.M., I stopped at her house, told her the apartment was ready, and handed her a key. She smiled, said, 'We'll talk about this later,' and returned the key to me. At that moment the bell rang and a certain Shklyarevich entered the room. I quickly hid the key in my pocket and started making small talk. As I prepared to leave together with Shklyarevich, she said to him loudly in the hallway, 'Come back to visit me on Monday,' while whispering to me, 'Come tomorrow at four.' The way she whispered made my head spin.

"I returned the next day promptly at four. And how surprised I was when the cook who opened the door handed me a letter and explained that Sosnovskaya could not receive me. She wrote that she felt unwell, that she was going to visit her mother at her dacha, that it was 'already late.' Beside myself, I went inside the first café I saw and wrote an angry letter in response, asking her to explain what she meant by the word 'late.' But the messenger I sent to her home returned almost immediately with my note: she wasn't there to receive it. I returned to my quarters and wrote another letter. In it I reproached her sharply for the games she'd played with me and requested that she return my wedding band, which, I wrote, I intended to take to my grave, for it was the one object I valued most in life, despite the fact that she almost certainly considered it a joke. With these words I wanted to show her that everything between us was finished, and that death alone remained for me. Together with the note I sent back her portrait, all her previous letters, and all the things she'd left with me—gloves, a hat, hairpins. . . . When the orderly returned, he informed me that he'd left my package and my letter with the yardman at Sosnovskaya's building, for she still was not at home.

"That evening I went to the circus, where I ran into Shklyarevich. I don't know him well, but we wound up drinking champagne together, for I was afraid to be alone. Suddenly he said, 'Listen, I can see you're hurt, and I know the cause of your suffering. Believe me, she isn't worth it. We've all been through this. She's led us all around by the nose.' I had the urge to draw my sword and split his head down the middle, but I was such a ruin that I did nothing. I didn't even break the conversation off; indeed, I was secretly glad to be talking with someone, to have found some source of empathy. I don't know what got into me then. . . . Of course I offered no response to his statements, didn't say a word about Sosnovskaya. But I took him to Starogradskaya and showed him the apartment I'd so carefully selected for our rendezvous. What a fool she'd made of me with that apartment! I felt so bitter, so ashamed. . . .

"From there we took a cab to the Nevyarovskoy Restaurant. A light rain was falling as the cab flew along the streets, and even the lights that hung before us, even that soft rain filled me with terror and pain. I returned with Shklyarevich to my house at about one in the morning; I was already getting ready for bed when the orderly brought me a note: she was waiting outside and asked that I come out immediately. She had driven there with her maid, she said, because she'd been so alarmed by my note that she couldn't stand to make the trip alone. I told the orderly to take the maid home and went with her in the cab to Starogradskaya. On the way there I reproached her, said that she was merely playing games with me again. She sat silently, staring ahead and occasionally wiping tears from her eyes. But she seemed quite calm, and as her frame of mind invariably influenced mine, I too grew quiet as we rode. When we arrived, her spirits rose dramatically; indeed, she became quite cheerful, for she liked the apartment very much. I took her hand, asked her forgiveness for my reproaches, and requested that she return the portrait that I'd had delivered to her house in all my anger earlier that day. We often fought, and it was always I who felt to blame and wound up asking for forgiveness. . . . At three in the morning I left to take her home. Again our conversation grew strained as we rode in the cab. She sat looking straight ahead; I couldn't see her face, only smelled her perfume, heard her cold and angry voice: 'You're not a man,' she said. 'You have no character at all. I can do whatever I want with you—enrage you one minute, pacify you the next. If I were a man, I'd cut a woman like that to pieces.' 'In that case, take back your ring!' I shouted, and violently thrust my wedding band onto her finger. She turned to me, smiling uncertainly. 'Come to see me tomorrow,' she said. I answered that I would not, under any circumstances. She began to plead, awkwardly, timidly, saying, 'No, no—you'll come, you'll come . . . to Starogradskaya.' And then she added with finality, 'No, I'm begging you to come. I'm going abroad soon, and I want to see you for the last time. I need to tell you something very important.' Then she began to cry again, saying, 'I'm just surprised—you say you love me, say you can't live without me, that you'll shoot yourself—and yet you don't want to see me for the last time.' Trying to sound distant and reserved, I said that if this was in fact the case, I would inform her of a time when I'd be free. My heart seemed to be bursting with love and tenderness for her when we parted in the rain outside her apartment. Then I went home, where I was appalled to find Shkl-yarevich sound asleep in my room.

"On the morning of Monday, June 18, I sent her a note, stating that I would be free after twelve o'clock that day. She answered: 'Six o'clock. Starogradskaya.' "

XI

Sosnovskaya's maid, Antonina Kovanko, and her cook, Vanda Linevich, both testified that on Saturday the sixteenth, after lighting a spirit lamp to curl her bangs, Sosnovskaya distractedly dropped a lit match on the hem of her peignoir, which quickly began to burn. Sosnovskaya shrieked and frantically tore the garment from her body, and later, still profoundly shaken by the incident, took to her bed and summoned a doctor. "It's a sign," she insisted. "Something terrible is going to happen."

Poor, unhappy woman! For me the story of that peignoir and her childlike horror is strikingly sad and moving. For me, that triviality casts a new light on Sosnovskaya; it ties together all those fragmented, contradictory stories we heard when she was alive and which, after her death, grew slightly passé from their constant retelling in both the courtroom and polite society. Above all else, it stirs in me a vivid sense of the genuine woman—the real Sosnovskaya—whom no one truly understood, just as no one understood Elagin—despite the intense interest in her daily life, the desire to decipher her, and the endless gossip of the past year.

I will say it once again: the poverty of human reason is astounding! It is always the same when people try to make sense of even the smallest events: we discover, once more, that they look without seeing, listen without hearing. To so thoroughly distort Elagin and Sosnovskaya and everything that occurred between them, one must disregard countless obvious facts—dismiss them all, as if deliberately. But it seems that everyone agreed to speak of nothing but vulgarities. There's nothing complicated here, they say. He's just a hussar—jealous, drunk, and reckless. And she's an actress who's become entangled in her own disordered and amoral way of life. . . .

Private rooms in restaurants, courtesans and wine, debauchery— this is how they saw Elagin. The rowdy excess of military life, they said, obliterated all his refinement, eradicated any higher feelings he might have had. . . .

They talk of wine and higher feelings! What was wine for someone like Elagin? "My soul seems to be filled with such agony and strength, it seems to strain and pull so hard toward the good and the sublime—toward the devil knows what!—that I fear my chest will burst. . . . I want to catch some delicate and fleeting melody which it seems I heard somewhere but can never hear again!" Drinking helps one breathe a little easier, a little deeper— makes that soundless melody seem clearer, closer. And what does it matter if music, drunkenness, and love are all the same deceptions, if they serve only to increase the strength of those impressions that the world and life create in us—those impressions that no human word can match in their abundance and intensity?

"She didn't love him," everybody said of her. "She was just afraid. After all, he constantly threatened to kill himself, and not only would his suicide have weighed down her soul, it would have put her at the center of a massive scandal." There was testimony that she even felt "a certain revulsion" toward the cornet. But didn't she willingly give herself to him? Suppose she did—does that really change anything? Who didn't possess her? It just happened that Elagin felt the urge to make a tragedy from that romantic farce in which she so enjoyed performing. . . .

And further:

"She was terrified by the pathological jealousy that he exhibited with growing frequency. Once the actor Strakun came to visit her while Elagin was there. At first he sat calmly and only blanched with jealousy. But then he stood and abruptly strode into the next room. She raced after him and, seeing a revolver in his hand, dropped to her knees before him, begging him to pity both himself and her. Such scenes were probably quite commonplace for the two of them. Is it surprising, then, that she would finally decide to try to get away from him—take a trip abroad, just as she'd prepared to do on the evening of her death? He brought her a key to the apartment on Starogradskaya—the apartment she'd arranged in order to avoid receiving him at home—and she refused to take it. When he insisted, she told him: 'There's no point—I'm leaving town. It's too late.' But then he sent her such a desperate letter that she drove off to see him in the middle of the night, terrified she'd find him dead."

Let's assume that all of this is true (though Elagin's confession completely contradicts such reasoning). Why, then, was Elagin so "pathologically" jealous? Why did he want to turn that comedy into a tragedy? Why didn't he just kill her in one of his fits of jealous rage? Why was there "no struggle between the victim and his killer"? And then there's the claim that she at times found him repellent: "She'd belittle him in front of people, make up insulting names for him. 'My bowlegged puppy,' she'd call him sometimes." But my God, this is absolutely typical behavior for Sosnovskaya. Even in her Lvov notes, she writes about feelings of revulsion: "He's still in love with me. . . . And what do I feel for him? Both love and revulsion. . . ." She insulted Elagin? No doubt. Indeed, in the midst of one of their many fights she called for her maid, then threw her wedding band on the floor, saying, "You can keep this bit of garbage for yourself." But what had she done before this scene? She'd run into the kitchen and said: "I'm going to call you in a moment and throw this ring on the floor. I'm going to tell you to keep it, but remember—this is only a little farce. Later you must give it back, because this ring makes me his wife—makes me the wife of that fool. And it matters more to me than anything on earth. . . ."

They were not at all mistaken in calling her an "easy woman," and the Catholic church had good reason to deny her Christian burial as a person of "corrupt morals and depraved behavior." Her character had much in common with that of prostitutes and devotees of "free love." What kind of character is that? One shaped by a sharp and irrepressible, indeed insatiable, sexuality. What produces such a character? This I cannot answer. But note what always seems to happen: unusual and complex men, men whose characters are somewhat atavistic, and whose sensitivities to both women and the world are unusually refined—these men are drawn by body and soul to such women as Sosnovskaya, and consequently they wind up heroes in a great number of romantic tragedies and dramas. Why? Are they impelled by their basest desires, driven by some sordid urge? Or is the mere awareness that these women are available sufficient to entice them? Of course not, no—a thousand times no: it is nothing like this. For these men know full well—they see, they sense—exactly what will come from their involvement with these women. They know the pain that these relationships will inevitably inflict on them, they know the genuine terror, the ruin they can bring. All of this they see, know, sense—and yet this awareness only adds to the attraction, only draws them more inexorably toward such women, toward their pain, and even ruin. Why?

Of course she was only playing a role in some farce when she wrote those little notes before death, trying to convince herself that her final hour had truly come. There's simply nothing to suggest otherwise—certainly not her banal and childish diaries or her visits to the graveyard. . . .

No one denies the theatricality of those walks among the graves or the naiveté of the notes she kept. And everyone recalls the way she liked to hint at similarities between herself and Mariya Bashkirtseva or Mariya Vechyora. But why did she decide to write such a diary? Why did she decide to emulate those women in particular? She had everything: beauty, youth, money, fame, hundreds of admirers—and she found all of this intoxicating, she reveled in it. And yet her life was one long, enervating search for something else, an incessant wish to leave behind this dull, repulsive world where nothing is the way it ought to be. Why? Because she liked this image. And why this image over all the other possibilities? It's a common choice among women who describe themselves as devotees of art. But why? What makes it so widespread?

XII

She woke up and summoned her maid much earlier than usual on Sunday: the little hand-bell that she kept beside her bed began to ring sometime near eight o'clock. The maid brought cocoa on a tray and drew open the curtains in her room. She sat up in bed and watched distractedly. As was her habit, she sat with her head slightly lowered and her eyes raised, her lips half parted.

"You know, Tonya, I fell asleep yesterday as soon as the doctor left," she said. "Dear Mother of God, what a shock! I was terrified! But as soon as he arrived I started to calm down, started feeling better. I woke up in the middle of the night and knelt in bed, prayed for an entire hour. Just imagine how I'd look all burned! My eyes would have burst. The flames would have scorched my lips. It would be horrible to look at me. . . . They would have wrapped my face in gauze. . . ."

She left her cup untouched on the tray and sat thinking for a long time. Then she drank her cocoa, bathed, put on a bathrobe, and, with her hair still undone, sat at a small desk, writing letters on stationery edged in black, like the paper used for funeral announcements: she'd ordered such stationery long ago. She then dressed, ate breakfast, and left to spend the day visiting her mother at her dacha. She returned near midnight with the actor Strakun, whom she always considered "one of my people."

"They were both in good moods when they arrived," the maid said. "When I met them in the entranceway, I immediately called her aside and gave her the note and those things that Elagin had returned while she was gone. 'Hide them quickly. Don't let Strakun see!' she whispered, hurrying to open the letter. She blanched as she read, then grew hysterical. 'For the love of God, run this second to get the carriage,' she shouted, no longer paying attention to the fact that her guest was sitting in the living room. I did as she requested and, returning in the carriage, found her on the steps to the house. The horses ran at a full gallop all the way to Elagin's while she sat crossing herself, repeating 'Dear Mother of God, please— just let me find him alive.'"

On Monday morning she visited the bathing houses on the river outside town. Later she was joined for lunch at home by Strakun and an Englishwoman (who came almost every day to teach Sosnovskaya her native language but practically never conducted an actual lesson). After lunch the Englishwoman left; Strakun stayed for another hour and a half He lay on the couch and smoked, his head on Sosnovskaya's lap, despite the fact that she was dressed "in nothing but a house coat and Japanese slippers." When Strakun finally began to leave, Sosnovskaya asked him "to come again at ten o'clock tonight."

"Aren't you getting tired of me?" he said, laughing as he looked for his walking stick in the hall.

IVAN BUNIN

"Oh no, not at all, you're very welcome," she said. "But if I'm not here, Lyusya, don't be angry. . . ."

Once her guest was gone, she spent a long time burning various papers and letters in the fireplace. She hummed to herself and joked with the maid: "I'll burn everything now," she laughed, "since I wasn't burned. . . . And really, it wouldn't be so bad to burn—but all of it, everything to ash at once!"

And then:

"Tell Vanda to have dinner ready at ten. . . . I'm going out."

She left after five, carrying "something wrapped in paper that resembled a revolver."

She was going to Starogradskaya, but she stopped en route at the seamstress Leshchinskaya's shop, where the peignoir that had begun to burn while she wore it on Saturday had been shortened so that she could wear it again. According to Leshchinskaya, she was in a "warm, happy mood." She looked at the altered peignoir, then wrapped it up with the package she'd taken from home and proceeded to sit for a long time with the girls who sewed in the shop, saying all the while, "Dear Mother of God, I'm so late. I have to leave right now!" but never rising from her seat. At last she stood up, sighed, and said in a cheerful voice: "Goodbye, Pani Leshchinskaya. Goodbye, sisters, my little angels. Thank you for letting me sit with you. It's such a pleasure to join this little circle of women after being surrounded by men for so long!"

She smiled once more at the doorway, nodded, and left. . . .

Why had she taken a revolver with her? It actually belonged to Elagin, but she kept it at her house, fearing he would shoot himself. "She intended at that time to return all his possessions to Elagin," the prosecutor said, "because she was leaving in a few days for an extended trip abroad. . . ." He continued:

"And so she headed off to that meeting which, unknown to her, would prove so fateful. By seven o'clock she was already inside house number 14 on Starogradskaya—had already entered the

[124]

apartment. And the door that was closed behind her would remain locked until the morning of June 19. What took place in those rooms during the night? Only Elagin can tell us. Let's listen, once more, to him. . . ."

XIII

And so the prosecutor read from the testimony of the accused, selecting those passages he wanted most to keep alive within our memories. And in that crowded, silent courtroom, we listened once again to the final pages of Elagin's story.

"On Monday, June 18, I sent her a note, telling her that I would be available after twelve noon. She wrote back: 'Six o'clock. Starogradskaya.'

"I was already there at a quarter til. I'd brought hors d'oeuvres as well as two bottles of champagne, two bottles of porter, glasses, and a bottle of perfume. But I wound up waiting for a long time. She didn't arrive until seven.

"She kissed me distractedly as she entered the apartment, then walked into the back room where she tossed the package she was carrying on the couch. 'Leave me,' she said in French. 'I want to get undressed.' I went into the next room and sat there alone for a long time. I was perfectly sober and utterly despondent, sensing, somehow, that everything was over—that everything was coming to an end. . . . It was a strange scene. I sat with the lamps lit, as if it were night, but I knew full well that a lovely summer evening was just beginning beyond the walls of those dark, windowless rooms. She didn't speak to me for a long time. I have no idea what she was doing—it was completely silent behind the door. Finally she called out, 'You can come in now.'

"She was lying on the couch in just a peignoir—no stockings, no slippers, nothing covering her legs. . . . She was looking up at the ceiling—at the lamp. Her head was slightly lowered, her eyes raised. She didn't speak. The package that she'd brought was opened: I saw my revolver. 'Why did you bring that?' I asked. She paused before answering. 'You know I'm leaving . . . it will be better if you keep it here. . . .' A terrible thought flashed through my head: 'No, it's nothing so simple! . . .' But I didn't question her. . . .

"We talked for quite a long time after that, but our conversation was cold and forced. In secret I was agitated: I wanted desperately to formulate and express some idea to her, and I thought, 'Now, now my thoughts will come together and I'll tell her something important, something vital,' for I knew that this could be our last meeting, or at least our farewell before a long separation—and still I said nothing, felt nothing but my lack of strength. 'Have a cigarette if you want,' she told me at some point. 'You don't like it when I smoke,' I said. 'It doesn't matter *now*,' she answered. 'And you can pour me a glass of champagne, too. . . .' This simple request made me wildly happy—you would have thought it was my personal salvation. In a few minutes we drank an entire bottle of champagne. I moved closer to her, began to kiss her hands, tell her how I couldn't bear our separation. She played with my hair and said distractedly, "Yes . . . what a tragedy that I can't be your wife. . . . Everyone's against us. Everyone and everything. . . . Only God, perhaps, is with us. . . . I love your soul, your *imagination*. . . .' I don't know what she wanted to express with those last words. I looked up at the umbrella above us. 'It's as if we're in a tomb,' I said. 'So quiet. . . .' She only smiled sadly in response.

"At about ten o'clock she said she was hungry, and we moved into the front room. But she ate very little—as did I. We drank more than anything. Suddenly she looked at the food I'd brought: 'Oh, you brought so much! You're such a schoolboy,' she exclaimed. 'Don't buy so much next time!' 'But when would I have the chance? When could I do this again?' I asked. She gave me a strange look, then lowered her head. 'Dear Jesus. Dear Mary,' she whispered, looking at me with raised eyes. 'What are we to do?. . . I want you, now. . . . Hurry. . . . Now. . . .'

"When I looked at the clock again it was already after one in the morning. 'Oh, it's so late,' she said. 'I have to go home right away.' But she made no effort to rise. 'You know—I realize that I have to go. Right away,' she said. 'But I can't move. I feel as if I'll never leave. You're my destiny, my fate—God's will.' I couldn't understand what she meant by those words, but I believe she wanted to express something similar to the message that she later wrote: 'I didn't choose to die.' You believe she wrote these words in order to express her helplessness before me. But I think she wanted to say something else—namely, that our unhappy meeting was destiny, was divine will—and she was dying not by her own choice but by God's. At the time, however, I didn't attach such importance to her words—I'd grown used to her eccentricities long ago. Then she asked, abruptly, if I had a pencil. This too surprised me: 'Why now?' But I hurried all the same to give her the pencil that I carried in my address book. Then she asked for my calling card. 'But wait, listen— you shouldn't write on it,' I said when she began to use it for her notes. 'No, it's all right. . . . This is just for me,' she answered. 'Give me some time alone, now, to think and take a little nap.' She laid the calling card on her chest and closed her eyes. It grew so quiet in the room that I too slipped into some kind of semi-conscious state. . . .

"At least half an hour passed. Then, suddenly, she opened her eyes. 'I forgot,' she said in a cold voice. 'I came here to return your ring. You yourself wanted to end everything yesterday.' She tossed her ring onto the ledge above the couch. 'Do you really love me?' she almost shouted. 'I can't understand it, then—how can you just calmly let me go on living? I'm a woman. I don't have the will to end it! It's not that I'm afraid of death—I'm afraid of suffering. But you could end my life with one shot. End my life—and then your own.' As she spoke, I understood with terrifying clarity all the horror, all the hopelessness of our situation. And I knew it had to be resolved, finally, somehow. But to kill her? No, this was more than I could bear. Something else had taken place: some other, equally decisive moment had arrived for me. I picked up the revolver and cocked it, 'What? Just you? No,' she shouted as she leapt up. 'I swear to God, never!' and she snatched the gun from my hand.

"Again that brutal silence filled the room. I sat while she lay motionless on the couch. She muttered something indistinctly to herself in Polish, then asked me to return the ring she'd earlier discarded. I gave it to her. 'Yours too,' she said. I gave her mine as well. She slipped her ring back onto her finger and told me to do the same. 'I always loved you and I love you now. I know that I've tormented you. I've brought you to the verge of madness. But that's my character. That's our fate. . . . Give me my skirt, please, and bring us some porter.' I did as she asked and left to get the porter. Coming back into the room, I saw that she'd taken out a little vial of opium. 'Listen,' she said firmly, 'we've reached the end of our little farce. Can you live without me?' I told her that I couldn't. 'Yes,' she said, 'I've taken all your soul. All your thoughts. You won't hesitate to kill yourself? If that's true, then take me with you. I can't live without you either. Kill me first, and then you'll know that I'm completely yours—for all eternity. And now, listen to my life. . . .' She lay down again in silence, and grew calmer. And then, unhurriedly, she began to tell me her entire life, beginning with her childhood. . . . I remember almost nothing of that story."

XIV

"I don't remember which of us started writing first. . . . I broke the pencil in two and we wrote, wrote without talking. I believe my first note was to my father. . . . You wonder why I reproached him—why I wrote that he 'didn't want me to be happy' when I never even asked him to accept her as my bride. . . . I don't know. . . . But it's all the same. . . . He wouldn't have allowed our marriage. Then I wrote to my friends in the regiment, wrote to say goodbye. And then—who else? The commander—I asked him to arrange a proper burial for me. You ask if this means that I was absolutely certain I would kill myself. Of course I was. Then how could I have failed to do so? I don't know. . . .

"I remember that she wrote very slowly, pausing, contemplating every phrase. She writes a word, stops, looks at the wall with raised eyes. . . . It was she who tore up the notes, not me. She did it herself: wrote them, tore them up, scattered the pieces. . . . I think the grave itself will be less terrifying than that hour we spent writing those superfluous notes in the silence beneath that lamp. . . . All of it was her idea. I did everything she asked that night. I did everything she wanted and I never questioned her, right up to the end.

" 'That's enough,' she said abruptly. 'If we're going to do this, we have to do it now. Give me some porter. . . . Mother of God, bless me.' I poured it for her. She sat up, dropped a few grams of powder into her glass, and drank more than half. The rest she gave to me, saying I should finish it. I did. Then she became disturbed and agitated, started pulling at my arm, begging me. 'Kill me,' she said. 'Kill me now. For our love. Do it—kill me.'

"How exactly did I do it? I think I held her with my left arm—yes, of course it was my left—and I brought her mouth close to mine. 'Farewell, farewell,' she said. 'But no—it should be hello. Hello—this time forever. If we didn't make it here—then there, above. . . .' I pressed myself to her and held my finger on the trigger. I remember how my body was trembling it seemed to jerk and twitch as I held her there, and then my finger twitched—as if it had its own will. . . . She managed to say three words in Polish: 'Aleksandr, my beloved. . . .'

"What time was it then? I think it was three. What did I do for the two hours that followed? It took me an hour to walk to Likharyov's quarters. The rest of the time I spent sitting next to her. And then I decided to clean up for some reason.

"Why didn't I shoot myself? Somehow I forgot about it. When I saw her dead, I forgot everything in the world. I just sat and looked at her. And then, in the same delirium, I started cleaning her, started straightening the room, putting everything in order. . . . I couldn't fail to keep my word, couldn't fail to follow through on that promise to kill myself after killing her. But I was seized by absolute indifference. . . . I feel the same indifference now toward the fact that I'm alive. . . . But I can't stand to think that you believe I'm a murderer—a butcher. No, no! I might be guilty according to the laws of man and God, but I'm innocent—innocent before her."

[Maritime Alps, 1925]

Tanya

SHE WAS a maid in the house of one of his relatives—a petty landowner, a widow named Kazakova. She was sixteen. She was small and thin, and this became quite noticeable when she went barefoot or, in winter, wore felt boots and walked with her skirt gently swaying behind her, her small breasts slightly raised beneath her blouse. Her features were pleasant and appealing, but not striking. It was their youth alone that made her grey peasant eyes so lovely. During those years—now long passed—he led a particularly dissipated and aimless life, wasting himself in foolish ways. He had many trysts and chance affairs—and she was just one more.

She quickly came to terms with that fateful and surprising encounter that had taken place so suddenly one autumn night. She wept for several days but at the same time grew more and more convinced that this occurrence was not a cause for sorrow but for joy—and that

[131]

he was growing ever closer to her heart. During moments of their intimacy, which soon began to repeat themselves with growing frequency, she even called him Petrusha, and sometimes she spoke of that first night the way she might have talked about a secret past they shared and cherished.

At first he both believed and didn't believe her version of events.

"You mean, you weren't just pretending to be asleep? You had to be pretending. . . ."

Her eyes widened with surprise.

"Couldn't you tell? Don't you know that boys and girls sleep heavy?"

"I wouldn't have begun to touch you if I'd known that you were really sleeping."

"Well, I didn't feel anything. Nothing. Almost to the very last minute. But what put it in your head to come to me? You didn't even look at me when you arrived. Didn't speak to me until the evening. 'You must be the maid they hired recently. Your name's Tanya, I believe. . . .' That's all you said. And after that you didn't give another thought to me—that's how it seemed, at least. Were you just pretending?"

He told her that of course he'd been pretending not to notice her. But he was lying: he'd expected none of this to happen.

He'd spent the early fall in the Crimea, then stopped to visit Kazakova while returning home to Moscow. He'd stayed two weeks, rested in the quiet calm of her estate and those barren days that mark the beginning of November, then decided it was time to leave. He had one last ride on horseback—took a hunting dog and roamed with a gun on his shoulder all day through the empty fields and the barren thickets, found nothing, came back tired and hungry to the manor house. For dinner he ate an entire pan of rissole in sour cream and drank a small carafe of vodka and several cups of tea while Kazakova spoke, as she so often did, about her dead husband

and her two sons, who were serving in Oryol. As usual, the entire house was dark by ten o'clock; just one candle burned in the study off the living room, where he always slept on an old ottoman when he visited. When he came into the room, she was kneeling on his bedding, running the candle's flame over the heavy, rough-hewn logs that formed the wall beside her. Seeing him, she thrust the candle back onto the nightstand, jumped to her feet, and bolted from the room.

"What's going on?" he said, almost dumbfounded. "Stop. What were you doing?"

"Burning a bedbug," she answered in a hurried whisper. "I was putting out your quilt and I saw a bedbug there, on the wall," she said—and laughing, ran away.

He stared after her, then took off his boots and lay down on the quilt without undressing, hoping to have another cigarette and do some thinking—he wasn't used to getting into bed so early—and immediately dozed off. Disturbed by its trembling light, he woke up long enough to blow out the candle, then dropped back into sleep. When he opened his eyes again, a bright autumn night stood outside the house, hushed and lovely in all its emptiness: he could see it through the two front windows that looked out on the courtyard, and the side window, which opened on the garden, and now was filled with brilliant moonlight. In its soft glow he found his slippers near the bed and went into the corridor beside the study. They had forgotten to give him everything necessary for the night, and now he had to step out onto the back porch. But the door had been latched shut from the outside: it was impossible to open it. He would have to go out through the *sentsy*, a large anteroom of rough-hewn logs that stood at the end of the main hall and opened onto the front porch. He started walking through the house, making his way carefully in that secret light from the courtyard. An old storage trunk stood below a high window in the main hall; across from it was a partition that formed the maids' room. The partition door had been left slightly ajar; beyond it there was only darkness. He lit a match and saw her sleeping there. She was lying on her back on a wooden bed, wearing just a shirt and cotton skirt. He could see the outlines of her small, round breasts beneath the shirt; her legs were bare up to her knees. Her face looked lifeless on her pillow, as did the arm she'd extended in her sleep toward the wall. . . . The match burned out. He stood there for a moment—then cautiously approached the bed.

He walked through the darkened *sentsy* to the front porch, thinking feverishly: How strange! How completely unexpected! Could she really have been sleeping?

He stood for a moment on the porch, then went out into the courtyard. . . . What a strange night. This courtyard spreading out beneath the high moon, all this empty space so brilliantly illuminated. Big sheds stood across from him—barns for horses and cattle, a carriage house, their thatch roofs turning hard as stone over time. The night's secret clouds were slowly parting in the northern sky, where they rose like lifeless mountains under snow. The clouds above his head, however, were thin and white, refulgent with that gemlike incandescence the moon poured into them as it slipped past, then plunged into the dark blue valleys, the starry depths of sky, its unobstructed light seeming to grow stronger on the courtyard and the roofs. All the objects that surrounded him seemed strange in their nocturnal forms, cut off from all human influence, shining with no purpose. He felt as if he'd never seen this before, as if he were looking for the first time at a world created by the night and the autumn moon. And this sensation only added to the strangeness of the scene surrounding him.

Near the carriage house he sat down on the footboard of a *tarantass* that was covered with dried mud. The air was filled with an autumnal warmth, all the scents of a garden in the fall. And the night was solemn, placid, beatific, linked somehow to all the feelings he had brought away from that sudden, unexpected joining with a being still half woman and half child. . . .

She'd sobbed quietly as she came to herself, seeming only then to grasp fully everything that had occurred. And perhaps she really hadn't understood until that moment?. . . Her entire body had surrendered to him, as if it were completely lifeless. He had intended to wake her with his whispering: "Listen, don't be afraid. . . ." But she hadn't heard him—or she had pretended not to. He'd kissed her hot cheek tentatively, and when she offered no response, he'd taken her silence as consent to anything that might follow such a kiss. He'd spread her legs, their tender warmth, their heat—and she had only sighed in her sleep, stretched weakly, tossed one arm behind her head. . . .

"But what if she wasn't just pretending?" he thought, getting up from the footboard and looking anxiously into the night.

He'd responded to the touching grief with which she wept by kissing her neck and breasts, inhaling her intoxicating scents of country life and girlish innocence. And there was something more to this than simple, animal appreciation for the unexpected happiness she'd unknowingly bestowed on him: he'd kissed her in a fit of ecstasy and love. And even as she sobbed, she'd suddenly responded with an unconscious rush of feminine emotion, pressing him more firmly to her body, embracing him with gratitude, cradling his head. She was still half asleep, did not yet understand exactly who he was—but it was all the same: he was the one with whom she'd been fated to first share this secret, blissful, mortal pairing. Now that it had happened, nothing could annul that shared intimacy. He would carry her inside himself forever. And the extraordinary night received him into its bewildering and brilliant realm together with her, with that link that lay between them.

How could he remember her only incidentally after his departure? How could he forget her sincere and tender voice, the devoted love her eyes expressed with sorrow and joy? How could he proceed

to love other women, even grant to some of them far more importance than he'd ever given her?

She served them the next day without raising her eyes.

"Why so troubled today, Tanya?" Kazakova asked.

She answered dutifully. "You know my troubles, *Barynya*. Are
they not enough?"

When she'd left the room, Kazakova said to him: "Of course,
she's an orphan. No mother—and her father's worthless. Just a
swindler."

Toward evening he passed her on the porch as she prepared
the samovar.

"I've loved you for a long time," he said. "Don't think otherwise. And stop crying. All this sobbing doesn't help. . . ."

"If you really loved me—if that was true—it would all be easier to bear," she answered, sniffling as she inserted the lit kindling
into the samovar.

Then she began to glance at him, as if asking, timidly: "Is it
true?"

When she came into his room to make his bed that evening,
he approached her, put his arms around her shoulders. She looked
at him with alarm. "Please, for God's sake move away," she whispered, blushing deeply. "The old lady's going to see."

"What old lady?"

"The old housekeeper! As if you didn't know."

"I'll come to you tonight. . . ."

It was as if he'd touched her with a flame—she'd been in horror of the old housekeeper the first time he found her in bed.

"What are you saying! No, no—you can't. I'll lose my mind
from fear."

"All right, calm down. I won't come," he told her hurriedly.

She began to serve with all her previous attentiveness and
speed, racing through the courtyard to the kitchen just as she had

done before, and now, from time to time, she'd seize an opportunity to glance at him with flustered joy.

One morning before dawn, while he was still asleep, she was sent to town for shopping.

"I'm not sure what to do," Kazakova said at lunch. "I sent the steward and his helper to the mill, and now I don't have anyone to pick up Tanya at the station. Could you, perhaps, drive there to meet her?"

He was careful to restrain his joy. "Well, all right. I don't mind a little drive," he said with affected nonchalance.

The old housekeeper was serving them at the table.

"Why, *Barynya*, do you want to stain a young girl's reputation for life?" she said, frowning. "What will they say about her in the village after this?"

"If you don't like it, go yourself," Kazakova told her. "What's the girl supposed to do, walk the whole way from the station?"

At around four he left in a cabriolet, drawn by a tall, black, aging mare. Fearing he'd be late for the train, he drove the horse at a hard run once he'd passed the village, the cabriolet leaping over bumps in the damp and slightly frozen surface of the road. The last few days had been wet and foggy, and now the fog was particularly heavy: even as he'd driven through the village, it had seemed that night was coming on, for smoky red lights were already visible in some of the windows of the peasant huts, glowing in the cold, dove-grey haze like preternatural fires. Farther on in the fields it grew almost completely dark, and the fog became impenetrable. Toward him streamed a cold, wet wind, but it didn't drive the fog away— just the opposite, it made that bluish, dark grey smoke so thick that he felt almost suffocated by its heavy scent of dampness, and soon it seemed that nothing lay beyond that murk, as if the world and every living thing were gone. His hat and coat, his moustache, his eyelashes—everything was covered with tiny beads of water. The black mare raced ahead with long, bold strides, and the cabriolet skipped over the road's slick ruts and bumps, its shuddering like a series of small blows to his chest. He managed to light a cigarette; the sweet, fragrant, warm and human smoke mixed with the primeval smell of fog, late fall, wet and barren fields. Straight ahead, behind, above, below—the darkness and the gloom grew deeper everywhere around him, and soon the horse was almost lost from sight: he could barely see her neck like a long, dark shadow, her ears turned forward apprehensively. And this spurred in him a deepening attachment to the mare, for she was the only living creature in that wasteland, engulfed by the lifeless enmity of everything around him—everything he couldn't see before him and behind him, to his left and right, hidden with such menace in the smoky darkness that raced toward him, growing only blacker and more dense.

When he drove into the next village where the train would stop, he exulted in the many signs of human habitation that surrounded him—the sad little lights in the impoverished windows of the huts, the gentle warmth that seemed to fill their rooms. With all its cheerful energy and city bustle, the station seemed like something from another world. He barely had time to tie his horse before the train came rumbling into the station, its bright windows flashing, the sulfurous smell of coal pouring from its engines. With the excitement of a man meeting his young wife, he ran into the station and immediately caught sight of her coming through the opposite doors. Well dressed for the city, she walked behind the stationmaster, who addressed her formally as "thou" as he carried her two large sacks of goods. The station was dirty and dimly lit by lamps that reeked of kerosene, but she was radiant, her eyes shining, her young face beaming with excitement from this rare outing to the city. And suddenly her eyes met his: she was so surprised and flustered that she stopped: What's happening? Why has he come here?

"Tanya," he told her hurriedly. "Hello, I've come to meet you. There was no one else to send."

Had there ever been, in all her life, an evening happier than this one? He came to meet me himself. And I am coming from the town, dressed up, prettier than he could ever have imagined after seeing me in nothing but an old skirt and a cheap cotton blouse. Now I look like a *modiste* with this headscarf of white silk. Now I'm here before him in a new brown dress of worsted wool, a cloth jacket, white cotton tights, new ladies' boots with copper on the heels. . . . Trembling inside, she spoke to him as if she were a guest as she picked up the hem of her skirt and followed him with the small steps of a refined lady.

"Oh, the floor's so slick," she said with almost condescending surprise. "The *mouzhiki* have tracked it up with mud."

She still quavered with joyful fear as she climbed into the cabriolet. To keep from wrinkling her dress, she raised it up and sat on her calico underskirt, then awkwardly arranged her legs around the two large sacks now lying on the floor beneath her. She sat beside him like his equal.

He flicked the reins without speaking and drove silently into the icy darkness of that foggy night, past the scattered, fleeting lights of the surrounding peasant huts and out along the bumps and ruts of that torturous November road. Terrified by his silence, she didn't dare speak: Was he angry about something? He understood this and deliberately kept silent. And then, once they'd passed the village and plunged deep into the total dark, he suddenly brought the horse to a walk and took the reins in his left hand. He slipped his free arm around her shoulder—her jacket already covered in tiny wet beads from the mist—and pressed her close to him, laughing, murmuring:

"Tanya, Tanechka. . . ."

All her body seemed to strain toward him. Against his cheek she pressed her silk headscarf, her flushed and tender face, her eyelashes filled with warm tears. When he found her lips, they too were wet from her joyful weeping, and for a long time he couldn't tear himself away from them. He stopped the horse. Seeing nothing in the fog and darkness, like a man completely blind, he climbed out of the cabriolet and threw his coat on the ground, pulled her toward him by her sleeve. She understood it all immediately, jumped down to him, carefully and quickly raised her new dress, her skirt, all her stylish garments, then felt her way onto the coat. She lay down and gave to him not only her entire body—which he possessed already—but all her soul as well.

He put off his departure yet again.

She knew she was the cause of his delay. She recognized the tenderness with which he treated her. She understood that he now spoke to her the way he would an intimate, a secret friend within the house, and thus she no longer trembled as she had at first whenever he came close to her. He grew calmer, simpler in the moments of their intimacy, and she adapted to him quickly. With that ease that youth allows, she'd changed completely, become carefree, routinely happy. It was easy now for her to call him Petrusha, and sometimes she even pretended to be tired of his kisses. "There's no getting away from you! The second you see that I'm alone, you come charging after me!"—such words gave her a particular rush of joy: this means he loves me; if I can speak to him this way, he must be mine! There was one more happiness: to express her jealousy, to assert her rights to him. "Thank God there's no work at the threshing barn. There'd be a crowd of girls there otherwise. And if you started in with them, well—I'd have to show you then," she said. And suddenly embarrassed, she added with a touching, tentative smile: "Maybe you need more than me?"

Winter began early. After the fogs came an icy northern wind that froze the muddy road's deep ruts and bumps, turned the ground to stone, scorched the last remaining grass in the courtyard and the garden. Whitish, lead-grey clouds began to fill the sky. The barren garden sounded agitated, ill-at-ease, as if it sought to run away. The white moon plunged in and out of cloud banks in the night with similar disquiet. The village and estate looked hopelessly run-down and poor. And then the snow began to fall, turning white the frozen mud, covering the grime with dry flakes like powdered sugar. The estate and all the fields that spread beyond it turned dove grey, seemed to grow broader in the snow. The peasants in the village were finishing their last work, sorting their potatoes for winter storage in the cellars. One day he decided to take a walk there; he put on a heavy winter coat lined with fox fur and a fur hat that he tugged down snugly over his ears. The northern wind whipped through his moustache, burned his cheeks. A morose sky hung over everything; the blue-grey fields that sloped beyond the river seemed strangely close. Mounds of potatoes lay on sacking on the ground beside the cellar of each hut. Young girls and women sat among the piles, sorting through them, removing all the rotten tubers. They were wrapped in hempen shawls and tattered coats, their feet in worn-out, broken boots of felt. Their faces and their hands were turning blue. "Their legs are bare under those skirts!" he thought with horror.

When he returned she was in the hallway, preparing a samovar for the table. The water inside it was already boiling as she wiped the surface clean with a cloth.

"You probably went out to the village," she said under her breath. "All the girls are there, sorting for the winter. . . . Well, what can I do? Go ahead. Just walk around and pick whatever one you like the best." And holding back tears, she ran out to the *sentsy*.

Snow began falling heavily toward evening. She glanced at him with unrestrained, childlike glee as she raced past him in the hall. "Still planning on another little walk?" she whispered teasingly. "This is nothing. You should see how the dogs are rolling on their backs in the courtyard. You know what that means, don't you? There'll be so much snow you can't even poke your nose outside!"

"My God," he thought. "How can I tell her that I'm leaving? Where will I find the strength?"

He longed to be in Moscow as soon as possible. To see the snowfall there. To feel its heavy frosts. A pair of horses pulling a sleigh. The muttering of harness bells as they approach and pass the square by Iverskaya Chapel. And on Tverskaya, those tall electric lamps still burning in the swirling snow. . . . The brilliant light of chandeliers in the Bolshoi Moskovsky. And him there, tossing into the doorkeeper's arms a fur-lined coat covered with snow, drying his moustache with his handkerchief, then walking cheerfully down the red carpet to the warm and crowded hall, the hum of countless conversations, the smell of tobacco smoke and food, the bustle of the maître d's. And over all of it, the notes of those strings pouring forth in waves—impetuous and blithe at times, languid and voluptuous at others. . . .

He couldn't raise his eyes during dinner, couldn't watch her serving them with cheerful, earnest energy, couldn't look at her untroubled face.

Later in the evening he put on felt boots and the old raccoon coat that Kazakova's deceased husband used to wear, jammed his fur hat squarely onto his head, and walked out from the back porch into the blizzard. He wanted to breathe a little and see the storm. But a deep drift had already piled up beneath the porch's awning. He stumbled in it, filled his sleeves with snow: a pure, white hell clawed and raged before him. He struggled around the house, wading through the deep snow, sinking with every step until he reached the front porch. Stamping his feet, brushing off his coat and hat, he hurried into the dark *sentsy*, where the storm still droned, and then into the foyer, where it was warm and a lit candle stood on the trunk. She ran out from behind the partition, barefoot, wearing the same cotton skirt she always wore.

"God in heaven!" she cried, clapping her hands together in alarm. "Where have you come from?"

Scattering snow, he threw his hat and coat on the trunk, and in a delirium of tenderness and joy, lifted her into his arms. Equally transported, she broke free from him, snatched up a broom and brushed the snow from his boots, then pulled them from his feet.

"My God, these are full of snow too! You'll catch a killing cold!"

In his sleep that night he sometimes heard it: a constant drone, a constant pressure on the house, and then a sudden, furious assault as the storm flung its full weight against the walls, shook the window shutters, blasted them with snow that rattled sharp and hard as sand, and then abated slightly, moved away, lulled him back to sleep. . . . The night seemed sweet and endless—the warm bed in which he lay, the warm old house, alone in the white darkness of that roaring snow-sea.

In the morning it seemed the night's wind was still beating at the shutters, banging them against the walls. He opened his eyes: no, it was already light. All the snow-streaked windows were filled with the brilliant white of drifts the wind had mounded to their sills. The snow and droning wind had not yet stopped, but they were less violent now, as if the daylight had reined them in. From where he lay, he could see two windows facing the ottoman, each of their double panes comprised of tiny squares, their frames blackened by the years; a third window, to the left of the couch, was white and lighter than the others. The ceiling too was bathed in the white, reflected light of the snow. The damper tapped and trembled as the stove began to draw with a steady hum in the corner—how good it was: he'd slept, heard nothing, and she—Tanya, Tanechka—steadfast and beloved, she had opened the window shutters, then softly come into the room in her felt boots, all her body chilled. With snow still covering the hempen shawl she'd wrapped around her shoulders and her head, she'd knelt and made a fire in the stove. He hadn't finished this thought when she came in again, this time with a tea tray, and no headscarf covering her hair.

She smiled almost imperceptibly as she set the tray beside the couch, glancing at his eyes, which looked both clear from such a good night's sleep and slightly startled by the light of morning.

"Are you going to sleep all day?"

"What time is it?"

She looked at the clock on the desk but didn't answer immediately. She still had trouble telling time. "Ten . . . ten minutes to nine."

He glanced at the doorway, then pulled her toward him by her skirt. She stepped back, pushed his hand away.

"No. . . . Not a chance. . . . Everyone's awake."

"Just for a minute."

"The old lady will come in. . . ."

"No one's going to come in—just for a minute."

"Oh, it's like some kind of punishment being with you."

She quickly slipped one foot and then the other out of her felt boots and lay down in the bed in her wool tights, carefully watching the doorway. . . . The cool, apple-skin chill of her cheeks! The scents of peasant life that mingled in her hair and breath!

"You're kissing with your lips squeezed shut again!" he whispered angrily. "When will you learn?"

"I'm not a *baryshnya*. . . . Wait, let me move down. . . . Hurry. I'm scared to death. . . ."

They stared into one another's eyes, expectant and intent, uncomprehending.

"Petrusha. . . ."

"Be quiet. . . . Why do you always start talking now?"

"When am I supposed to talk to you, if not now? I won't squeeze my lips together anymore, I promise. . . . Swear to me you don't have anyone in Moscow."

"Don't press on my neck like that. . . ."

"No one in this life will love you the way I do. You fell in love with me. But it's like I fell in love with myself. . . . My joy in myself is almost more than I can bear. . . . But if you leave me. . . ."

Her cheeks were still flushed and hot when she hurried from the couch onto the back porch. She squatted for a moment beneath its awning, as if gathering her strength, then threw herself forward into the white whirlwind, sinking past her bare knees in the snow as she made her way around the house to the front porch.

The foyer smelled of charcoal from the samovar. Slurping tea from a saucer, the old housekeeper sat on the trunk under the high window, now plastered by the storm.

"Where have you been carried off to? All covered in snow . . .," she said, glancing askance at Tanya as she continued her noisy drinking.

"I took some tea to Pyotr Nikolaevich."

"Did you give it to him in the servants' quarters? Everybody knows what kind of tea you serve!"

"Well then—you know. May God grant you health. . . . Has the *Barynya* gotten up yet?"

"Now she remembers the *Barynya*!. . . She was up before you!"

"Always angry. . . . Angry all the time. . . ."

She sighed contentedly as she went behind the partition for her cup, singing in a voice that was barely audible:

One day into the garden I will go,
In the green, green garden I will walk
And there I'll meet my darling love at last . . .

Sitting in the study with a book that afternoon, he listened to the storm. It seemed to fade at times, only to resurge, turn menacing again, as it swirled around the house, which was sinking ever deeper in that milky whiteness, that constant snow that flew at it from every side. Once it settles down, he thought, I'll leave.

He managed to speak to her secretly in the evening. He told her to come to him much later, when everyone would be sound asleep. He wanted her to stay all night, until the morning. She shook her head, then thought it over and finally agreed. It was a terrifying prospect, and that terror made it even sweeter.

He was no less apprehensive. And at the same time a deep regret weighed heavily on his mind: she had no reason to suspect this night would be their last.

He periodically dozed off during the night, then woke up with alarm: will she make up her mind to come?. . . Darkness in the house. A constant noise surrounding it. The shutters bang. Again the wind begins to sough in the stove. . . . Suddenly he awoke in alarm. He hadn't heard her—she moved with such criminal stealth through the heavy darkness of the house that it was quite impossible to hear her—but he had somehow sensed that she now stood invisibly beside the ottoman. He stretched out his hand. Silently she slipped beneath the covers. He could hear the beating of her heart; he felt her chilled, bare feet. He whispered the most perfervid words he could find.

For a long time they lay facing each other, pressed close together, kissing so intently that their teeth began to hurt. She recalled that she was not allowed to squeeze her lips together, and in the hopes of pleasing him she held her mouth open like a fledgling jackdaw.

"You didn't sleep all night, no doubt," he said.

"Not a minute. I was waiting the whole time," she answered in a joyful whisper.

He groped around the nightstand for his matches, then lit a candle. She gasped in terror.

"Petrusha, what are you doing! What if the old lady wakes up and sees the light?"

"To hell with her," he said, looking at her small, flushed face. "To hell with her—I want to see you. . . ."

He took her in his arms and stared at her intently.

"I'm afraid," she whispered. "Why are you looking at me that way?"

"Because there is nothing on this earth that's better than you," he said. "That little braid wrapped around your head. Like the braid of Venus when she's young. . . ."

Her eyes shone with happiness and laughter. "Who's that—Venus?"

"No one, really. It doesn't matter. . . . And this sad little shirt of yours. . . ."

"Buy me a good one then, one made of calico. . . . It seems like you really love me, after all."

"I don't love you in the least. . . . You smell like quail again. . . . Or something. It's like dry hemp."

"Why do you like that so much?. . . You said I always start talking when we're together like this. But look—now it's you who's doing all the talking."

She began to press his body harder against hers. She wanted to say more, but now, already, it was impossible to speak. . . .

Later he put the candle out and lay silently for a long time, smoking in the dark and thinking: I have to tell her, all the same. Horrible . . . but I have to do it now.

His voice was practically inaudible when he began to speak. "Tanechka. . . ."

"What?" she answered, her voice as soft and secretive as his.

"You know . . . I have to leave. . . ."

She sat up in the bed. "When?"

"Soon, I'm afraid. . . . Very soon. There's something pressing that I have to tend to. . . ."

She fell back on the pillow. "My God!"

The idea of some important affair in some distant city known as Moscow produced in her a certain veneration. But how could they be parted for the sake of such affairs? She fell silent, searching desperately in her mind for some solution to this insoluble horror. There was none. She wanted to shout, "Take me with you!" But she didn't dare—was that even possible?

"I can't live here forever, after all. . . ."

She listened and agreed: yes, yes.

"And I can't take you with me. . . ."

Suddenly she spoke out of despair. "Why not?"

He thought quickly. Why not? Why not?

"I have no house, Tanya. All my life I've been moving constantly from one place to another," he answered hurriedly. "I live in a hotel room in Moscow. . . . And I'll never marry anyone."

"Why not?"

"Because I wasn't born that way."

"And you won't ever marry anyone?"

"No one, never. And I swear to you, I give you my honest word—there's something very important there that I have to do, something urgent. I'll come back at Christmas. Absolutely."

She pressed her face against him. Her warm tears fell on his hands. "Well, I'll go now," she whispered. "Soon it will be light."

She rose and made the sign of the cross over him in the darkness.

"Mother of God, protect him. Mother of God, keep him safe."

She ran back to her room behind the partition and sat there on the bed, pressing her arms to her chest, licking the tears from her lips.

"Heavenly father! Mother of God!" she whispered to the droning of the wind in the *sentsy*. "Please, let the storm continue now. Let it not pass for two more days. Two more days at least!"

Two days later he left. The weakening blizzard still swirled in the courtyard, but he couldn't stand to have their secret misery drag on any longer, so he refused all of Kazakova's urging that he wait.

The house and all the estate were empty then, abandoned, dead. And it was utterly impossible for her to imagine Moscow, him there, his life, the things that occupied his time.

He didn't come at Christmas. What days those were! Each one passed, from morning until night, in an agony of unresolved expectation while she performed a sad charade, pretending even to herself that she awaited no one. And from Christmas Eve until New Year's Day she put on her best clothes—the brown dress and ankle boots with copper on their heels that she was wearing when he met her at the station on an autumn night, a night she'd now carry forever in her memory.

For some reason on the day of the epiphany she fervently believed that he'd appear at any moment, cresting the last hill before the house in a *mouzhik*'s sleigh that he'd hired at the station, having sent no word of his arrival so that Kazakova didn't specially send her horses out for him. All day she sat on the trunk in the front hall, staring at the entranceway until her eyes began to ache. The house was empty—Kazakova had driven out to a neighbor's house, and the old woman had gone to eat lunch in the servants' hall; she was still sitting there, enjoying some bit of vicious gossip with the cook. Tanya didn't even go to eat, told them that her stomach hurt. . . .

And so the dusk began to fall. She looked again at the empty courtyard covered in a brilliant skein of ice, and told herself: It's over. I need no one now. I don't want to go on waiting anymore! Then she rose and strolled in all her finery through the main hall and the drawing room, the yellow light of winter sunset falling through the windows. She began to sing in a loud and carefree voice, a voice lightened by the knowledge that her life had passed:

> One day into the garden I will go,
> In the green, green garden I will walk
> And there I'll meet my darling love at last . . .

And just as she sang those words about her darling love, she stepped into the study, saw his empty couch, the empty armchair by the desk—that armchair that he used to occupy with a book in his hands—and collapsed into it, laid her head against the desk, sobbing, shouting.

"Mother of God, please, send death to me!"

He arrived in February, when she'd already buried all vestiges of hope, resigned herself to never seeing him again.

And everything, it seemed, came back.

He was shocked when he saw her—how thin she'd grown, how thoroughly she'd faded, how sad and timorous her eyes had turned. And she had been astounded when he first arrived: he seemed to be some other person, older, unfamiliar—unpleasant, even. His moustache seemed to have grown larger, his voice coarser; when he was taking off his coat inside the foyer, she found both his laughter and his speech exceedingly contrived and loud. Every time his eyes met hers, she felt uncomfortable. But they sought to hide these thoughts from each other, and soon their past revived.

And then those awful days drew near—those days preceding his new departure. He swore on an icon that he could come at Holy Week and stay for the entire summer. She believed him. But she also wondered what would happen in the summer. Would it be the same as now? That was not enough for her anymore. She needed either a complete and absolute return to their first time together—instead of this attempted repetition—or a constant life with him, one with no more separations, no more vain hopes leading to humiliations, no more new agony. She tried to drive these thoughts away, tried to imagine the joy of summer when freedom would surround them . . . night and day in the garden, in the fields, in the threshing barn, and he would be beside her then for a long, long time.

His last evening at the estate was light and breezy, hinting at the first approach of spring. Behind the house the garden stirred and rustled anxiously. Kazakova's forestkeeper had trapped a fox earlier that day and brought it to the courtyard; he was keeping it now in a pit among the fir trees. The dogs couldn't reach it, but the fox's close proximity had brought them to a desperate frenzy. The wind was filled with their helpless, fitful barking as it streamed up from the grove toward the house.

He was lying on his back on the ottoman with his eyes closed. She lay on her side next to him, her cheek resting sadly on her palm. Neither of them spoke.

"Petrusha, are you asleep?" she whispered finally.

He opened his eyes and looked at the dusk that had gathered in the room, the golden light that still fell through the side window. "No, why?"

"It's all changed, though. . . . Both of us, after all, we know it. You don't love me anymore. You ruined me, in the end, for nothing," she said calmly.

"What do you mean for nothing? Don't say ridiculous things."

"It will be your sin. . . . But what will I do now?"

"Why should you do anything?"

"You're leaving again. Leaving for your Moscow—but what will I do here, all alone?"

"You'll do everything you did before. And then—I already told you positively—at Holy Week I'll come for the entire summer."

"Yes. Maybe you'll come for the summer. Only, before you never would have said, 'Why should you do anything?' like that. You really loved me then. You said you'd never seen a sweeter girl. . . . But I was different then"

"Yes, you were," he thought. "So very different. How changed you are. Terribly. In almost every way."

"My time's passed," she said. "It used to be, when I snuck out to you, I was terrified to death and full of joy: Thank God the old woman's still asleep! But now I'm not afraid. Not even of her. . . ."

He shrugged. "I don't really understand you. Give me my cigarettes, could you? On the table there. . . ."

She passed them to him, and he lit one. "I don't know what's wrong. You're just unwell. . . ."

"That must be why I've grown so dull for you. But tell me, what is it? What made me unwell?"

"You don't follow me. I'm saying that you're unwell emotionally. Because just think for a moment, please—where did this come from? What made you decide all of a sudden that I don't love you anymore? And why repeat the same thing over and over again: 'before, before, before. . . .'"

She didn't answer. The golden light hung in the window. The garden rustled in the wind. The hopeless whines of the ravening dogs rose again. . . . She got up quietly and wiped her eyes with her sleeve, tossed back her head in a momentary shudder, softly walked in her wool socks toward the doorway of the living room.

He called out to her softly, sternly: "Tanya."

She turned and answered in a voice almost inaudible: "What do you want?"

"Come here."

"What for?"

"I said come here."

She went to him compliantly, lowering her head to hide her tearful face.

"Well, what do you want?"

"Sit down. Come on, don't cry. Kiss me."

He raised himself on the couch; she sat down and hugged him, sobbing softly. "My God, what am I to do?" he thought with despair. "Again these warm childlike tears. This childlike face. She lacks the slightest understanding of my love for her, has no inkling of its strength. But what can I do? Take her with me? Where? To what kind of life? And what will come of it? Tie yourself down . . . destroy yourself for good?" He began to whisper rapidly, feeling his own tears trickle down his nose and lips.

"Tanechka, my darling. My joy. Don't cry. Listen, I will come in the spring and stay all summer. And then we really will go walking in the 'green, green garden.' I heard you singing that song and will remember it forever. . . . We'll take the cabriolet out to the forest. Remember how we drove the cabriolet from the train station?"

"No one will let me go with you!" she whispered bitterly, addressing him for the first time with informal "you." She shook her head against his chest. "And you won't go anywhere with me."

But in her voice he already heard a timid note of joy and hope.

"I will, I will go with you, Tanechka! And don't you dare speak to me with formal 'thou' again. Don't you dare weep anymore. . . ."

He put his arms under her legs and lifted her light frame onto his lap.

"Now repeat after me: 'Petrusha, I love you.'"

She repeated the words vacantly, still shuddering with sobs: "I love you very much. . . ."

That was in February, in the terrible year of 1917. He was in the countryside for the last time in his life.

[October 20, 1940]

Sukhodol

W_{E WERE} always amazed by Natalya's attachment to Sukhodol.

She grew up there with our father. She was the daughter of his wet nurse and lived with him in one house. And for a full eight years she lived with us in Lunyovo—lived with us as a relative, not a former slave, not a house serf. She herself called each of those years a reprieve, a rest from Sukhodol and all the suffering it had caused her. But there's a reason why they say a wolf is always looking to the woods no matter what you feed it: as soon as she had finished raising us, Natalya headed back to Sukhodol.

I remember bits of our childhood conversations with her.

"You're an orphan, aren't you, Natalya?"

"An orphan, sir, an orphan. Just as my master was. Your grandmother, Anna Grigoryevna, after all, was practically a girl when they folded her fair arms across her breast. . . . My father and my mother were no different."

"Why did they die so young?"

"Death came, and so they died."

"But why—why did it happen so early?"

"God made it so. . . . The masters wanted to punish my father, so they sent him to be a soldier. And then my mother died early on account of turkeys—newborn turkeys. I don't remember any of this myself, of course—where would I have been at such a time? But this is how the other serfs in the household said it happened. She was the birdkeeper. And there was no counting all the hatchlings she was to care for. One day a hailstorm caught them in the open pasture, beat them all to death. Killed them all. She ran out to save them there, and when she looked and saw them dead, her soul flew out from terror."

"Why didn't you get married?"

"My groom's still growing up."

"But really . . . seriously."

"They say the young mistress, your aunt, made it so I'd never marry. And that's how it got started in the household—the teasing. They began to call me 'miss,' just like her—as if I too was a young lady."

"What do you mean? How could they say you're a lady?"

"But I am sir, I am indeed a lady," she said, a slight smile creasing her lips. She ran her dark, old woman's hand over her mouth. "My mother was your father's wet nurse, after all. The milk we shared makes me his sister. I'm your second aunt."

Growing up, we listened ever more attentively to any talk of Sukhodol at home. And as it grew easier to explain those things that had once perplexed us, all the oddities of life at that estate became more and more conspicuous. We had once been convinced that Natalya was one of us—that she too was a Khrushchyov of ancient noble lineage! No one could have believed this more earnestly than we did, for we knew that she had lived a life identical to our father's during the past half-century. But now we learned that members of our noble family had driven her father into the army and terrified her mother so intensely that the woman's heart exploded at the sight of some turkey hatchlings killed by hail.

"Of course!" Natalya had said. "Who wouldn't die from terror, seeing such a thing? They'd have sent her somewhere next to hell."

And then we learned even more strange facts about Sukhodol. We learned that there was "no one on this earth" as kind and simple as the owners of that estate—but there was also no one "more explosive." We learned that the old manor house at Sukhodol was dark and gloomy. We learned that our deranged grandfather, Pyotr Kirillych, was killed in that house by his bastard son, Gervaska, Natalya's cousin and a friend of our father. We learned that a tragic affair had driven our aunt Tonya out of her mind, and that she now lived in a serf's old hut near the decaying manor house, ecstatically playing country dances on a piano so old its keys rattled and droned. We learned that even Natalya had suffered a period of madness, for as a young girl she fell inexorably in love with our late uncle, Pyotr Petrovich, who banished her to the farm at Soshki. . . . Our passionate dreams of Sukhodol were understandable: for us it was a poetic image of the past. But what could such a place be for Natalya? As if answering a question she'd been mulling over silently, she once said to us with great bitterness:

"Well, what more is there to say?. . . They used to carry whips with them to meals at Sukhodol. Just the memory brings me terror."

"Whips?" we asked. "Do you mean hunting crops?"

"It's all the same, sir."

"But why?"

"In case a fight broke out."

"Did everyone fight at Sukhodol?"

"God save us, sir, not a day passed without some kind of war! Everyone was ready to explode—every day was pure gunpowder."

We glanced ecstatically at one another as Natalya spoke. Her words enthralled us, and the scene that then took shape in our imaginations remained for many years: a huge estate and garden, a house of rough oak beams beneath a thatch roof turned black with age—and meals in the dining hall, everyone sitting at the table, everyone eating and throwing bones on the floor for the hunting dogs, everyone watching from the corners of their eyes, whips lying in their laps. We dreamed of that golden age when we would be adults, when we too would dine with whips in our laps! But we also understood full well that those whips had never brought Natalya any joy. And still she left Lunyovo for Sukhodol, that source of her dark memories. She had nowhere to live there, no family, no corner to call her own. And since ownership of Sukhodol had changed, she couldn't serve Aunt Tonya after her return. Instead she had a new mistress—Klavdiya Markovna, Pyotr Petrovich's widow. But it didn't matter: Natalya couldn't live away from that estate.

"What can you do, sir?" she said modestly. "Habit. The thread must follow the needle. . . . You're needed where you're born. . . ."

She was not alone in suffering a deep attachment to Sukhodol. Everyone who'd ever lived there seemed to be enthralled. My God, what fervent acolytes they were! How ardently they loved their memories of that place!

Aunt Tonya was completely destitute. She lived in a peasant hut. Her happiness, her sanity, her chance to live a normal life had all been lost to Sukhodol. My father tried repeatedly to talk her into joining us in Lunyovo, but she refused to hear of it. She would not give up her ancestral home: "I'd rather hack the stones out of a quarry!"

Our father was a carefree man. For him, it seemed, there were no bonds, no troubling attachments. But you could hear a deep sadness in his stories about Sukhodol. He'd left it long ago—moved to Lunyovo, the country estate of our grandmother, Olga Kirillovna. But he complained until the very end:

"Only one Khrushchyov left on this entire earth—just one! And still he doesn't live at Sukhodol!"

[157]

But then, of course, he often fell to thinking after making such pronouncements. He'd pause and look at the fields outside the window, and taking a guitar down from the wall, he'd add:

"Sukhodol. A lovely place, all right—may the earth swallow it whole!"

And these words were no less sincere than those he'd spoken just before them.

But the soul inside him came from Sukhodol—a soul immeasurably affected by the weight of memory, the steppe and its inertia; a soul shaped by an ancient sense of clan that merged the village huts and the servants' rooms with the manor house of Sukhodol. It's true that we can trace our lineage back to early history—the name Khrushchyov is entered in the Sixth Book of noble families, and among our legendary ancestors there were many noblemen of ancient Lithuanian descent as well as a few little Tatar princes. But the Khrushchyov blood has also mixed with that of household serfs and laborers since time immemorial. Who gave life to Pyotr Kirillych? There are many different versions of this legend. Who fathered his killer, Gervaska? We had heard from early childhood that it was Pyotr Kirillych himself. Why were there such sharp differences between my father and my uncle? We'd heard many different stories about this as well. My father nursed at the same breast as Natalya. He traded crosses with Gervaska. . . . It was long past time for the Khrushchyovs to face the fact that they had relatives among the village serfs and household menials.

My sister and I lived for a long time in the steady tow of Sukhodol, lived under the spell of its antiquity. Together with the owners of the manor house, the domestic serfs and villagers formed one large family there. But it was always our ancestors, of course, who ruled that family, and we felt this through the ages. The history of family, kin and clan, is always subterranean, convoluted, mysterious, often terrifying. But it's that long past, those dark depths and legends, that often give a family strength. Sukhodol had no more written record of its ancient history than some Bashkir encampment in the steppe, for legends took the place of all such writing in those early days in Rus. But legends and old songs are a sweet poison for the Slavic soul! Our former serfs from Sukhodol were ardent idlers and dreamers—and where could they indulge their souls more freely than they did on our estate at Lunyovo? Our father, after all, was the last, true heir to Sukhodol. The first words we spoke were words of Sukhodol. The first songs and stories that moved us were those our father and Natalya brought from Sukhodol. And who could sing "My True Love's Airs" the way my father had learned to sing it from the household serfs? Who could match those notes of idle sorrow and tender reproach, that tone of unresisting candor? Could anyone tell a story like Natalya? Was anyone closer to us than the *mouzhiki* of Sukhodol?

Like so many families living over generations in close isolation, the Khrushchyovs gained notoriety in history through their fights and brawls. When we were still quite small, a particularly violent quarrel erupted between my father's house at Lunyovo and our relatives at Sukhodol. As a result, my father didn't cross the entrance to his boyhood home for almost an entire decade. And thus we didn't know Sukhodol as children. We were there only once, briefly, while en route to Zadonsk. But sometimes dreams are more powerful than any reality: our memories of that long summer day were dim, but they remained indelible. We remembered undulating fields and a large, overgrown road that fascinated us with its broad expanse; we remembered the hollow trunks of a few surviving white willows that rose occasionally along its side—and one that stood farther off in the fields, a beehive hanging in its limbs above the wheat, a beehive left completely to the will of God near a road buried in the weeds. We remembered a wide turn in the road and a long, slow rise; a huge plain dotted with little huts that had no chimneys. We remembered the rocky yellow ravines that opened beyond those huts, and the white crushed stone lying at the bottom of those barren cliffs. . . . It was a part of Sukhodol's past—Gervaska's murder of our grandfather—that first acquainted us with horror. And when we heard that story, we were haunted by the yellow ravines we'd seen that day—those ravines leading to some secret place. We were convinced Gervaska had used them to escape, having carried out his terrible crime and vanished "like a key flung into the sea."

Like those who served inside the manor house, serfs who worked the fields at Sukhodol came periodically to visit us at Luny-ovo. They were driven by a need for land rather than nostalgia, but they still entered the manor house as if arriving at a relative's. They bowed below the waist to my father, kissed his hand, straightened their hair, then kissed each of us—my father, me, my sister, and Natalya—three times on the lips. They brought honey, eggs, and homespun towels as gifts. Having grown up in the fields, we were well attuned to the scents of country life; indeed, we craved such smells the way we longed for Sukhodol's songs and its legends, and thus we savored the unique and pleasant, slightly hempen scent of Sukhodol's *mouzhiki* as they kissed us. Their gifts were also laced with the smells of an ancient village in the steppe: we tried to learn them, tried to keep them in our memories—the heavy scent of haylofts and smoke-filled huts that came from the towels, the aroma of blooming buckwheat and beehives in rotting oaks that lingered in that honey. The *mouzhiki* who came from Sukhodol never told us any stories. After all, what stories could they tell? Even legends did not exist for them. Their graves were anonymous, their lives al-most identical. Traceless. Gaunt. All their labor and their struggles brought only bread—bread that's eaten up. They dug out ponds in the rocky riverbed where the Kamenka once flowed. But ponds are unreliable—they too go dry. They built huts and shacks. But these cannot last for long: the smallest spark will burn them to the ground. . . . So what was it, then, that so stubbornly drew us all to-ward that barren pasture, to those huts and ravines, the ruined manor house at Sukhodol?

II

We were well into our adolescence when we finally reached that estate we'd heard so much about, that estate which stamped Natalya's soul and ruled her life.

I remember it like yesterday. As we approached Sukhodol toward evening, a torrential storm broke out with violent claps of thunder and lightning bolts that snaked across the sky in sudden, blinding streaks. A black-and-violet thunderhead drifted ponderously into the northwest and blocked out half the sky. The fields of green wheat covering the plain turned smooth, precise, and deathly pale beneath its mass, while the sparse grass along the road became fresh and unusually bright. The horses looked emaciated from the rain as they slopped down the road, the *tarantass* splashing behind them, their iron shoes glinting in the dark blue mud. . . . And suddenly, at the turn to Sukhodol, we saw a strange figure in the tall, wet rye—a figure that at first seemed neither male nor female. Wearing a bathrobe and a headscarf like a turban, it was beating a skewbald, hornless cow with a switch. As we approached, the beating grew more vigorous and the cow, flicking its tail, jogged clumsily onto the road while the old woman shouted something, ran toward the *tarantass*, and thrust her pale face toward us.

We glanced apprehensively into her black madwoman's eyes as this strange figure kissed us, the sharp, cold tip of her nose touching our cheeks, the heavy scent of a peasant hut rising from her clothes. Could she be the witch Baba-Yaga? But then, a grimy scarf rose like a turban from this Baba-Yaga's head, and her naked body was wrapped in a wet bathrobe so badly torn it didn't even cover her thin breasts. She shouted as if she were deaf, as if she wanted to curse and berate us—and from that shouting we understood: Aunt Tonya had come to meet us.

Plump and short, with a few grey whiskers and unusually animated eyes, Klavdiya Markovna shouted too—but hers were happy shouts, like those of an excited schoolgirl. She'd been knitting a cotton sock as she sat by an open window and now, with her glasses perched on her head, she looked past the house's two large porches, toward the courtyard and the fields. Standing on the right side porch, Natalya made a low bow, smiling modestly: kindhearted as ever, darkly tanned, she wore bast shoes, a red wool skirt, and a grey blouse with a low-cut collar that revealed her wrinkled neck. And I remember how, looking at her neck and her sharp collarbones, her sad and tired eyes, I thought: this woman grew up with our father long, long ago in this very place, where in lieu of the great manor home that our grandfather built from oak—and which burned to the ground many times—an ordinary house now stands, where the garden's been reduced to this ordinary assortment of old birches, a few bushes and poplar trees, and where nothing remains of the servants' quarters and the outbuildings but a peasant hut, a barn, a clay shed, an icehouse buried under amaranth and wormwood. . . . Earnest questions and the smell of smoke from a samovar began to fill the air while from the hundred-year-old cabinets came crystalline dishes for jam and sugar biscuits specially kept for guests, gold spoons worn thin as maple leaves. And while the conversation warmed—it had been solicitous and friendly after such a long falling-out—we went to explore the house's dark chambers, search for the balcony with a view of the orchard.

Everything was black with age, simple, rough in those empty, low-ceilinged rooms; they'd been built from the remains of chambers that our grandfather himself once occupied, and they were arranged according to his original plan for the house. In one corner of the servants' quarters hung a large dark icon of St. Merkury, the same saint whose iron sandals lie before the iconostasis in the ancient cathedral in Smolensk. We had heard the story: Merkury was a man of great renown; a voice from the icon of the Guiding Virgin called on him to free the lands of Smolensk from the Tatars. When he had driven out the Tatars, Merkury slept, and was beheaded by his enemies. The saint then rose and, with his head in his hands, came to the gates of Smolensk to tell of these events. It was terrifying to look at that scene, painted by an icon-maker, long ago, in the ancient city of Suzdal: it showed a decapitated man holding in one hand the icon of the Guiding Virgin and, in the other, his own lifeless head, still helmeted and blue. This image of St. Merkury was said to be our grandfather's most cherished icon; heavily encased in silver, it had survived several terrible fires, one of which had cracked its board. The genealogical table of the Khrushchyov family was written out in Old Church Slavonic on its back. The painting's aura seemed to be matched perfectly by the large iron deadbolts that secured the top and bottom halves of the heavy divided door leading to the dining hall. Although it had been built to replicate that room where the Khrushchyovs once gathered to eat meals while holding whips in their laps, the current hall was only half the size of the original. It had small sash windows and inordinately wide, slick, dark floorboards. We passed through it on our way to the drawing room. There, across from the balcony doors, once stood the piano that Aunt Tonya played when she was in love with the officer Voitkevich, a friend of Pyotr Petrovich. Farther on, the doors had been left wide open to the den, which in turn led to the corner rooms of the house where our grandfather once had his private apartment. . . .

It was a gloomy evening. Summer lightning flashed in the distance, revealing thunderheads that hung like pink and gold mountains beyond the remnants of the orchards, the silver poplars, and the stripped-out barn. Evidently the storm had not passed over Troshin Forest, which now was going dark far beyond the orchard, on the hillsides past the ravines. From there descended the warm, dry smell of oaks mingled with the scent of green leaves, and a light, damp breeze that passed across the tops of the remaining birches in the avenue, the tall nettles, the overgrown weeds and shrubs near the balcony. Over everything reigned the deep silence of evening, the silence of the steppe and all the distant, unknown lands of Rus. . . .

"Come for tea now, please," a quiet voice called out to us. It was she—the witness and survivor of this entire life, the vital narrator of its events—Natalya. And behind her came Aunt Tonya, Natalya's former mistress: her back was slightly hunched as she glided ceremoniously across the smooth, dark floor, peering around the room with her madwoman's eyes. She still wore her grimy headscarf, but the dressing gown had been replaced by an old-fashioned *barege* dress and a shawl of faded gold silk.

"*Ou etes-vous, mes enfants?*" she shouted, smiling affectedly. Sharp and precise as a parrot's, her voice echoed strangely in the empty, dark rooms.

III

The sad remains of that estate which gave Natalya life still retained a delicate allure, just as she herself possessed a natural charm with her peasant's candor and simplicity, her pitiable and lovely soul.

It smelled of jasmine in the old drawing room with sloping floors. The decaying balcony had turned blue-grey with time and now was sinking into the tall nettles, the honeysuckle, and the staff shrubs. If you wanted to get down from it, you had to jump, for it had no steps. On hot days, when its wood baked in the sun and the sagging doors were left open, their shimmering glass reflected in the dingy oval mirror that hung inside the drawing room, we always thought of Aunt Tonya's piano, for it once stood below that mirror. She used to play it, reading yellowed sheets of music with titles written in elaborate script, while *he* stood behind her, clenching his jaw and frowning, his left hand resting firmly on his waist. Wonderful butterflies flew into the drawing room, their bodies and their wings like something made from Japanese kimonos, bright cotton prints, or shawls of black-and-lilac-colored velvet. Before he left, he crushed one with his palm—lashed out in rage as it alighted timidly on the piano lid. Only a silvery dust remained, but when the maids stupidly wiped it away several days later, Aunt Tonya grew hysterical. . . . We went out onto the balcony, sat on the warm floorboards—and thought, and thought. Wind rose in the orchard, brought to us the sound of birches rustling like silk, their green branches spread wide, their trunks like white satin paper flecked with black enamel; wind blew in from the fields, whispering and sighing loudly. A gold-green oriole cried out sharply, joyfully, then shot like an arrow above the white flowers, following a flock of chattering jackdaws that lived with all their relatives in the ruined chimneys and dark lofts, where it smelled of old bricks and sunlight fell through the dormer windows, sloped in golden strips across mounds of grey-and-violet ash. The wind settled down. Bees crawled sleepily among the flowers by the balcony, carrying out their measured work. And only the poplars' silvery leaves stirred amid the silence—lightly, evenly, like a small and constant rain. . . . We roamed through the orchard and wandered to its outskirts where the undergrowth was wild and heavy, bordering the fields of wheat. And there, in the bathhouse that our great grandfather built—that bathhouse where Natalya once hid a mirror that she'd stolen from Pyotr Petrovich, and which now lay in ruins, its ceiling half collapsed—we discovered white rabbits. How softly they leapt out to the steps. How strangely they sat there, twitching their whiskers and their divided mouths, squinting with their wide-set, bulging eyes at tall spring onions and nightshade, blackthorn and cherry trees choked by high nettles. . . . And an eagle owl lived in the stripped-out threshing barn. He'd searched for the gloomiest place he could find and settled on a pole for holding haystacks; perched there with his ears stuck up like horns, his blind and yellow pupils aimed fiercely at the world, he resembled a small, pugnacious demon. . . . The sun descended far beyond the orchard in the sea of wheat; a bright and peaceful evening settled in. A cuckoo called in Troshin Forest; the birch-bark pipes of the old shepherd, Styopa, sounded plaintively somewhere above the meadows. . . . The eagle owl sat and waited. Night came and sleep descended on the fields, the village, the manor house. And then the eagle owl screeched and cried. Noiselessly he'd sail around the barn and through the orchard, softly settle on the roof of Aunt Tonya's hut— and begin to wail as if in pain, waking Aunt Tonya on her bench beside the stove.

"Jesus. Beloved. Dearest. Pity me," she'd whisper.

Flies buzzed with sleepy dissatisfaction along the ceiling. Something woke them every night. Sometimes a cow scratched its flank against the hut. Sometimes a rat ran fitfully across the rattling keys of the piano, then toppled with a crack into the pottery shards that Aunt Tonya carefully stacked in the corner of the room. Sometimes the old black cat with green eyes returned late from one of its outings and lazily called to be let in—and sometimes that owl flew onto the roof and began its screaming like a prophet of doom. Then Aunt Tonya would overcome her drowsiness, brush away the flies that crawled around her eyes as she slept, grope her way past the benches to the door, throw it open with a bang, and step outside. And then, aiming by sheer guesswork, she would fling a rolling pin into the starry sky. The owl's wings would rustle softly against the thatch as he launched himself into the darkness, descending almost to earth as he glided back toward the barn, then shooting up to settle on its roof. And from there, once more, his cries would reach the manor house and drift through the estate. He'd sit as if remembering something, let out a startled wail, and pause, go silent. Then, without the slightest warning, he'd launch into a frenzied laughing, hooting, squealing—only to break off, go silent once again—but not for good: he'd soon burst out with moans and sobs and keening cries. . . . And the warm, dark nights, with their lilac-colored clouds, were calm, calm. The steady, drowsy stirring of the poplars' leaves was like a languid stream.

Summer lightning flashed cautiously above dark Troshin Forest, and the warm, dry scent of oaks lingered in the air. Near the forest, drifting in a glade of sky between the clouds, Scorpio hung above the plains of wheat like a silver triangle, like the little roof they put above a graveyard cross to protect it. . . .

We often came back late to the manor house. Having breathed our fill of dew and wildflowers, grass and fresh air from the steppe, we'd carefully cross the porch and enter the dark foyer. And there we'd often find Natalya praying at the icon of St. Merkury. Barefoot, small, her hands clasped together, she stood and whispered, crossed herself, bowed low before the saint, who was hidden by the dark. All of it was simple, as if Natalya were engaged in conversation with someone no less gracious and benign than she.

"Natalya?" we called out quietly.

"Yes, it's me," she answered softly, simply, breaking off her prayers.

"Why are you still up so late?"

"The grave will give us all the time we need to sleep."

We sat on the window seat while she stood before us, her hands clasped together. Summer lightning flickered in the distance and secretly lit up the darkened chambers of the house. We opened a window. A quail was calling far away in the heavy dew of the steppe. A duck stirring on the pond began to quack uneasily.

"The two of you have been out walking, sir?"

"Yes."

"And so it ought to be. Walking's for the young. We used to walk all night as well. Dusk would bring us out, and dawn would send us home."

"Did you live well back then?"

"Yes, sir. It was good, our life."

A long silence fell.

"*Nyanechka*, why does the owl shout so much at night?" my sister asked.

"For no good reason, dear. There's no getting at him, though. Gunshots, even. Nothing makes him stop. And he brings us all a terror. Everyone believes he's promising some doom. How your aunt is terrorized by him! And it takes almost nothing, after all, to stop her heart with fear."

"What made her ill?"

"Well, everybody knows, sir—it was tears and tears, black grief. . . . Then she started praying. She grew fierce with us—with all the girls in the house. And she was always angry with her brothers. . . ."

Remembering the whips, we asked: "It wasn't very friendly then, among the family?"

"Friendly? There were no friends anywhere! Especially once your aunt was taken ill and your grandfather died. That's when the young masters came into their own, and Pyotr Petrovich wed. Everyone was hot—pure gunpowder!"

"Did they whip the house serfs often?"

"No, sir, that was not the custom here. I was guilty in so many ways! And all they did to me—all Pyotr Petrovich ordered—was to cut my hair with sheep shears and dress me in a shirt of twill, then ship me to the farm. . . ."

"What was it you were guilty of?"

But there was no guarantee of a quick and simple answer. Sometimes Natalya told her stories with surprising detail and direct-ness. But at other times her speech grew halting; she fell to thinking and lightly sighed. And even though we couldn't see her face in the darkness, we knew from her voice that she was smiling sadly.

"Well, I was to blame. . . . I've told you before . . . I was young. Foolish, sir. '*In the garden sang a nightingale—a song of sins and suffering.*' Everyone knows, sir. It was a girl's foolishness. . . ."

"Nyanechka," my sister said tenderly, "tell us that poem all the way—to the end."

Natalya was embarrassed. "It's not a poem, dear, it's a song. . . . I don't remember all the words now."

"That's not true—you do know all the words."

"Well then, all right. Here you are," Natalya said, and quickly ran through the refrain without emotion: "*'In the garden sang a nightingale—a quiet song of sins and suffering; and in the dark of night, her head still full of dreams, a foolish girl lay listening. . . .'*"

"Were you very much in love with uncle?" my sister asked, overcoming her embarrassment.

"Very much, dear."

"Do you always remember him in prayers?"

"Always."

"They say you fainted when they took you away to Soshki."

"I fainted, yes. . . . All of us who served the house—we were awfully tender. Couldn't take real punishments. Our skin was soft—nothing like those *odnodvortsy* who have leather hides. . . . When Yevsey Bodulya drove me away in the cart, fear and sorrow were like a fog in me. . . . He brought me to a town, and I felt like I was suffocating there—I'd never breathed such air! And then we drove out to the steppe, and I felt so sad and helpless. An officer who looked like him rode past: I shouted, fainted dead. And when I came back to myself, still lying in that cart, I thought: 'Everything is better now. . . . It's like I've gone to heaven now.'"

"Was he strict?"

"God preserve me! He was strict."

"But Aunt Tonya was the most difficult of all?"

"She was, sir. I'll tell you: they even took her to a saint's remains. What we've gone through with her! She could live now, live just fine—it's time, after all. But she was proud, and wound up touched. . . . How he loved her, that Voitkevich! But what can anybody do!"

"Well, and grandfather?"

"Well, what of that?. . . His mind was weak. But he could blow up too. They all were flint and fuel. . . . But for all that, the old masters didn't act like we were grime. They didn't wipe us from their

[169]

hands. Sometimes your father would punish Gervaska for some-thing at dinner—punish him with good reason—and then, in the evening, you'd look outside and see them playing balalaikas in the yard together. . . ."

"But tell us, was he handsome, that Voitkevich?"

Natalya thought it over. "No, sir, I don't wish to lie: he looked a bit like a Kalmyk. And so serious! Insistent. Always reading poems and scaring her—'I'll die,' he'd say, 'I'll die and then come back for you.' . . ."

"But then, grandfather lost his mind from love as well, didn't he? . . ."

"It was because of your grandmother. But that was a different kind of story. And the house was gloomy. . . . Not at all a happy place. . . . I'll tell you, if you want to listen. If you want to hear about it in my clumsy words."

And Natalya began a long narrative, whispering unhurriedly.

IV

According to legend our great grandfather, a rich man, moved from somewhere near Kursk to Sukhodol in his later years. He didn't like the place—its isolation and its endless forests. It's become a cliché to say that there were forests everywhere in the old days, but evi-dently it was true two hundred years ago, when people traveling our roads fought their way through dense woodlands. Everything was lost in those forests—the Kamenka River and its upper banks, the village, the estate and all the hilly fields surrounding it. But it wasn't like this in my grandfather's time. By then the picture had already changed: bare hills and rolling steppe, fields of buckwheat, rye, and oats; a few hollow white willows along the big road; and on the rise where the manor house stood, nothing but flat white stones. Only Troshin Forest remained of all the woodland. But, of course, the or-chard and the garden were still lovely: a wide avenue of seventy spreading birches; cherry trees sinking in the nettles; dense thickets of raspberry cane, acacia, and lilac; and almost a full grove of silver poplars at the orchard's edge, bordering the fields. The house had a thick, dark, solid roof of thatch. It looked out on a courtyard with long outbuildings and servants' quarters extending in sections along its sides. Beyond the courtyard sprawled the estate's village — large, poor, ramshackle — amid an endless expanse of green pastures.

"The village was all of a piece with the master," Natalya would say. "And the master didn't pay much mind to things. Couldn't handle money well. Didn't follow farming. Semyon Kirillych, your grandfather's brother, had already taken for himself whatever was largest and best in their inheritance, including their father's house. All he left your grandfather was Soshki and Sukhodol, and another four hundred souls, half of which ran away."

Our grandfather died at around the age of forty-five. Our father always said that he'd lost his mind when a sudden storm caught him sleeping on a carpet in the garden and rained an entire treeload of apples down on his head. But among the menials, Natalya told us, there was another explanation. They said that Pyotr Kirillych lost his mind from grieving over the loss of his beautiful wife, who died the day after a huge thunderstorm passed through Sukhodol. Pyotr Kirillych had dark hair, sloped shoulders, and black eyes that looked out at the world with affectionate attention; he looked a little like Aunt Tonya, and he lived out his life in a quiet, peaceful state of madness. According to Natalya, the family had more money in those days than anyone knew what to do with; and so, wearing boots of Moroccan leather and a florid caftan, Pyotr Kirillych wandered noiselessly through the house, nervously looking around him and stuffing gold coins in the cracks between the oak beams that formed the walls.

"It's for Tonya's dowry," he muttered when they caught him. "This is far more reliable, my friends. Far more reliable. . . . But even so, it's a matter of your will. If you don't want me to, I won't. . . ."

And then he went right back to hiding coins inside the cracks. Some days he would rearrange the heavy furniture in the drawing room, expecting, all along, some kind of visit despite the fact that the neighbors almost never came to Sukhodol. On other days he would complain of hunger and prepare *tyurya* for himself—inexpertly crushing and grinding green onion in a wooden cup, crumbling bread into the mush, then pouring in a foamy mix of water and fermented flour, and, finally, adding so many large, grey grains of salt that the *tyurya* was bitter, impossible to eat.

Life on the estate slowed to a halt after lunch, and all the people in the manor house wandered off to some quiet napping place where they would doze for hours. During those long afternoons, Pyotr Kirillych was at loose ends: he slept little even during the night, and now had nothing to do. And so, unable to endure his loneliness, he would quietly approach the bedrooms, the foyers, and the female servants' hall and call out to the sleepers:

"Arkasha, are you asleep? Tonya, are you sleeping?"

Upon receiving an infuriated shout—"For the love of God, *papenka*, leave me in peace!"—he would hurriedly begin to soothe his listener—"Well then, sleep, sleep, my soul, my dear. I'm not going to wake you"—and then proceed to the next room, avoiding only the footmen's quarters, for the lackeys at Sukhodol were extremely churlish. Ten minutes later, however, he would appear again in the doorway and call out in a still more cautious voice, pretending that he'd just heard the harness bells of a private cab passing through the village—"Maybe Petenka has come home on leave from his division?"—or seen a massive thunderhead looming in the distance.

"And the master truly was terrified of thunderstorms, poor lamb," Natalya told us. "I was still a girl, still young enough to go without a headscarf then, but I remember well, sir. There was a kind of blackness to the house. . . . An unhappy place, God be with it. And a summer day was like a year. There were more serfs tending to those rooms than anyone knew what to do with. . . . Instead of one footman, they had five! And everybody knew—the young masters, after lunch, they go to sleep—and we, loyal serfs and upright servants, we went along to nap ourselves. And Pyotr Kirillych better not come to wake us! Especially not Gervaska. 'Lackeys! Hey, lackeys, are you sleeping?' he calls out. And Gervaska lifts his head from the trunk where he's been dozing, says: 'Would you like me to stuff your crotch with nettles?' And Pyotr Kirillych starts: 'What! Who do you think you're speaking to, you damned idler, you do-nothing!' Gervaska answers back: 'I was talking to the house spirit, sir—I was half asleep. . . .' And so Pyotr Kirillych again goes roaming around the hall and the drawing room, all the time peering out the windows, looking at the garden: isn't there a cloud out there? It was true, though—thunderstorms came often then. And those were powerful storms. Sometimes after lunch it would happen—an oriole begins to shriek, and suddenly, over the orchard, thunderheads come rolling in. . . . The house goes dark inside and all the weeds, the thick beds of nettles, they start to rustle and sway. The turkeys and their poults go to hide under the balcony. . . . And you feel such a menace in the air. Such black loneliness! And he, the old master, how he sighs and crosses himself, climbs up to light the wax candle in front of the icons, hangs up the towel from his father's burial— that towel I feared like death itself. Either that, or he throws a pair of scissors out the window. That helps, of course. Scissors—just the thing for turning back a thunderstorm!"

Sukhodol was happier when it was home to two citizens of France. First there was a certain Louis Ivanovich, a man with a long moustache and dreamy blue eyes, strands of hair combed carefully from ear to ear across his balding pate, and pants that ballooned around his hips in extraordinary ways, then tapered past his knees. He was followed by the middle-aged, forever cold and shivering Mademoiselle Sizi. And everything seemed livelier when they were there;

when Tonya had piano lessons; when Louis Ivanovich's voice rumbled through all the rooms as he shouted at Arkasha, "Go, and do not returning be!"; when in the classroom could be heard, "*Maître corbeau sur un arbre perché.*" The French contingent stayed at Sukhodol for a full eight years. Even after the children had been sent to school in the province's main town, they remained at the estate to save Pyotr Kirillych from ennui. It was only when the children were about to come home for their third holiday of the year that the French finally departed. And at the end of that school holiday, Pyotr Kirillych decided it was more than adequate to send Petenka back alone: Tonya and Arkasha were to stay with him. And so they stayed for good, untended and untaught. . . .

Natalya used to say, "I was younger than all the rest. But Gervaska was almost the same age as your *papasha*, and that made them best friends from the start. Only, it's right what they say: 'Wolves and horses can't be in-laws.' They befriended each other, swore for all time on their friendship, even traded crosses—and then Gervaska almost right away does this: he almost drowns your papa in the pond! He was just a dirty scab of a thing, but he was full of fiendish little plans. A nasty little plotter. 'So,' he says to your papa, 'you going to beat me when you grow up?' 'Yes,' your papa answers, 'I am.' 'Oh no,' Gervaska says. 'Why not?' asks your papa. 'Just because,' he says. And then he thinks up something. We had a barrel on the hill near the pond. He saw it, made a little note inside his head. And then he gave Arkady Petrovich the idea—climb inside and roll right down. 'You sail it down here first, then I'll take a ride,' he says. And so the young master climbs inside, shoves off, and goes rolling, banging down the hill so hard he hits the water. . . . Mother of God, there was just a cloud of dust where he'd been! Thank God the shepherds were nearby. . . .

The house still looked and felt inhabited when the French were there. During grandmother's day there had been authority and order. A master and an overseer. Power. Subordination. Formal rooms where guests were entertained, and private rooms where the family gathered. Ordinary working days and holidays. All of this remained in evidence while those two citizens of France resided there. But when they went away the house was left without a master. When the children were still small, Pyotr Kirillych seemed to have the upper hand. But what could he really do? Who owned whom? Did he command the serfs, or did they rule him? Someone closed up the piano. The tablecloth disappeared from the dining room. They ate lunch at random at the bare oak table. The *sentsy* was so crowded with borzois that no one could walk through it to the porch. There was no one left to think of cleanliness, and the dark log walls of oak, the dark ceilings and floors, the dark and heavy doors and frames, the old icons that filled a corner of the house with their stark figures painted in the ancient Suzdal style—soon all of it had gone completely black. The house was frightening at night, especially during thunderstorms, when the garden raged under heavy rain, when the mystic visages of the icons were lit up every minute in the hall, when the pink and golden, trembling sky suddenly flew open, yawned above the garden trees, and then, in blackness, blows of thunder split the air. And during the day it was sleepy, empty, dull. Pyotr Kirillych grew weaker every year, went more and more unnoticed. His wet nurse, the decrepit Darya Ustinovna, eventually emerged as the house's overseer, but her power was just as minimal as his. And the steward Demyan simply refused to be involved in the household, saying he knew only how to run the fields. "I'm not doing anything to hurt the master," he would say with a lazy smirk. My father had no time for Sukhodol in his youth: he was completely carried away by hunting, balalaikas, and his love for Gervaska, who was counted among the footmen but disappeared for entire days with his young master to places like Meshchersky's Marshes, or to the carriage house where he gave lessons in the subtleties of birch-bark pipes and balalaikas.

"We knew perfectly," Natalya would say, "they used the house only for sleeping. And if they aren't asleep, it means they're in the village or the carriage house—or else they're out hunting: rabbits in the winter, foxes in the fall, quail and ducks and bustards in the summer. They climb into the *drozhky*, throw a gun over their shoulders, shout to Dianka—and that's it, they're gone: today it's Srednaya Mill, tomorrow it's Meshchersky's, the day after that the steppe. And always with Gervaska. Everywhere they went, it was always his idea. But he'd pretend the young master was dragging him along. Arkady Petrovich loved him, truly loved Gervaska, his enemy, like a brother. But that one—he just jeered at Arkady Petrovich. The more they were together, the more vicious was his jeering. Arkady Petrovich would say, 'Gervaska, come on, let's practice balalaikas. Please—teach me 'Red the Sun Went Down.' And Gervaska looks at him, exhales cigarette smoke through his nose, says with a smirk: 'First, kiss my hand.' Arkady Petrovich goes all white, jumps up, and *bam!*—slaps Gervaska in the face with everything he's got. And that one, he just jerks his head back, turns even blacker, scowls like a killing brigand. 'Get up, you bastard!' your *papasha* shouts. He gets up, stands all straight, like a borzoi, but with his baggy pants hanging down. . . . Says nothing. 'Ask my forgiveness.' 'My fault, sir.' And the young master—he just chokes on anger, doesn't even know what else to say. 'You hear that—"sir"! That's right—"sir" he shouts. 'I try to get along with you like an equal, you bastard. Sometimes I even think, "I'd give up my soul for him." And you—what are you doing? You try to set me off! You want me in a rage!'

"It's enough to make you wonder, though," Natalya said. "Gervaska mocked the young master and your grandfather while your aunt, the young mistress, she mocked and jeered at me. But Arkady Petrovich—and really, the truth be told, your grandfather too—they worshipped Gervaska. They could forget their souls looking at him! And I was just the same with the mistress. I worshipped her . . . when I returned from Soshki, came back a little to my senses after those misdeeds. . . ."

V

They began to bring whips to the table after our grandfather died and Gervaska fled Sukhodol, after Pyotr Petrovich married, after Tonya lost her mind and declared herself a bride of "sweetest Jesus," and after Natalya returned from the farm called Soshki. It was love that made Aunt Tonya lose her mind; love that sent Natalya into exile.

The dull isolated days of our grandfather were being replaced with a time of young masters. Pyotr Petrovich returned to Sukhodol, having unexpectedly resigned his post. His homecoming proved to be the ruin of both Natalya and Aunt Tonya.

They both fell in love. They didn't notice when it happened. At first it simply seemed that life had grown happier.

As soon as he returned, Pyotr Petrovich brought a new order to Sukhodol, a festive, stately way of life. He came with a friend, Voitkevich, as well as a cook—a clean-shaven alcoholic who looked with contempt upon the tarnished, ribbed molds for jelly, the crass and ugly cutlery of Sukhodol. Pyotr Petrovich wanted to appear generous, carefree, and rich before his friend, and he tried to come across this way through awkward, adolescent gestures and displays. And indeed he was, in many ways, a boy—a boy with both delicate and handsome features as well as a harsh, cruel temperament; a boy who seemed self-confident but who in fact was easily embarrassed to the point of tears—and then long harbored bitter malice toward the cause of his discomfiture.

"Brother Arkady," he said on his first day back at Sukhodol. "I seem to recall us having a few bottles of Madeira that weren't bad."

Our grandfather flushed. He wanted to say something but couldn't find the courage, and instead began tugging at the front of his caftan. Arkady Petrovich was confused.

"What Madeira?"

Gervaska gave Pyotr Petrovich an insolent look and smiled.

"You forget, if you will permit me, sir," he said to Arkady Petro-vich, making no attempt to hide his ridicule. "We did have a stock of that wine. More than anyone knew what to do with! But us drudges in the yard, we took care of it, sir. Fine wine, really—fit for a master. We gulped it down like *kvass*. . . ."

"What is this?" shouted Pyotr Petrovich, flushing darkly. "Don't open your mouth!"

Grandfather joined in ecstatically. "That's right, Petenka, that's right! Bravo!" he cried in a thin, joyful voice. "You can't imagine how he mocks me! So many times I've thought—I'll just sneak up right now and shatter his skull with a copper pestle! . . . God knows I've had that thought! I'll plant a dagger to its hilt in him!"

But Gervaska suffered no loss of words.

"I hear, sir, that the punishment for that kind of thing is quite painful," he answered with a scowl. "And besides, I have an idea too—it just keeps crawling into my head: the master's overdue in heaven!"

Pyotr Petrovich would later say that after such a shockingly im-pudent answer, he managed to control himself only on his guest's account. He spoke just three more words to Gervaska: "Leave. This instant." And then he even felt embarrassed for this flash of anger. He hurried to apologize to Voitkevich, smiling as he raised to him those charming eyes that always lingered for a long, long time in the memory of anyone who knew Pyotr Petrovich.

For too long those eyes lingered in Natalya's memory.

Her happiness was stunningly brief. And who could have thought that it would end in a trip to Soshki, the most remarkable event of her entire life?

Soshki farm is still intact today, though its ownership long ago passed to a merchant from Tambov. It consists of a long peasant hut in the middle of an empty plain, a storehouse, a shadoof and a well, and a barn in the middle of some melon fields. It was just the same in grandfather's day; even the town along the road from Sukhodol has hardly changed over the years. Natalya's crime was theft: to her own surprise she'd stolen a small folding mirror in a silver frame from Pyotr Petrovich.

When she saw that mirror she was so astonished by its beauty—as she was by everything that Pyotr Petrovich owned—that she could not resist. And for several days, until they noticed that the mirror was missing, she lived in a daze, stunned by her crime, spellbound by her terrifying secret and her treasure, like the girl in the tale of the scarlet flower. Lying down to sleep, she asked God to let the night pass quickly, to let morning come as soon as possible: the manor house had come to life, turned festive; something new and wonderful had entered all the rooms since the arrival of the handsome master, so elegantly dressed and pomaded, with a high red collar on his military jacket, with a dark complexion and a face as tender as a girl's. A festive atmosphere had even filled the entranceway where Natashka slept, and where, at dawn, she jumped up from the trunk on which she made her bed and immediately remembered that the world contained great joy because a pair of boots light enough for the tsar's first son to wear now stood outside the door, waiting to be cleaned. That festive mood, together with her giddy fear, grew strongest out beyond the garden—there, in the abandoned bathhouse, where the double mirror in a heavy silver frame was hidden. While everyone was still asleep, she'd run there through the dewy brush, and in that secret place she'd savor her possession of this mesmerizing treasure—carry it out to the bathhouse steps, unfold it in the hot morning sun, stare at her reflection until her head began to spin—and then she'd hide it, bury it once more, run back to the manor house where all morning she would tend to him, that man to whom she couldn't raise her eyes, he for whom she stared so long at her reflection, hoping, crazily, that he might find her pretty.

But the fairy tale about the scarlet flower ended quickly, very quickly. It ended in disgrace and shame that had no names in

Natashka's mind. . . . It ended in an order from Pyotr Petrovich that they cut off all her hair, make hideous that girl who used to wear her nicest things for him, who darkened her eyebrows in that little mirror, who created in her mind the sweet illusion that she had shared with him some secret intimacy. He discovered her crime himself and turned it into a simple theft, the stupid escapade of a serf girl whom they dressed in a shirt of coarse twill and whom—disgraced, suddenly cut off from everything she knew and cherished, her face still swollen from her sobbing—they sat on a manure cart and, with all the other house serfs gathered round to watch, drove away to some frightening and unseen farm somewhere in the distant steppe. She knew that there she'd have to tend to turkeys, chickens, fields of squash and melon; that she would burn in the sun, utterly forgotten by the world; that the long steppe days would be like years; that the horizons would sink in sheets of shimmering heat, and it would grow so silent, so sultry that she'd long to sleep a dead sleep for days but would be forced instead to listen to the careful crack of dried peas, the deliberate scratching of the brood hen in the hot dirt, the measured exchange of sad calls among turkeys—be forced to watch out for the cruel shadow of the hawk as it sailed across the land, and then leap up, scream "Shoo!" in a thin and drawn-out voice. There an old Ukrainian woman would have complete control over Natashka's life and death, and now, already, she was waiting impatiently for her victim to arrive! The only advantage that Natashka had over someone being driven to his execution was that she might still decide to hang herself. And this alone gave her comfort as they drove to her exile, which she assumed would be eternal.

The sights were endless as they traveled from one end of the district to the other. But none of it was for her. She thought, or rather felt, one thing alone: life is over. Your crime and your disgrace are far too great for you ever to hope for a return! For now there remained one person who was close to her: Yevsey Bodulya.

But what would happen once he gave her into the hands of the old Ukrainian, spent the night, then left her behind forever in that strange land? She wept, and then she wanted to eat. To her surprise, Yevsey looked on this quite simply, and while they ate together he spoke to her as if nothing had occurred at all. Then she fell asleep and woke up in the town. It stunned her with its dreariness, its dry and stuffy air—and something else, something vaguely harrowing and mournful, like a troubling dream you can't explain. From that entire day she would remember only that the steppe is hot this time of year, that nothing on this earth is longer than the big district roads or more endless than a summer day; she would remember that there are places in a certain town where the wheels of a cart rattle strangely over the paving stones; she would remember that the town smelled of tin roofs in the distance, but in the middle of the square, where they stopped to rest and feed the horse among rows of closed-up eating sheds, the air was filled with the scents of tar and dust and rotting hay, which lay mixed with manure in clumps where other carts and *mouzhiki* had stopped. Yevsey unharnessed the horse and led it to the wagon to eat. He pushed his hat back on his head, wiped the sweat from his forehead with his sleeve, and, looking blackened by the raging heat, set off for an inn. He'd given Natashka the strictest orders "to look around" and, if anything went wrong, to raise the entire square with her shouts. Natashka stared at the cupola of a newly built cathedral, which burned like a huge, silver star somewhere far away, above the houses. She sat without taking her eyes from it, sat without moving until Yevsey returned. Looking livelier, still chewing something, he led the horse back into the cart shafts while holding a *kalach* under one arm.

"You and I are a little late now, my princess," he mumbled with new animation, addressing either Natashka or the horse. "No cause for hanging, though, I hope. It's not like there's a fire burning somewhere. . . . I'm not going to race back, either. The master's horse, brother, means more to me than your damn mouth," he said, already imagining Demyan, the steward. "He opens that hole of his, starts talking. 'You watch it with me,' he says. 'Something happens—I'll see what you've got in your pants!' 'Akh,' I think. 'His insult is like a blow to my stomach. The masters never even dropped my pants. Never once beat me! And you? You're like a dog with black gums.' 'Watch it,' he says. What's for me to watch? I'm no slower than you. I won't come back at all if I don't feel like it. Take the girl to the farm, make the sign of the cross—and that's the last they see. . . . And really, I mean—I'm surprised at this girl! What's the little fool grieving for? Is all the world in Sukhodol? The cart drivers will come through, or some wanderers. They pass the farm—just say a word, and next thing you know, you're past Rostov. . . . And there, well, no one knows a thing. Let them try to guess your name!"

Plans for hanging herself were momentarily displaced by thoughts of flight in Natashka's cropped head. The cart began to squeak and shake. Yevsey stopped talking and led the horse to the well in the middle of the square. The sun was going down behind them now, slowly sinking past a large garden outside a monastery. Across from it stood a jail with yellow walls: all of its windows had turned golden in the fading light. The sight of the prison further spurred her thoughts of flight. People do it—run away and live! But they say the wanderers steal children and burn their eyes out with hot milk, then pass them off as cripples to help their begging. And the cart drivers, they say they take children to the sea, sell them to the Nogais. And it happens—sometimes the masters catch their runaways, bring them back in chains, lock them in the prisons. It's not animals locked up in there, after all—just like Gervaska said. Those are people in there too. . . .

The light disappeared from the jail's windows. Natashka's thoughts grew confused. No, running away is even more terrible. Worse than hanging yourself. . . . Yevsey's bold talk had stopped. He was silent now, pensive.

"We're a little late, my girl," he said, his voice already sounding worried as he jumped onto the side of the cart.

And again the cart began to roar over the paving stones, shuddering and knocking loudly as it made its way toward the district thoroughfare. "It would be best to turn this cart around," Natashka half felt, half thought. "Race back to Sukhodol, fall at the master's feet!" But Yevsey kept driving on. There was no star above the buildings anymore. Ahead stood bare white streets, white houses, white paving stones—all ending in that huge white cathedral with its new cupola of white tin beneath a dry and pale blue sky. But back there, at home, the dew had already fallen; fresh cool air lingered in the garden; the scent of a warming stove began to rise from the cook's quarters; far beyond the plains of wheat, beyond the silver poplars at the garden's edge, beyond the old and cherished bathhouse, the dusk was slowly dimming. In the drawing room the doors were open on the balcony, and a scarlet glow was mixing with the twilight in the corners of the room while a girl who resembled both grandfather and Pyotr Petrovich with her black eyes and her dark, slightly sallow complexion adjusted the orange silk sleeves of her light, wide dress. Sitting with her back to the sunset, she stared at the sheets of music, struck the piano's yellowing keys, filled the room with the solemn and melodious notes of Oginsky's polonaise—filled the room with all those sounds of sweet despair, and seemed to pay no attention at all to the stocky, dark-complexioned officer who stood behind her, his left hand resting firmly on his waist as he frowned and intently watched her quick, light hands.

"It's happened to us both . . . her and me," Natashka half thought and half felt on those evenings, her heart going still. She would run into the cold, damp garden, step into the deep underbrush, and stand, half hidden, among the nettles and strongly scented burdock, waiting for that moment that would never occur—that moment when the young master would come down from the balcony, start walking down the avenue, see her, suddenly turn from the path and draw close with quick steps—and she would not utter a sound from terror and joy. . . .

The cart was rattling down the street. She'd thought the town might hold something magical, but it was only hot and odorous. Natashka looked with painful wonder at the well-dressed people walking along the paving stones among the houses, the gates, and the small shops with open doors. . . . "Why did Yevsey come this way?" she thought. "Isn't he embarrassed to rattle past them all so loud?"

They left the cathedral behind and began to descend toward the river along a bumpy, dusty incline that took them past a charred-looking blacksmith's shop and the rotting little shacks of craftsmen. The shallow river smelled of warm, fresh water and silt, clean spring air—familiar scents. The first light began to burn in a distant, lonely little house that stood on the opposite hill near the signal arm at the railroad tracks. . . . They were in the open now, completely on their own. They crossed a bridge and drove up to the signal arm—an empty road of white stones stared at them, its chalky surface receding far into the dark, fresh, and endless blue of evening in the steppe. The horse broke into a little trot until it passed the signal arm, then slowed back to a walk. Again you could hear how quiet it was, how silent the earth and sky became at night: only a little bell was ringing softly somewhere far away. It steadily grew stronger, more melodious, flowed into the rhythmic rattling of a *troika*, the steady clatter of carriage wheels as they raced along the road and drew near. . . . A young, free driver held the *troika's* reins, and in the carriage sat an officer, his chin buried in the collar of his hooded officer's coat. He lifted his head for a moment as the *troika* drew level with the cart, and Natashka saw a red collar, a black moustache, a young man's eyes shining under the visor of a helmet. . . . She gasped, went numb, and fainted. . . .

The senseless thought that this was Pyotr Petrovich had flashed through her mind, and the sudden jolt of pain and tenderness that surged like lightning through her simple, nervous, menial heart suddenly revealed exactly what it was she'd lost: all proximity to him. . . . Yevsey rushed to douse her lolling head with water from a wooden jug they carried in the cart.

A wave of nausea brought her back to consciousness, and she hurriedly leaned over the cart's side. Yevsey held her cold forehead in his palm. . . .

And then, her collar damp, her body unburdened and chilled, she lay on her back and looked at the stars. Alarmed, Yevsey sat silently, thinking and shaking his head, believing she was asleep as he drove faster and faster. The shuddering cart raced forward, and the girl felt as if she had no body anymore, just soul. And that soul was content, "as happy as it would have been in heaven."

Her love had bloomed like that scarlet flower in the garden of a children's tale. And now she rode away with it, took it to the steppe, a place even more remote than the deep woods of Sukhodol, so that there she could overcome in solitude and silence the first sweet agony of that love—and then, for years, for all her life, for eternity—bury it within the soul that Sukhodol had given her.

VI

Love was strange at Sukhodol. And so was hate.

Our grandfather was killed in that same year. His death was as senseless as that of his killer—as senseless as the death of anyone who died at Sukhodol.

Pyotr Petrovich invited guests to celebrate the feast of Pokrov—always a big holiday at Sukhodol—and worried terribly: would the marshal of the nobility come as he had promised? Grandfather was overjoyed but also worried for some reason no one understood. The marshal came, and the dinner was a great success. It was lively and loud, and no one had a better time than grandfather. Early in the morning of October 2, they found him dead on the floor in the drawing room.

When he resigned from the military, Pyotr Petrovich had made no effort to conceal the fact that he was sacrificing himself to save the Khrushchyov family's honor and ancestral home. He did not hide the fact that he was taking the estate into his hands "against his will." But he thought it essential to become acquainted with those more educated members of the local gentry who might prove useful, while avoiding any kind of rift with the others. At first he met these obligations flawlessly, even visiting all the small estate owners and the farm of Aunt Olga Kirillovna, a monstrously fat woman who suffered from sleeping sickness and cleaned her teeth with snuff. By fall no one was surprised that Pyotr Petrovich ran Sukhodol like an autocrat. He no longer resembled a handsome officer who'd come to visit while on leave; instead he looked like the true owner of an estate, a young master. He no longer flushed darkly when upset. He grew sleek, filled out, wore expensive caftans. He pampered his small feet with red Tatar slippers, adorned his small hands with turquoise rings. Arkady Petrovich was embarrassed to look into his brother's light brown eyes. He didn't know what to talk about with him. He went out hunting as much as possible and, at first, simply deferred to Pyotr Petrovich in everything.

At the feast of Pokrov, Pyotr Petrovich wanted to charm each and every one of his guests, show them all that he was master of the house. But grandfather bothered him terribly. He was blissfully happy but also tactless, garrulous, and pathetic in his velvet hat, his new, inordinately wide, navy blue coat, which the family tailor had sewn. He too imagined himself to be the gracious host, and he fussed around the house from early morning, determined to turn the initial reception of the guests into some kind of stupid ceremony. Half the double doors between the vestibule and the main hall were never opened. But grandfather himself pulled up the iron catches—carried in a chair by himself and climbed onto it, his entire body shaking from the effort. With both doors now flung back, grandfather stationed himself on the threshold and, exploiting the silence of Pyotr Petrovich—who had resolved to endure all of this and now seemed paralyzed by embarrassment and rage—he remained there, in the entranceway, until the very last guests had arrived. With his eyes fixed constantly on the porch—where it was also necessary to open all the doors as if in keeping with some odd custom—he stood and shuffled his feet with excitement until he saw a new arrival, then rushed toward him, throwing one foot over the other as he leapt up and executed a little *pas de chat*, followed by a low bow and a breathless, sputtering stream of words, which he repeated before everyone:

"How glad I am! How delighted! It's been so long since you visited me! Please, please come in!"

It enraged Pyotr Petrovich too that grandfather informed each and every new arrival of Tonya's departure to Lunyovo, the estate where her aunt Olga Kirillovna lived. "Tonechka's fallen sick with melancholy. She's gone to her aunt's for the entire fall,"—what could the guests possibly make of this unsolicited announcement? Of course everyone knew the story of Voitkevich. He might have had truly serious intentions, sighing as he did, enigmatically, whenever he was near Tonya, playing duets with her on the piano, reciting "Lyudmila" in a muffled voice, or telling her with gloomy pensiveness, "Your sacred word has bound you to a dead man." But even his most innocent attempts to express his emotions—giving her a flower, for instance sparked a rage in Tonya, and Voitkevich left abruptly. Once he had gone, Tonya stopped sleeping at night, sitting instead near an open window in the dark, waiting for a particular moment—known only to her—when it was time to burst out sobbing and rouse Pyotr Petrovich from his sleep. He would lie in bed for a long time, clenching his jaw, listening to those sobs and the constant patter of the poplars, which sounded like a small, incessant rain in the dark garden beyond the windows. And then he went to try to soothe her. Half asleep, the house girls came as well, and sometimes grandfather would come running in alarm, at which point Tonya would begin to pound her feet and shout: "Leave me alone! Savages! My enemies!"—and the entire business ended in shameful abuse, almost violence.

Pyotr Petrovich would drive out grandfather and the girls, slam the door, and stand there, still holding its handle. "Just imagine, you little snake," he'd whisper in a rage. "Just imagine how this looks to them!"

"Ahhh!" Tonechka would squeal furiously. "Papenka! He's shouting that I'm pregnant!"

And clutching his head in his hands, Pyotr Petrovich would fly from the room.

At the feast of Pokrov he was deeply worried about Gervaska: a few incautious words could trigger an embarrassingly rude response from him in front of the guests.

Gervaska had grown terribly. Huge, ungainly, he was both the smartest and most prominent of the servants, and now he too was dressed in a long, dark blue coat; wide trousers; and soft kid boots without heels; a worsted, lilac-colored scarf tied around his neck. His dark, coarse and dry hair was parted on the side, but Gervaska didn't want it cropped close to his scalp; instead he kept it in an even bowl-cut all the way around his head. There was nothing for him to shave other than two or three tough little curls on his chin and at the corners of his mouth, which was so big that people joked about tying it shut with ribbon. All bones and sharp angles, with an exceedingly wide, flat chest, with a small head and deep-set eyes, with thin, ashy-blue lips and large bluish teeth, this ancient Arian, this Persian of Sukhodol, had already been given a nickname: Borzoi. Looking at his bared teeth, hearing his intermittent coughing, many people thought to themselves: "Soon, soon, Borzoi, you'll drop dead." But unlike all the other serfs, they dignified this overgrown child with a patronymic: Gervasy Afanasyevich.

Even the masters were afraid of him. Their mind-set was the same as that of their serfs: you either rule a man or fear him. Much to the surprise of all the other menials, Gervaska had received no punishment at all for his impudent answer to grandfather on the day of Pyotr Petrovich's arrival. "You're an absolute swine, brother," Arkady Petrovich told him succinctly, to which he received an equally concise response: "I can't stand him, sir!" But Gervaska went to Pyotr Petrovich of his own accord. He stood in the doorway, presumptuous as usual, one knee cocked forward while he leaned back on his disproportionally long legs in enormous, wide trousers, and asked to be flogged:

"I'm a lout, sir, and I have a terrible hot temper," he said nonchalantly, widening his gaze as he looked into the room.

Believing the phrase "terrible hot temper" to be a hint at something, Pyotr Petrovich took fright.

"There will be plenty of time for that, my friend, plenty of time," he shouted with feigned severity. "Now go away, I can't stand seeing your impudence."

Gervaska stayed where he was without speaking. Then he said: "As you wish."

But he continued standing there a little longer, twisting one of the tough little hairs above his upper lip, baring his bluish teeth like a dog, all emotion eradicated from his face—and then he went away. From that time on he was firmly convinced of the advantage such a manner afforded: show no expression and be as brief as possible in your answers. Pyotr Petrovich began to avoid not only talking to Gervaska but even looking him in the eye.

Gervaska behaved with the same inexplicable nonchalance at Pokrov. Everyone in the house was run ragged preparing for the holiday, giving and receiving instructions, cursing, arguing, washing floors, cleaning the heavy dark silver of the icons with bluing chalk, kicking the dogs away as they tried to crowd back into the *sentsy*, worrying that the jellies wouldn't set, that the pastries and the cakes would burn, that the forks would not suffice. Only Gervaska smirked calmly and said to Kazmir, the alcoholic cook, who was now in a frenzy: "Take it easy, father deacon, or your cassock's going to split a seam!"

"Watch you don't get drunk," Pyotr Petrovich said to Gervaska distractedly, worrying about the marshal.

"I haven't drank since I was born," Gervaska shot back, as if speaking to a peer. "Not interesting."

And then, when all the guests had arrived, in a voice loud enough for everyone to hear, Pyotr Petrovich called out ingratiatingly:

"Gervasy! Don't disappear, please. It's like I have no hands without you near!"

And Gervaska answered with utmost courtesy and poise: "Don't worry for a moment, sir, I wouldn't dare to leave you."

And he served as never before, fully justifying the words that Pyotr Petrovich had spoken to the guests:

"You can't imagine the nerve of that gangly fellow. But he's an absolute genius! Hands of pure gold!"

How could he have known that these words would be the drops that overfilled the cup? Hearing them, grandfather began to pull at the breast of his coat and suddenly, across the entire table, he shouted at the marshal:

"Your Excellency! I beg your hand in aid! Like a child to its father, I run to you now with a complaint against my servant. Against that one, there! Against Gervasy Afanasyevich Kulikov! At every step he mocks me! He. . . ."

They interrupted him, implored him, calmed him down. Grandfather was distraught to the point of tears, but they began to soothe him with such affection and esteem—all of it, of course, tinged with a mocking irony—that he yielded to their supplications, was filled once more with the happiness of a child. Gervaska stood silently by the wall, his eyes lowered and his head turned slightly to the side. Grandfather saw that this Vulcan's head was extraordinarily small—and would be even smaller if the Vulcan's hair were trimmed; he noticed that the back of that head was pointed, almost sharp, and there the hair was particularly thick—coarse, black, crudely cut, it formed a kind of protuberance that stuck out over the back of his thin neck. All the sun and wind of his hunting trips had made Gervaska's skin begin to peel, and now his face was marked by several pale, violet-colored splotches. Grandfather cast his glances at Gervaska with fear and alarm, but all the same shouted joyfully to the guests:

"Very well, I forgive him! But for this I will not allow you to leave, dear guests, for three entire days! I won't let you leave for anything! Most of all, I beg you not to leave this evening. How disturbed I feel when the sun goes down! It's all so sad and lonely, so frightening. The sky starts to fill with storm clouds. And they say they caught two more French soldiers again—Bonaparte's men!—in Troshin Forest!. . . I'm bound to die in the evening—mark my words! Martyn Zadeka already predicted this in my future. . . ."

But he died early in the morning.

He insisted, and "for his sake" many guests stayed the night. They drank tea all evening. There were so many different kinds of preserves that you could come and go several times to try them all. Then they opened up the card tables, lit so many spermaceti candles that their reflected light spilled from all the mirrors, and the rooms of Sukhodol—filled with noise and conversation and the fragrant scent of Zhukovsky tobacco—took on a golden glow, like the incandescence of a church. But most important was the fact that many guests had decided to stay the night, for this meant not only another happy day but more chores, responsibilities. After all, if not for him, Pyotr Kirillych, they never would have managed such an entertaining party, such a rich and lively dinner, such a grand assembly of guests.

"Yes, yes," grandfather thought worriedly as he stood without his jacket late that night in his bedroom and looked at the blackening

icon of St. Merkury, a row of wax candles burning on the lectern before it. "And death will be savage to the sinful. . . . Let the light of
our anger burn without ceasing!"

But just then he remembered that he had wanted to think
something else; hunched over, whispering the fiftieth psalm, he
moved across the room, pausing to trim the pastille that smoldered
on his nightstand, and picked up his Psalter. He opened it with a
deep sigh of contentment and raised his eyes once again to the
headless saint—and suddenly struck on the idea he'd been meaning
to pursue. A smile lit up his face:

"They say, 'Have it—hate it; lose it—love it.' Well, it will be
the same with this old man when he's gone. . . ."

Fearing he would wake up late and fail to issue some essential
order, grandfather hardly slept. And early in the morning, when
that silence that comes only after a holiday still hung with the scent
of tobacco smoke in all the disordered chambers of the house, he
stole into the drawing room with nothing but slippers on his feet,
fastidiously picked up several small pieces of chalk that lay on the
floor near the open green tables, and then let out a faint gasp of
pleasure as he glanced at the garden through the glass doors, saw
the bright cold light of the azure, the silver rime that had covered
the balcony and the handrails, the brown leaves of the bare thicket
below the balcony. He opened the door and sniffed deeply: a bitter,
almost astringent scent of autumnal decay still rose from the
bushes, but now it was mixed with a winter freshness. And everything was motionless, calm, almost solemn. The sun was just rising
over the village, and it lit the tops of the birches that lined the main
path to the house like a painting, revealing a subtle, joyful lilac tint
that the azure sky created as it gleamed through the white, half-bare
limbs and branches still flecked with golden leaves. A dog ran to the
cold shade beneath the balcony, its feet crunching sharply over the
brittle grass, which seemed to be laced with salt. That crisp sound
reminded him of winter, and a shiver of pleasure passed through

the old man's shoulders. Then grandfather came back into the drawing room, took a deep breath, and began to rearrange the heavy furniture, which scraped loudly along the floor as he worked, glancing occasionally at the mirror, where the sky was reflected. Suddenly Gervaska entered the room, moving noiselessly and quickly. He was without his coat, half asleep, and "evil as the devil," as he would later say.

"Quiet, you! Who told you to move the furniture!" he shouted in an angry whisper.

Grandfather raised his excited face and answered with a tenderness that had come to him the previous day and stayed through the entire night.

"You see what type you are, Gervasy," he whispered. "I forgave you yesterday, and you, instead of showing gratitude to your master. . . ."

"I'm sick of you, you slobbering fool. You're worse than fall," Gervaska interrupted him. . . . "Let go of the table!"

Grandfather looked with fear at the back of Gervaska's head, which jutted out even more than usual above the thin neck that rose from the collar of his white shirt, but that fear was not enough to stop him from flaring with anger. He stepped in front of the card table that he'd planned to move into the corner.

He paused for a moment to think it over. "You let go!" he shouted, but not loudly. "It's you who must defer to the master! You're going to wear out my patience! I'll bury a dagger in you!"

"Akh," Gervaska said with annoyance, baring his teeth and hit the old man on the chest with a backhanded blow.

Grandfather slipped on the smooth oak floor, flailed his arms, and struck his temple on the sharp edge of the card table as he fell.

Seeing the blood, the old man's gaping mouth, his skewed and lifeless eyes, Gervaska tore from grandfather's still warm neck a small gold icon and an amulet on a worn-out cord. . . . He looked hurriedly around, tugged grandmother's wedding ring from the old man's pinky . . . and then Gervaska went quickly and soundlessly from the drawing room—vanished into thin air.

The only person from all of Sukhodol who saw him after that was Natalya.

VII

Two major events occurred at Sukhodol while she was still living at Soshki: Pyotr Petrovich married, and the brothers left as volunteers in the Crimean War.

She returned only after two full years had passed: they'd forgotten about her. And when she returned, she did not recognize Sukhodol, just as Sukhodol did not recognize her.

On that summer evening when a cart sent from the master's estate began to squeak outside the hut in Soshki, and Natashka hurried down the steps, Yevsey Bodulya exclaimed with surprise:

"Is that really you, Natashka?"

"Who else would it be?" she answered with an almost imperceptible smile.

Yevsey shook his head.

"You've turned out badly here."

But in fact she simply didn't look the way she had before. The round-faced girl with short cropped hair and clear eyes had turned into a calm, reserved young woman with a petite, graceful figure and a gentle manner. She wore a wraparound skirt of checkered wool and an embroidered blouse; although her headscarf was tied in the Russian style, it was dark, and Natashka's face, tanned from the sun, was covered in small freckles the color of millet. Born and raised in Sukhodol, Yevsey naturally objected to the dark headscarf, the freckles, and the suntan.

As they drove home, Yevsey said:

"Well now, my girl, you're old enough to have a husband. Do you want to marry?"

She only shook her head.

"No, Uncle Yevsey. I won't ever go to the altar."

Yevsey even pulled the pipe out of his mouth. "Why? What good could come of life alone?"

She began to explain unhurriedly: it wasn't meant for everyone to marry, after all. At Sukhodol they'd give her to the young mistress, most likely—and the young mistress had promised herself to God. She wouldn't want her servant girls getting married. And besides, she'd had many dreams lately. It was clear what they meant.

"What do you mean?" Yevsey asked. "What did you see?"

"No, well. . . . Nothing, really," she said. "Gervaska scared me to death then. He told me everything, and I started thinking. . . . And then the dreams came."

"Is it really true that he sat down and ate with you, Gervaska?"

Natashka thought for a moment:

"He ate breakfast. He came and said: 'I'm here on important business from the masters. Only, let's have a meal first.' We set the table for him as an honest man. He ate his fill, went outside the hut—and winked at me. I ducked out and he talked to me around the corner. Told me all of it in truth. And then he just went off on his own. . . ."

"Why didn't you call for the bosses?"

"No chance, no way. . . . He promised he would kill me. Said to keep quiet until evening. He told them he'd go down to sleep along the storehouse, and just kept on going."

All the house serfs looked at her with great curiosity at Sukhodol; her girlfriends from the servants' quarters pestered her with questions. But she answered with such brevity that Natashka seemed to be playing some kind of role that she had specially taken on.

"It was good," she told them repeatedly.

And once she said, like some kind of old pilgrim woman, "God's will is in everything. It was good."

And simply, without delay, she entered the daily working life of the estate, seemingly unsurprised by the fact that grandfather was gone, that the young masters had gone to war as volunteers, that the young mistress "had been touched" and now wandered among the rooms in emulation of her father, that Sukhodol was now controlled by a new, completely unfamiliar mistress who was lively, small, plump, and pregnant.

At lunch the new mistress shouted:

"Call in that one—what's her name? Natashka!"

Natashka came into the room quickly and noiselessly. She crossed herself and bowed to the icon in the corner, then to the mistress and Miss Tonya, and stood waiting for questions and instructions. Of course, only the mistress questioned her—Tonya, who had grown very tall, thin, and sharp-nosed, stared vacantly with her fantastically black eyes and never uttered a word. The mistress decided that Natashka should serve the young lady. Natashka bowed and said simply:

"Very well, ma'am."

The young mistress continued to stare at Natasha with the same indifferent attention, then suddenly attacked her that evening, her eyes crossed in a savage fury as she pulled out Natashka's hair with violent pleasure because the young serf had clumsily tugged on her leg as she removed her stockings. Natashka wept like a young child but said nothing, and later, as she sat on a bench in the servants' quarters and removed the many strands of hair that Tonya had torn loose from her scalp, she even smiled with tears still hanging on her lashes.

"Awfully fierce," she said. "This isn't going to be easy. . . ."

Tonya lay in bed for a long time after waking up the next morning. Natashka stood in the doorway with her head lowered, glancing sidelong at her mistress's pale face.

"What did you see in your dreams?" the young mistress asked. Her face and voice were so completely disengaged that someone else might have been speaking for her.

Natashka answered:

"Nothing, it seems, miss."

The young mistress leapt up as suddenly as she had attacked the night before, and flung her cup of tea at Natashka in a rage, then collapsed back onto the bed and began bitterly to sob and shout. Natashka managed to avoid the cup as it sailed toward her, and she soon learned to move out of the way of flying objects with unusual skill and speed. It turned out that the young mistress would sometimes shout, "Then make something up!" at those stupid girls who answered her questions about dreams by saying they'd seen nothing in their sleep the night before. But as Natashka was an ungifted liar, she was forced to develop a different skill: dodging.

A doctor was finally brought to see the young mistress. He left her with a wide array of pills and drops. Fearing they might poison her, Miss Tonya forced Natashka to try all her medicines first: she took them one after the other without a word of protest. Soon after her return to Sukhodol, Natashka learned that the young mistress had been waiting for her "like the light of day." Miss Tonya, it turned out, had remembered her for some reason, and she all but wore her eyes out looking for the cart on the road from Soshki while ardently assuring everyone that she would be completely well the moment Natashka returned. And Natashka did return—only to be met with absolute indifference. But perhaps it was her bitter disappointment that made the young mistress cry? Natashka felt her heart constrict with sorrow and regret when she realized this. She went into the corridor, sat down on a trunk, and wept again.

"Well now, feeling better?" the young mistress asked when Natashka came back into the room with swollen eyes.

The medicine had made her head spin and her heart skip beats, but Natashka whispered, "Better, miss," as she approached her, took her hand, and kissed it ardently.

For a long time after that she felt such pity for the young mistress that she couldn't look at her directly, and walked everywhere with her eyes lowered.

"There she goes—a little Ukrainian snake in the grass!" Soloshka shouted at her from the servants' quarters one day. More than any of her other girlfriends, Soloshka had tried to become the confidante of Natashka's innermost thoughts and feelings. But she repeatedly ran up against Natashka's brief and simple answers to her questions—answers that left no room for any of the charms and pleasures of girlish intimacy.

Natashka smiled sadly.

"Well, maybe so . . .," she answered thoughtfully. "It's true what they say—we bond to those we're near. I miss them, those Ukrainians. More than my own father and mother even."

At first she'd given no meaning to her new surroundings in Soshki. They'd arrived near morning. And nothing seemed strange that morning other than the fact that the peasant hut was very long and white and clearly visible from far away in the plains; that the Ukrainian woman greeted them in a friendly way as she heated the stove, while the Ukrainian man did not listen to Yevsey. And Yevsey rambled on and on without stopping. He spoke about the masters, about Demyan, about the blazing heat they'd encountered on the road, about the food he'd eaten in town, about Pyotr Petrovich, and of course about the mirror. But the Ukrainian man, Shary—or, as they referred to him in Sukhodol, the Badger—only shook his head and, when Yevsey finally fell silent, looked at him distractedly and began to sing under his breath in a happy, nasal tone: "Whirl, little snowstorm, whirl . . ." Then she began, little by little, to come to herself—and to wonder at Soshki, to discover more and more charm in it as well as ever more dissimilarities with Sukhodol. Even the Ukrainians' hut was remarkable with its white walls, its smooth and level roof of thatch made from rushes. How clean and wealthy it seemed in comparison to the poor and slovenly huts of Sukhodol! What expensive foil icons hung in the corner! And how lovely were the bright towels displayed above them, the paper flowers arranged around their frames! And the patterned cloth on the table, the rows of dark blue pots on the shelf near the stove! But most remarkable of all were the keepers of that hut.

What it was that made them so exceptional Natasha couldn't say, but she felt it constantly. She had never seen a *mouzhik* who was so calm, well kept, and agreeable as Shary. He wasn't tall, his head was shaped like a wedge, and his thick, full, greying hair was cut short. He had no beard, only a narrow moustache, like a Tatar's, which was also grey. His face and neck were tanned and deeply creased from the sun, but even his wrinkles seemed agreeable, neatly defined, somehow necessary. He wore pants of coarse, bleached canvas folded into the tops of his boots, which were so heavy they seemed to weigh down his feet. His shirt, also made of bleached canvas, had a low-cut collar and extra width in the arms; he wore it neatly tucked into his trousers. He hunched his shoulders slightly as he walked, but neither this nor his deep wrinkles nor his grey hair made him seem old: his face had none of that weariness, that torpor that fills our men. His small, sharp eyes looked at the world with keen and delicate laughter. He reminded Natashka of an old Serb who once appeared at Sukhodol from out of nowhere with a boy who played the violin.

The Ukrainian woman was named Marina, but they always called her the Spear at Sukhodol, for she was tall, thin, and gracefully built despite her fifty years. She had wide-set cheekbones and a coarse face. Her complexion was much darker than that of anyone who lived at Sukhodol, and years of sun had added an even, slightly yellow hue to her fine skin. But the candor of her eyes, their unyielding ebullience, made her almost pretty: they contained the grey of both amber and agate, and they changed like a cat's eyes. A large black-and-gold kerchief with red polka dots covered her head, resembling a high turban; a short, wraparound skirt of black wool clung tightly to her long waist and legs, sharply accentuating the whiteness of her blouse. On her bare feet she wore shoes with steel strips lining their heels; her bare calves were shapely and thin, and

the sun had turned them the color of light lacquered wood. Sometimes when she worked she would narrow her eyes and sing in a
deep, strong voice about the infidels laying siege to Pochaev, and
the Mother of God defending the monastery as "the evening sunset
burned above the walls," and there was such despair in her voice,
such keening sorrow—and yet, at the same time, such majesty and
power, such a mighty threat of retribution, that Natashka couldn't
take her eyes from her for fear and ecstasy.

The Ukrainians had no children; Natashka was an orphan. If
she'd lived with a family in Sukhodol they would have called her
their adopted daughter, and they would have pitied her on certain days while denouncing her as a thief and brandishing her
debts to them on others. The Ukrainians were almost cold by
comparison, but they treated Natashka with temperance and
equanimity, saying little and asking almost nothing. In the fall,
Russian peasant women from Kaluga were brought in for the harvest and the threshing, but Natashka stayed away from these
"Kaluga girls," for they were known to be debauched and shame-
fully diseased. Busty, impudent, and mischievous, they wore
bright *sarafans*, swore with pleasure and obscene proficiency,
scattered flippant phrases throughout their speech, straddled
horses like men, and rode as if possessed. Her grief might have
been dispersed by daily life and new confidantes, by tears and
shared songs. But to whom was she to tell her story? With whom
was she supposed to sing? If one of the Kaluga girls began a song,
all the others would immediately join in, erupt with their coarse,
shrill voices, their whistling and their little yelps. Shary sang only
humorous little songs that were meant for dancing. And even in
her love songs, Marina was stern and proud, somber, meditative:

The willows that I planted
Stir softly now
Beyond the weir

she'd sing, forlornly drawing out the words, and then, lowering her voice, she'd add with absolute despondency:

And still my darling love
Is nowhere near.

And so it was in solitude that Natashka slowly drank in the bittersweet poison of unrequited love, suffered through her shame and jealousy, the terrible and tender dreams that often came to her at night. Every day she struggled with the dead weight of her impossible hopes and expectations in the silence of the steppe. And the searing pain of her injury often gave way to tenderness within her heart; passion and despair became humility—a simple desire for some modest and discrete existence close to him, a love that she'd conceal from everyone forever, a love that demanded nothing, expected nothing. News and messages from Sukhodol helped to sober her, but for a long time there was no news, no sense of daily life at home—and Sukhodol began to seem so wonderful, so necessary that she felt she couldn't bear her loneliness and sorrow. . . . Then, suddenly, Gervaska appeared. He quickly and offhandedly related all the news from Sukhodol, covering in half an hour events that others might require entire days to describe, including the fact that he had killed grandfather with a shove.

"And now—goodbye for good!"

He went out to the road and turned; his eyes seemed to burn right through her as she stood there, stunned by his confession:

"And it's time for you to get the pap out of your head!" he shouted. "He's getting married any day. And he won't need you at all, not even on the side. Open your eyes!"

She did open her eyes. She lived through the terrible news, came to herself—and opened her eyes.

Then the days began to pass steadily and slowly, like the pilgrims who walked and walked on the highway past the farm and often carried on long conversations with her as they rested. They

IVAN BUNIN

taught her patience and reliance on God, whose name they pronounced with dull despondency. Above all else, they taught her
one rule: don't think.

"Think, don't think—nothing changes. Nothing will occur by
our will," the pilgrims would say as they retied the laces of their bast
shoes and squinted wearily into the distant steppe, their weathered
faces creasing deeply. "God's will is in everything. . . . Now sneak us
a little onion from the garden, there, won't you dear?"

There were others, of course, who frightened her with talk of
sin and promised her far greater woe and suffering in the world
that lies beyond this one. And then she had two terrible dreams, almost in a row. She was thinking all the time about Sukhodol—at
first it was so hard to keep from thinking!—about the young mistress, about grandfather, about her future. Sometimes she would
try to guess when she'd marry, and if she would, with whom. It was
in the midst of such a reverie that she slipped imperceptibly into a
dream: with utter clarity she saw herself running to a pond with
buckets as the sun set on a sultry, dusty day, and a troubling wind
swept across the land. Suddenly a hideous dwarf with a large head
and torn-out boots appeared on a hillside of dry clay. He had no
hat; the wind blew his red, disheveled hair into clumps, and his
unbelted fire-red shirt billowed around him. "Grandfather!" she
shouted with alarm and horror. "What's burning!" "Now it will all
be blown away! Not a trace will remain!" the dwarf shouted back,
his voice drowned out by the hot wind. "An untold storm is coming! Don't dare to take a groom!" The other dream was even more
terrible. She seemed to stand at noon on a hot day inside a peasant
hut. The door had been bolted shut from outside. She was waiting
for something, her heart going still—and suddenly a huge grey
goat jumped out from behind the stove. It reared back onto its
hind legs and came at her, obscenely aroused, with ecstatic and
imploring eyes that burned like coal. "I'm your groom!" it shouted
in a human voice, tapping its hind legs in shallow little steps as it

502

awkwardly drew close, then toppled forward onto her, its front legs striking hard against her breasts. . . .

Lurching up from her bed after this dream, she almost died from the pounding of her heart, the terror of the dark, and the thought that she had no one she could turn to.

"Lord Jesus," she whispered hurriedly. "Holy Mother of Heaven! Holy saints!"

But she imagined all the saints were dark and headless like Merkury, and thus they only added to her fear.

As she began to contemplate her dreams, she realized that her girlhood years had passed. She became convinced that many trials awaited her and that her fate was already determined, for it was not in vain that something so unusual as love for the young master had fallen to her lot! She believed it was essential that she learn restraint from the Ukrainians and obedience from the pilgrims. And since the people of Sukhodol liked to play roles—since they convinced themselves that certain events were inevitable, even though they themselves had invented these events from the beginning—Natashka too took on a role to play.

VIII

Her legs went weak with joy when Natashka ran out on the steps and understood that Bodulya had come for her; when she saw the dusty, battered cart from Sukhodol stopped outside the hut on the eve of St. Peter's Day; saw the torn hat on Bodulya's shaggy head; saw his tangled, sun-bleached beard; saw his animated, weary face—prematurely aged and indistinct, almost enigmatic in its amorphous incongruity; saw the familiar shaggy dog that looked not only like Bodulya but all of Sukhodol, with dingy grey fur covering its back and black hair matted to its chest and neck as if stained by the heavy smoke of peasant huts. . . . Quickly she composed herself. As they drove home, Bodulya sang whatever came into his head about the war in the Crimea, seeming to rejoice one minute and grieve the next, while Natashka said in a judicious tone:

"Well, it's obvious—we've got to force them back, those French."

All day while they drove toward Sukhodol, she had an eerie feeling: she was looking at the old and familiar with new eyes; she seemed to reenter her former self as they drew closer to her home. Soon she noticed little changes that had taken place along the road, recognized the people they passed. At the turn from the big road into Sukhodol, a three-year-old colt was running in a fallow field overgrown with wart cabbage. Standing with one foot on a rope lead, a young boy clutched at the colt's neck and tried to climb onto its back, but the colt refused to let him, shaking and running. Natashka felt an odd thrill of joy when she recognized the child as Fomka Pantyukhin. They passed the old man Nazarushka, who was now at least a hundred, and so wasted away "there'd be nothing left to put in his coffin"; even his eyes were colorless and sadly faded. He sat in an empty cart like a woman instead of a man, his legs stretched straight out in front of him, his frail shoulders raised high and held tense. Hatless, he wore a long, threadbare shirt that had turned dove grey with ash from his constant lying on the stove. Natashka's heart contracted, went still as she remembered once again that the kind and carefree Arkady Petrovich had wanted to flog this Nazarushka three years ago when he was caught with a radish in the vegetable garden and stood weeping, barely alive from fear, among a crowd of house serfs who shouted with raucous laughter:

"No, no, old man—whining won't do you any good. You'll have to drop your pants for this one! There's no getting out of it now!"

But how that same heart raced when she saw the pastures, the row of peasant huts—and then the estate: the garden, the high roof of the manor house, the back walls of the servants' quarters, the storage sheds, the stables. Yellow fields of rye filled with cornflowers ran right up to those walls, ran up to the tall weeds and the spring onions. Someone's white calf with brown spots had waded deep into the oats and stood there now, eating tassels from the stems. All of the surroundings were peaceful, simple, ordinary; they grew ever more alarming and remarkable only in Natashka's mind, which now turned turbid as the cart rolled briskly into the courtyard, where white borzois lay sleeping like headstones in a country churchyard. For the first time after two years in a peasant hut, she entered the cool interior of the manor house with all its familiar smells—wax candles and linden flowers, the open pantry, Arkady Petrovich's leather saddle lying on a bench in the vestibule, empty cages in which quail are kept above the window. Timidly she looked up at St. Merkury, moved now from grandfather's room to a corner of the entranceway. . . . Sunlight from the garden was streaming cheerfully through small windows, as it had before, into the gloomy hall. A chick that had appeared inside the house for some odd reason wandered around the drawing room, cheeping forlornly. A sweet scent came from the linden flowers drying on the hot, bright windowsill. . . . Everything old that surrounded her seemed to have grown younger, as always happens in a house after a burial. In everything, in everything—but especially in the flowers' scent—she felt a part of her soul, her childhood, her adolescence, first love. And she was sorry for those who had grown up, those who had died, those who had changed—as she herself, and the young mistress, had changed. Her peers were now adults. Many of those old men and women who would occasionally appear in the entranceway of the servants' quarters and look uncomprehendingly at the world, their heads wobbling with decrepitude—many of them had disappeared forever from this earth. Darya Ustinovna had disappeared. Grandfather had disappeared—he who'd feared death like a child, believing it would slowly take him into its grip and prepare him gradually for that terrible hour, but was instead mowed down with lightning speed by its scythe. It was impossible to believe that he no longer existed, that it was he rotting beneath that burial mound near the village church in Cherkizovo. It was impossible to believe that this thin, black-haired, pointy-nosed woman—she who was indifferent one moment and furious the next; she who chatted openly with Natashka as she would with a girlfriend and then began ripping out her hair—was the young mistress Tonya. And it was impossible to understand why the household was now run by some Klavdiya Markovna, who was small, had a little black moustache, and tended to shout. Once, Natashka looked timidly into the new mistress's bedroom and saw the fateful little mirror in a silver frame—and it all came flooding sweetly back into her heart, the fear and joy she'd felt, the tenderness, the expectation of happiness and shame, the heavy scent of burdock wet with dew at dusk. . . . But she stifled all those thoughts and feelings deep within herself, snuffed them out. Old blood—old blood from Sukhodol ran in her veins. She had eaten too much bitter bread from the loamy soil of that estate. She had drunk too much brackish water from those ponds her ancestors dug in the dried-up river beds. She was not daunted by that ordinary, everyday life that exhausted her with its predictable demands—it was the unusual, the extraordinary that she feared. Even death did not frighten her. But dreams, the darkness of night, thunderstorms, fire—these things made her tremble. She carried within herself the vague expectation of some inevitable disaster the way another woman caries an unborn baby below her heart.

This expectation made her old. And she told herself every day that her youth had passed, looked constantly for proof of her old age. The year had not yet rounded out since her return to Sukhodol, and already not a trace remained of that youthful feeling with which she'd crossed the threshold of the manor house.

Klavdiya Markovna gave birth. Fedosya the birdkeeper was promoted to nanny—and Fedosya, who was still young, put on the dark dress of old age, became humble, God-fearing. The new

Khrushchyov could barely bug out its milky, senseless little eyes; it produced streams of drool and bubbles, toppled forward helplessly under the overwhelming weight of its own head, screamed viciously—and already they called him *barchuk*, "little master"; already the old, old pleas and admonitions could be heard from the nursery:

"There he is, there he is—the old man with the sack. . . . Old man, old man! Don't you come to us. We won't let you take the little master. He's not going to shout anymore. . . ."

Natashka imitated Fedosya, considering herself a nanny as well—a nanny for the ailing young mistress. In the winter Olga Kirillovna died, and Natashka asked to go to the funeral with all the old women who were living out their final years in the servants' quarters. There she ate frumenty, and its bland, cloyingly sweet flavor filled her with revulsion; but later, when she returned to Sukhodol, she spoke sentimentally about Olga Kirillovna, saying that she'd "looked like she was alive," though even the old women hadn't dared to glance at that monstrous body in the coffin.

In the spring they brought to the young mistress a sorcerer from the village of Chermashnoe, the renowned Klim Yerokhin, a wealthy and appealing *odnodvorets* with a big grey beard and curly grey hair that he parted in the middle. He was a very capable farmer, and his speech was ordinarily simple and direct, except for those moments when, in the presence of the ailing, he transformed himself into a sorcerer. His clothes were unusually neat and well made: a tight little jacket sewn from coarse cloth the color of steel; a red sash and good boots. His little eyes were artful and astute; piously they sought an icon as he came into the house with his fine figure slightly hunched forward, and began a perfectly pragmatic conversation. He talked about crops, about rains and drought, and sat for a long time, meticulously drinking his tea. Then he crossed himself once more and finally asked about the patient, altering his voice the moment he spoke of her.

"Twilight. . . . Darkening. . . . Time. . . .," he said enigmatically.

The young mistress was shaking as if gripped by a violent fever. Sitting in the dusk in her bedroom, waiting for Klim to appear at the threshold, she was prepared to collapse onto the floor in convulsions. Natalya too was seized from head to foot with horror as she stood beside the young mistress. The entire house had gone quiet—even Klavdiya Markovna had ordered a crowd of servant girls into her bedroom, where she spoke with them in whispers. No one dared to light a single lamp, raise a single voice. The usually cheerful Soloshka was ordered to stand in the corridor outside Tonya's room and wait for instruction or a call from Klim. Her heart was beating in her throat, and her mind was going dark when he walked right past her, untying a little handkerchief that held some sort of sorcerer's bones. And then his loud, strange voice resounded in the deathly quiet of the house.

"Rise, slave of God!"

His grey head suddenly popped out of the doorway.

"A board." He threw the words out lifelessly.

Cold as a corpse, her eyes bulging out with terror, the young mistress was placed standing on the board as it lay on the floor. It was so dark that Natalya could barely make out Klim's face. Suddenly he began in a strange, distant sort of voice:

"Filat will come in. . . . Open the windows. . . . Open wide the doors. . . . Shout and say: 'Grief! Grief!'

"Grief, grief!" he exclaimed with sudden force and threatening power. "You must go now, grief—into the darkening forest—it's there you sleep—it's there you rest! On the ocean, on the sea," he muttered now, rapidly repeating the words in an ominous, muffled stream: "On the ocean, on the sea—on the Island of Buyan—lies a bitch, and on her back—there spreads a full grey fleece . . ."

Natalya felt there could be no words more terrible than these, which sent her back to the edge of some savage and fantastic world, some still unformed, primeval place. And it was impossible not to believe in the power of those words, just as Klim himself could not fail to believe in them, having brought about miracles among those possessed by disease—the same Klim who sat in the entranceway after his sorcery and spoke so simply, so modestly as he wiped the sweat from his forehead with a handkerchief and once more settled into his tea.

"Well, two more twilights now. . . . If God allows, it will ease a bit. . . . Did you sow buckwheat this year, madam?. . . They say it's good this year, the buckwheat. Strapping good!"

They expected the young masters to return from the Crimea in the summer. But instead Arkady Petrovich sent a registered letter with the news that they could not return before the end of the fall due to a wound that Pyotr Petrovich had suffered and which, though minor, required extensive rest. They sent someone to the soothsayer Danilovna, in the village of Cherkizovo, to ask if the wound would heal safely. Danilovna began to dance and snap her fingers, which meant, of course, that it would. Klavdiya Markovna was reassured. But Natalya and the young mistress had little time to think of the brothers. At first the young mistress had improved. But after St. Peter's it all began again: misery and fear—fear of thunderstorms and fires, and something else that she kept hidden. All of it was so consuming that she could think of nothing else. Nor could Natalya turn her attention to the men. Of course she asked for Pyotr Petrovich's health and salvation every time she prayed, just as later she would ask for his soul's repose as part of every prayer she uttered until she too reached her grave. But the young mistress was closest to Natalya now, infecting her more and more with her fears, her expectations of disaster, and that secret terror she explained to no one.

The summer was fiercely hot, dusty, windy; each day brought another thunderstorm. Dark, disturbing rumors spread among the people—rumors of some kind of new war, of riots and fires. Some said that any day now the *mouzhiki* would have their freedom; others said just the opposite—everyone would be pressed into the army. And as so often is the case, a countless array of vagabonds, monks, and fools appeared. Tonya almost came to blows with Klavdiya Markovna because of them, for the young mistress was determined to present them all with bread and eggs. Dronya came to the estate—he was tall, red-haired, exceedingly ragged. He played the role of a holy fool, but in fact he was just a drunk. He would become so lost in thought as he walked across the courtyard that he'd bang his head into the wall of the manor house, then jump back with a joyful look on his face.

"Birdies! My small birdies!" he would squeal in a falsetto, contorting his entire body and raising his right arm, as if to shield himself from the sun. "My birdies flew and flew across the sky!"

Emulating all the married women, Natalya watched him with the dull compassion one is supposed to show when looking at a holy fool. But the young mistress rushed to the window and cried out in a tearful, piteous voice:

"Holy Droniye! Little St. Droniye—pray to God for me, a sinner!"

Hearing such shouts, Natashka's eyes widened with terrible misgivings.

From the village of Klichin came Timosha Klichinsky: yellow-haired, small, effeminately fleshy with large breasts and the face of a cross-eyed baby, he labored both to breathe and comprehend beneath his suffocating bulk. Wearing a white calico shirt and short calico pants, he shuffled his ripe little legs in quick, mincing steps with the tips of his shoes pointed down, and as he approached the porch of the manor house his small narrow eyes looked as if he'd just surfaced from a deep pool of water, or saved himself from certain death.

"Ooful," he muttered and panted. "Ooful."

They calmed him down, fed him, waited for him to say something. But he didn't speak, just breathed noisily through his nose and made a chomping sound with his lips and tongue. And then, having chomped his fill, he tossed his sack back over his shoulder, looking anxiously for his walking stick.

"When will you come again, Timosha?" the young mistress called to him.

He answered with a shout, his voice an absurd, high alto:

"At holy week, Lukyanovna!" he called, mangling, for some reason, the mistress's patronymic.

And the mistress wailed mournfully:

"Holy Saint! Pray to God for me, a sinner, Mariya of Egypt!"

Reports of calamities—storms, conflagrations—came from all directions every day. The ancient fear of fire grew more and more extreme in Sukhodol. The moment storm clouds rose from behind the estate and darkened the sandy-yellow fields of ripening wheat, the moment the first gust of wind sailed across the pasture, all the women in the village rushed to carry the small, dark boards of their icons to the doorways of their huts, hurried to prepare those special pots of milk that everyone knew was best for pacifying flames. And at the manor house, scissors sailed through windows into beds of nettles; the dreadful, venerated towel made its appearance, and with trembling hands the people lit wax candles, covered up the windows. Even the mistress was consumed by some kind of fear, either genuine or contrived. She used to say, "Thunderstorms are natural occurrences," but now she crossed herself and squeezed her eyes shut, shrieked at the lightning. And in order to deepen her alarm and that of those around her, she spoke incessantly of some kind of fantastic storm that erupted over Tirol in 1771 and instantly killed 111 people. Her listeners would then join in, hurrying to tell their own stories about a white willow burnt to nothing on the highway, about a woman in Cherkizovo knocked dead by a thunderbolt a few days earlier, about a *troika* so deafened on the road that all three horses fell to their knees. . . . And then a certain Yushka—"a wayward monk," as he liked to call himself—began to join these revelries of fear and panic.

IX

Yushka had been born a peasant. But he never dirtied his hands with work. Instead he lived where God provided, paying for his bread and salt with stories of his constant loafing and his "wayward-ness." "Brother, I'm a *mouzhik* with brains, and I look like a hunch-back," he would say. "Why should I work?"

And he really did look like a hunchback; there was a kind of caustic intelligence to his completely hairless face, and he kept his shoulders slightly raised from the rickets in his chest. He chewed his nails; his fingers—which he used constantly to push his long strands of reddish-brown hair back from his face—were thin and strong. He considered plowing both "boring" and "obscene." And so he entered the Kiev Monastery, "grew up there," and was soon thrown out "for an offense." Then Yushka realized that posing as a man who seeks to save his soul—a pilgrim wandering among the holy sites—was old and tired, and often quite unprofitable. He de-cided to adopt a different guise: without removing his cassock, he began to boast of his idleness and lust, to smoke and drink (there never seemed to be enough to make him drunk), to ridicule the monastery, and to explain exactly how, by means of obscene ges-tures and body movements, he'd had himself thrown out.

"It's no surprise," he'd tell the *mouzhiki* with a wink. "No sur-prise at all they slapped me, slave of God that I am, square on the neck for that! So I headed home, to Rus. . . . I'm not going to waste away, I said. . . ."

And indeed, he didn't waste away: Rus took him in, a shame-less sinner, with the same consideration that it gave those pilgrims struggling to save their souls: it fed him, gave him drink, let him stay the night, listened to his stories with delight.

"Did you really swear off work for good?" the *mouzhiki* always asked, their eyes shining with the expectation of some new and poi-sonous revelation.

"The devil couldn't make me work," Yushka answered back. "Not now. I'm spoiled, brother! And I'm rutting like a monastery goat. I don't need women—even if it's offered up for free, I don't care much about those older ones—but girls, well, they're afraid of me like death, and they love it. And why wouldn't they? You don't come across my type just anywhere! Maybe my feathers aren't the prettiest, but my bones are shaped just right. . . ."

Already savvy to the world, Yushka came straight through the main entrance to the manor house when he appeared at Sukhodol. Natasha was there, sitting on the bench and singing to herself, "As I swept I found a piece of sugar." She leapt to her feet in terror when she saw him.

"Who are you?" she cried.

"A man," Yushka said, quickly looking her over from head to foot. "Go and tell the mistress."

"Who's there?" the mistress called out at that moment from the hall.

But Yushka immediately reassured her: he told her he was a former monk, not at all a runaway soldier, as she quite likely feared. He explained that he was returning to his native land and asked that they search him, then let him stay the night and rest a little. His directness so disarmed the mistress that she allowed him to move into the servants' quarters the next day, and he soon became a regular member of the household. Thunderstorms came ceaselessly, but he never tired of entertaining the mistress; he thought up a way to block the dormer window and better protect the roof from lightning; he even ran onto the porch during the loudest claps of thunder just to prove that they were not so terrible. When he helped the house girls heat the samovars, they watched him from the corners of their eyes, feeling his quick, lascivious glances passing over them, but they still laughed at his jokes, while Natashka—whom he had already stopped more than once in the dark corridor with the whispered words, "I'm in love with you, girl!"—could not bear to raise her eyes to him. The stench of shag tobacco that had seeped into his cassock made him foul to her, and he was terrifying, terrifying.

She knew what would happen. She slept alone in the corridor, near the door of the young mistress's bedroom, and Yushka had already told her point blank: "I'll come to you. You can stick me with a knife, and I'll still come. And if you scream, I'll burn this whole place to the ground." Above all else, her strength was sapped by the knowledge that something *inevitable* had been set in motion, that the realization of her dream—that terrible dream about a goat in Soshki—had now drawn near, and she was clearly destined to suffer ruin with her mistress. Everyone understood by now: the devil dwells in the house at night. Everyone knew exactly what it was besides thunderstorms and fires that drove the young mistress from her mind, what it was that spawned in her those shameless and voluptuous moans as she slept, then drove her to leap up with a wailing cry, a howling beside which even the most deafening blows of thunder seemed like nothing. "I'm being strangled!" she would scream. "By the snake of Eden! By the serpent of Jerusalem!" And who was that snake, if not the devil, if not the grey goat that came into the rooms of girls and women at night? And is there anything in the world more terrifying than his appearance on those nights when storms rage, when thunder rolls ceaselessly above the house, and lightning flickers constantly across the blackened surface of the icons? The urgency, the lust with which that charlatan whispered to Natashka—it too was inhuman. How was she to fend it off?

In the corridor at night, contemplating her fateful, inevitable hour as she sat on a horse cloth on the floor, Natashka peered into the darkness with a pounding heart, listened for the faintest creak, the slightest rustling in the sleeping house. Already she felt the first attacks of that painful illness that would torment her far into the future: suddenly an itch began in her foot, followed by a sharp, prickling spasm that bent all her toes toward her cramping sole, and then—painfully, sweetly twisting all her sinews—traveled up her legs, spread through her entire body, came right up to her throat until Natashka longed to scream, release a cry even more frenzied, even more voluptuous and tortured than the wails of her young mistress.

The inevitable occurred: Yushka came, precisely during one of those terrifying nights at the end of summer. It was the eve of St. Ilya, the ancient fire-thrower's day. There was no thunder that night, and no sleep for Natashka. She dozed—and suddenly woke up, as if she had been pushed. The insane beating of her heart told her that it was the dead of night, the latest hour. She jumped up and looked to one end of the corridor, then to the other: the taciturn sky was filled with fire and secrets; from all directions it flashed, burst into trembling flames, swelled with blinding sheets of pale blue and gold lightning. Every few seconds the entranceway turned as bright as day. She began to run, then stopped, rooted to the floor: the cut logs of aspen that had been lying for a long time in the courtyard now turned a blinding white with each flash of lightning. She stepped into the hall: one window was raised, and she could hear the steady rustling of the garden. It was darker there than in the entranceway, but this made all the brighter those flames that flashed beyond the windows, and as soon as blackness poured back into the room, everything would jump and twitch once more as another random flare began to burn, and the garden rose, trembling in its momentary light, the sky's massive backdrop—gold one instant, violet-white the next—gleaming through the lacy edges of the foliage, through poplars and pale green birches that loomed like ghosts. "On the ocean, on the sea—on the Island of Buyan," she whispered, rushing back, certain she would utterly destroy herself with this sorcerer's incantation, "Lies a bitch and on her back— there spreads a full grey fleece . . ."

And as soon as she spoke those dreadful, primordial words, she turned and saw Yushka standing two steps from her with his shoulders raised. The lightning lit up his pale face, the black circles of his eyes. He lunged silently toward her, seized her waist with his long arms, locked his grip; he flung her to her knees in a single motion, then shoved her onto her back on the cold floor of the entranceway. . . .

Yushka came to her the next night as well. He came to her for many nights, and she, losing consciousness from horror and revulsion, gave herself submissively to him. She didn't dare to contemplate resisting, or appealing to the masters or the other serfs for help, just as the young mistress did not dare resist the devil as it satisfied itself with her at night—just as, they said, even grandmother, a powerful and beautiful woman, had not dared to resist her house serf, Tkach, an utter villain and thief who finally was banished to Siberia. . . . At last Yushka grew bored with Natashka, grew bored with Sukhodol—vanished as abruptly as he'd appeared.

A month later she felt that she was with child. And in September, the day after the young masters returned from war, the manor house caught fire: for a long and terrifying time it burned. Her second dream had come to pass. The fire began at dusk, under a heavy rain. According to Soloshka, it was caused by a golden ball of lightning that flew out of the stove in grandfather's room and bounded through the house. But Natalya would later recount how, seeing the flames and smoke, she bolted from the bathhouse—where she'd spent several days and nights in tears—and began to race toward the house, only to run into a stranger in the garden, a man in a red jerkin and a tall Cossack hat with a galloon. He too was running as fast as he could through the wet bushes and burdock. . . . Natalya could never say with complete certainty if the man was real or some kind of vision, but one fact was clear: the horror that seized her when she saw him had freed her from her future child.

After that she faded. Her life began to run along the rails of simple, quotidian existence, and she did not veer from those tracks until her final days. They took Aunt Tonya to a saint's remains in Voronezh. Afterward the devil no longer dared come close to her, and she grew calmer, began to live like everyone else. Only the gleam of her almost feral eyes, her extreme slovenliness, her violent irascibility, and her mournful sadness during thunderstorms revealed the disturbance of her mind and soul. Natalya was with her during the visit to the saint's remains, and from that trip she too gained a certain calm, a release from everything in her life that seemed inescapable. How she had trembled at the mere thought of meeting Pyotr Petrovich once again! She'd lacked the strength to think about it calmly, regardless of how long she tried to steel herself. And Yushka, her shame, her ruin! But the very singularity of that ruin, the unusual depth of her suffering, the apparent ineluctability of her misfortune—for surely it was not a mere coincidence that the shock of the fire would so closely follow her ruin and disgrace—all of this, together with the pilgrimage to the saint's remains, gave her the right to look simply, calmly into the eyes not only of those around her but even into the eyes of Pyotr Petrovich. God himself had marked her and the young mistress with the tip of his annihilating finger: why should they fear people! When she returned from Voronezh, Natalya entered the manor house at Sukhodol as placidly as a nun, like a simple and humble servant of everything light and good, like a woman who'd received her final communion before death. She approached Pyotr Petrovich calmly, and her heart contracted with tender, youthful, girlish sentiment only for a moment as she touched her lips to his small, dark hand with its turquoise ring. . . .

Life became mundane at Sukhodol. Various rumors surfaced about emancipation, triggering alarm among the house serfs and the field hands: What lies ahead? Will it all be worse? How easy it is to say, "Begin your new life!" The masters too were confronted by the prospect of a new life—and they had managed poorly with the old one. Grandfather's death, followed by the war, the comet that plunged the entire country into terror, the fire, and finally rumors of emancipation—all of this changed the masters' faces and their souls, deprived them of their youth and their insouciance, their quick tempers and their readiness to make amends, while fostering ennui, malice, a constant captiousness with one another. "Disharmonies began," as our father said, and eventually they led to whips at meals. Necessity stubbornly reminded the young masters that they had to find some means of reviving the estate, which their long absence at the war, the fire, and the family's debts had utterly destroyed. But the brothers only bothered each other as they sought to manage their affairs. One was ridiculously greedy, stern, and suspicious; the other was ridiculously generous, kind, and trusting. Finally they managed to agree on a venture that was sure to bring big gains: they mortgaged the estate and bought nearly three hundred bedraggled horses, gathering them from almost every corner of the district with the help of a certain Ilya Samsonov, a gypsy. They hoped to get the horses fat and healthy over the winter, then sell them at substantial profit in the spring. But after consuming huge quantities of flour and straw, the horses for some reason began keeling over one by one; almost all of them were dead by spring. . . .

The discord between the brothers now grew more and more severe. At times it reached a point where they would snatch up guns and knives. There's no saying how it would have ended if a new misfortune had not befallen Sukhodol. In the winter, four years after his return from the Crimean War, Pyotr Petrovich went to visit Lunyovo, where he had a lover. He spent two days on the farm, drinking constantly, and then, still drunk, left for Sukhodol. There was a great deal of snow on the ground; two horses were harnessed to the wide sledge, which was covered with a heavy rug. Pyotr Petrovich ordered that the outrunner—a young, high-strung filly that sank to her belly in the loose drifts—be unharnessed and tied to the back of the sledge. Then he stretched out to sleep, his head apparently lying back toward the horse in tow. A misty, dove-grey dusk began to fall. As he often did, Pyotr Petrovich had taken Yevsey Bodulya with him on the trip instead of Vaska Kazak, the regular driver, for his constant beatings had embittered all the house serfs, and Pyotr Petrovich feared that Vaska would one day kill him. Settling back to sleep, Pyotr Petrovich shouted, "Get going!" at Yevsey and kicked him in the back. The shaft horse, a strong bay, its coat already damp and steaming, went plowing through the loose, deep snow and the murky gloom of the empty fields, carrying them into the winter night as it grew ever darker and more lowering. . . . But at midnight, when everyone at Sukhodol was already sleeping like the dead, an anxious rapping at the window of the entranceway woke Natalya. She leapt up from the bench and ran out barefoot to the porch. The dark forms of the horses and the sledge stood out dimly; Yevsey was standing there with a whip in his hand. "Disaster, girl—disaster!" he muttered indistinctly, strangely, as if he were asleep. "The horse killed the master. . . . She was tied . . . she ran up, stumbled—and her hoof . . . His face is all smashed. . . . He's already cold. . . . It wasn't me. Not me. By Christ, not me!"

Silently she descended from the porch and approached the sledge, her bare feet pressing down the snow. She crossed herself and fell onto her knees. She cradled the icy, bloody head in her arms and began to kiss it, began to shriek and fill the house with a savage, joyful wailing, struggling to breathe between her laughter and her sobs. . . .

X

Whenever we happened to leave the cities behind and came to rest in the quiet, impoverished backwoods of Sukhodol, Natalya repeatedly unfolded the narrative of her broken life. Sometimes her eyes darkened and stared blankly; sometimes her voice became a sharp and clear half-whisper. I always remembered the crude icon that hung in a corner of the lackeys' quarters in our old house: the decapitated saint sought out his countrymen; he carried his lifeless head in his own hands to demonstrate his story's truth.

Even those slight physical traces of the past that we briefly glimpsed at Sukhodol have vanished now. Our fathers and our grandfathers left us no portraits, no letters, not even the mundane artifacts of their everyday existence. And those few small possessions that did remain were ruined in the fire. Some kind of trunk stood for a long time in the entranceway: a hundred years ago it had been covered in sealskin, but only a few stiff rags and worn-out clumps of that upholstery remained. It belonged to our grandfather once, and its movable drawers of Karelian birch were stuffed with charred French dictionaries and church books spattered in candle wax. Eventually, however, it too disappeared, just as the heavy furniture that once stood in the living room also broke apart and disappeared. More and more the old house sagged and wore away. And all the long years that followed the events depicted here—those years saw nothing but the slow and steady dying of the house. . . . Its past seems more and more a myth.

The residents of Sukhodol led remote and gloomy lives, but they still seemed substantial, wealthy, intricate. And judging by the sheer inertia in that way of life, judging by the people's fierce adherence to its principles, one could easily believe there'd be no end to it. But those descendants of the nomads from the steppe proved weak and pliant, ill-prepared for punishment! And so the sheltered homes of Sukhodol's inhabitants disappeared as tracelessly, as quickly as those little mounds of earth above the hamsters' passageways and burrows vanish under the plow when it cuts across the field. The occupants all died or scattered; only a few hung on and struggled to live out their last remaining days. We did not witness their true lives and mores; we encountered, instead, the memory of that earlier time combined with some stark, half-savage existence. And we visited that region of the steppe less and less often over the years. It seemed more and more remote to us; we felt more and more removed from both the blood and custom that once gave shape to us. Many of our fellow noblemen, like us, were born of heralded and ancient families. Our names are entered in the history books and chronicles; our ancestors were courtiers and governors in ancient Russia, "distinguished gentlemen," close associates and even relatives of the tsars. Had we been born farther to the west, had our ancestors been known as knights, how much more conviction would have come into our voices when we spoke of them, how much longer would our way of life have persevered! No knight's descendant could ever say that in half a century an entire class of people vanished from the earth. He could never speak of such great numbers of people who deteriorated, who committed suicide and drank themselves to death, people who went mad, let go of everything, just disappeared. He could never admit, as I confess here, that the lives of not only our ancestors but even the lives of our great grandfathers are a complete and utter mystery to us now, and every day it grows more difficult for us to gain the vaguest understanding of events that happened only fifty years ago!

Long ago they plowed over and seeded that place where Lunyovo once stood, just as many other estates have been plowed and seeded. Somehow Sukhodol held on. But after chopping down the last birches in the garden and selling off the last of the arable land in small plots, its owner, Pyotr Petrovich's son, abandoned the estate and went to work as a conductor on the railroad. The last, old inhabitants of Sukhodol—Klavdiya Markovna, Aunt Tonya, and Natalya—lived out their final years in hardship. Spring became summer, summer became fall, fall became winter. . . . They lost track of the many changes. They lived on memories, dreams, quarrels, worries about daily meals. Those grounds on which the estate once spread expansively now sank beneath the peasants' rye in summer, and the house was visible from far away, surrounded by those plains. All that remained of the garden were bushes, and they grew in such a riot that quail called directly from the balcony. But what is there to say of summer! "Summer is our paradise," the old women would declare. Long and hard were the rainy falls, the snowy winters in Sukhodol. Cold and hunger gripped the ruined house. Blizzards mounded snow across its walls; the freezing wind of Sarmatia blew right through its rooms. And the heat—they heated it very rarely. In the evening a tin lamp burned dimly in the window of the mistress's room, the only inhabitable space in the house. The old mistress wore a short fur coat, felt boots, and glasses as she leaned toward the lamp and knitted a sock. Natalya dozed on a cold bench by the empty stove. And Aunt Tonya, like some Siberian shaman, sat and smoked a pipe inside her peasant hut. When they were not quarreling, Klavdiya Markovna would place her lamp on the windowsill instead of the table. And on those nights Tonya sat in a strange, weak half-light that reached her from the house, reached inside her freezing hut, cluttered with broken furniture and pottery shards and the great mass of the piano that had heaved onto its side. The hut was so cold that chickens, whose care consumed all of Tonya's strength, would often suffer frostbite to their feet while sleeping on those ceramic shards and ruined bits of furniture.

And now the Sukhodol estate is completely empty. All those mentioned here have died, as have their neighbors and their peers. And sometimes you think: Is it true? Did they really live on this earth?

It's only at the graveyard that you feel they really did exist—feel, in fact, a frightening proximity to them. But even for that you must make an effort; you must sit and think beside a family headstone—if you can find one. It is shameful to say, but impossible to hide: we don't know where the graves of grandmother, grandfather, and Pyotr Petrovich lie. We know only that their place is somewhere here, near the altar of the old village church in Cherkizovo. You won't make it there in winter: the drifts are waist deep—just the tops of a few bushes, some branches, an occasional cross can be seen sticking out from the snow. In the summer you ride along a hot and dusty, quiet street in the village, tie your horse up at the churchyard fence. Spruces stand baking in the heat beyond it, dense as a dark green wall. And behind the open gate, behind the white church with a rusty cupola, you find a whole grove of small and spreading ash trees, elms, and lindens—it's cool and shady everywhere. For a long time you wander among the bushes, the small mounds and hollows covered by a thin graveyard grass, the stone slabs sinking into the earth, porous from the years of rain and overgrown by black, crumbling moss. . . . Here there are two or three monuments of iron. But who are they for? They're tarnished such a heavy green and gold that it's impossible to read the inscriptions. Under what mounds lie grandmother, grandfather? God alone knows! You know only that they're somewhere here, somewhere close. And so you sit and think, try to imagine all those forgotten Khrushchyovs. At one moment their time seems endlessly far away; at the next, impossibly close at hand. And then you say to yourself:

"It's not so hard. . . . It's not so hard to imagine. You only have to remember that the same crooked, gold-plated cross rose into the blue summer sky when they were here. Then, just as now, there were hot and empty fields of rye that yellowed and turned ripe, while here the bushes and the shade were cool. . . . Then, just as now, a white nag like this one wandered grazing in the bushes, with slightly green and scruffy withers, with pink and broken hooves."

[Vasilyevskoe, 1911]

The Scent of Apples

T HE EARLY DAYS of a lovely autumn come back to me. In August there were warm and gentle rains—rains that seemed to fall deliberately to help the sowing, coming in the middle of the month, near the holiday of St. Lavrenty. People in the country always say that fall and winter will not quarrel if the water's still and the rain is soft on St. Lavrenty's Day. During the warm days of *babye leto*, the gossamer was thick in the fields, and this too is a good sign— another promise of fine weather in the fall. . . . I remember a fresh and quiet morning. . . . The big garden, its dry and thinned-out leaves turning golden in the early light. I remember the avenue of maples, the delicate smell of the fallen leaves, and the scent of autumn apples—*antonovkas*, that mix of honey and fall freshness. . . . The air's so clear it seems there is no air at all. The sounds of squeaking carts and voices drift distinctly through the garden: it's the traders from the city. They've hired some of the local *mouzhiki* to pack up apples that they'll send to the city during the night—invariably the trip is made at night, when it's so wonderful to lie on a pile of apples and stare at the stars, smell the scent of tar in the fresh air, listen to the cautious squeaking of the loaded carts as they move in a long line through the darkness on the big road. The *mouzhik* who loads the apples eats them one after another with a crisp and succulent crunching, but the trader never tries to change such habits. Instead he says, "Go ahead, eat your fill! Everyone deserves a little of the extra honey!"

The morning's cool silence is broken only by the sated, throaty calls of thrushes from a mountain ash that's turned as red as coral in the garden thicket, and the muffled rumbling of apples being poured into measuring boxes and barrels. Through the thinned-out trees you can see far down the big road that's strewn with straw. It leads to the hut where the trader has set up an entire household for the summer. The scent of apples hangs everywhere, but there the smell's especially strong. They've set up beds inside the hut. A single-barreled shotgun leans against a wall not far from a tarnished samovar. Dishes are stacked in the corner. In the yard outside lie bits of matting, crates, and tattered cloth; a fireplace for cooking has been dug into the ground. Here a splendid pork-fat stew simmers at midday, and the samovar is heated in the evening, its long ribbon of blue smoke stretching out among the trees. On holidays the yard beside the hut is like a market square; every minute customers in bright attire flit past the trees. Wearing *sarafans* that smell of dye, the daughters of the *odnodvortsy* gather in a lively little group; servants from the manor houses come dressed in coarse and pretty, almost atavistic suits. The young wife of the village elder appears as well. Pregnant, with a wide, sleepy face, she projects the self-importance of a pedigreed cow. Each of her two braids has been wrapped around the sides of her headdress, then covered with several scarves. It's a style known as "horns," and it makes her head appear enormous. Wearing half-boots with strips of steel along the heels, she plants her feet and stands with dumb placidity, her figure draped in a long apron and a sleeveless gown of velveteen, a violet skirt with brick-red stripes and golden lace (which she pronounces "lice") along its hem.

"Now there's a little lady with real presence!" the trader says of her, shaking his head. "You don't see many like that anymore. . . ."

Hatless, towheaded boys in short pants and white canvas shirts come steadily in groups of twos and threes, shuffling their feet in rapid, light succession while watching from the corners of their eyes the shaggy German Shepherd tied to a nearby apple tree. Only one of them, of course, buys anything, and even he spends just one kopeck, or offers up an egg as barter. But there are many customers, and the buying's brisk: in his red boots and long frock coat, the consumptive trader is happy. His brother, a burring, lively semi-imbecile, lives with him "out of charity," and together they trade jokes and silly phrases as they sell their wares; sometimes the trader even "fingers out a tune" on his accordion. And so a crowd remains all day around the hut, and you can hear among the garden trees the laughter and the voices, sometimes the rhythmic tread of dancing until dusk. . . .

In fair weather the air turns sharply colder as night comes on; dew weighs down the grass. Having breathed your fill of the rye scent that rises from the new straw and the chaff in the threshing barn, you head home to dinner, walking briskly past the garden's earthen wall. Voices in the village, the squeak of a closing gate — everything resounds with rare and sharp precision in the freezing final glow of dusk. Then full dark falls. And still another smell: someone's lit a fire in the garden. The sweet smoke of burning cherry limbs wafts heavily toward you. And in the darkness, in the depth of the garden, you witness something from a childhood tale: crimson flames blaze like a corner of hell near the hut, surrounded by the gloom. And like something carved from ebony, the black silhouettes of people move around the fire while their gigantic shadows lurch across the apple trees. One's almost completely covered by a massive arm that's several meters long; then the shadows of two legs appear like huge black columns. And suddenly it all slips from the trees—the shadows seem to merge and fall straight down the avenue, stretching from the trader's hut to the front gate. . . .

Late at night, when all the village lights are out, and the seven stars of the Pleiades hang like gems in the sky, you run once more into the garden. Rustling among the fallen leaves, you blindly make your way toward the hut. In the clearing there it grows a little lighter; the whiteness of the Milky Way spreads out overhead. . . .

"Is that you, *barchuk*?" someone calls out from the dark.

"Yes, it's me. . . . Aren't you sleeping, Nikolay?"

"Sleep's not for us, sir. . . . But it must be late already. . . . Seems the night train's coming now."

We listen for a long time, eventually discern a trembling in the ground. The trembling turns into a noise, and soon it seems the train wheels are pounding out their rapid measure just beyond the garden: rumbling and knocking, the engine flies toward us . . . closer, closer, ever louder and more furious . . . until its roaring suddenly subsides, dies off, as if the cars had sunk into the earth. . . .

"Where's your gun, Nikolay?"

"Here, sir, beside the crate. . . ."

You point the single-barreled shotgun up—it's as heavy as a crowbar—and pull the trigger on an impulse: a crimson flame shoots toward the sky with a deafening bang, blinds you for a moment, puts out all the stars—and then a cheerful echo comes crashing out, rolls along the horizon like a wheel, slowly, slowly fades away in the sharp, clean air. . . .

"Well done!" says the trader. "Give them a jolt, *barchuk*! Give them a good scare! That's the only thing they understand! They shook down all the pears already at the garden wall!"

Falling stars etch their paths with burning streaks into the sky's blackness. For a long time you look into its blue-black depths, its dense array of constellations—and then the earth begins to drift beneath your feet. You rouse yourself. Hide your hands inside your sleeves, run fast along the avenue toward the manor house. . . . How cold it is! How heavy the dew! How good it is to live on earth!

II

"Good *antonovkas* bring good years." Everything's in order in the village if there's a healthy crop of *antonovkas*: it means the wheat is also healthy, and the coming harvest will be plentiful. . . . I remember a year of rich harvests.

In the early dawn, while roosters are still crowing and black smoke rises from the chimneys of the peasant huts, you throw open the window that looks out onto the garden: it is filled with a lilac shade, through which falls the morning sun in random, brilliant spots. It's impossible to wait: you order that a horse be saddled, then run down to the pond to wash. The willows on the banks have lost almost all their leaves, and now the turquoise sky shines through their empty branches. The water below them is icy, limpid, somehow heavier than usual: immediately it takes away the sluggishness of night. And then—after washing, after joining the workers in the servants' hall to eat black bread and hot potatoes with large, damp grains of salt—how good it is to feel the leather saddle shift beneath you as you ride through Vyselki on your way to hunt. Autumn is a time of many holidays and festivals. People put on their best clothes; they appear well kept and satisfied. The village looks completely different than it does at other times of year. And if the harvest has been good, if mounds of grain have risen on the threshing floors like golden cities on a plain while the early-morning cackling of geese continues sharp and clear upon the river, village life is far from bad. And Vyselki has been known throughout the ages as a place of great prosperity; since grandfather's days it's been famous for its "riches." Old men and women lived long lives there—the first true sign that a village is well off—and they were always tall and strapping, their hair as white as down. "Oh yes," you'd overhear a person saying. "Agafya just finished off her eighty-third year." Or a conversation along these lines:

"When will you die, Pankrat? You must be getting on toward a hundred."

"What's that you say, sir, if you'll permit me?"

"I was asking your age—how old are you?"

"I don't know, sir."

"Well, do you remember Platon Apollonych?"

"Oh yes, of course. Like yesterday."

"Then—you see?—you have to be at least a hundred."

A sheepish smile passes briefly across the old man's face as he stands rigidly before the master. What can he say, after all? He's guilty. He's lived far more than his fair share. And if he hadn't stuffed himself with onions on St. Peter's Day, he'd probably go on living even longer.

I remember his old wife. She always sat on a little bench on the porch, hunched over, shaking her head, gasping for breath as she clung to her seat with her hands—and always, it seemed, thinking about something. "About her valuables, I'll bet," the village women liked to say, for she did indeed have quite a few possessions locked away in trunks. She would act as if she hadn't heard a word, stare blindly off into the distance with her eyebrows sadly raised, shake her head and struggle, evidently, to revive some distant memory. She was tall and dark. Her skirt was almost from another century; her rope shoes were strictly for the dead. The skin around her neck had turned dry and yellow, but she always kept her blouse—with its little, inlaid triangles of colored linen—a perfect, flawless white. "Good enough for getting buried in." A large stone lay near the porch: she'd bought it herself for her grave, just as she had bought a shroud, a lovely one, with angles and crosses, prayers inscribed along its edges.

The peasant houses in Vyselki were well suited to those older residents, for they'd been built of brick back in the days of our grandfathers. It wasn't customary for married sons to split off land from their fathers' plots in Vyselki, and therefore wealthy peasants—Savely, Ignat, Dron—had cottages comprised of two or three large sections to hold their growing families. They raised bees, kept their estates in careful order, took pride in their steel-grey stallions. Their threshing floors were often packed with thick bundles of rich, dark hemp. They had barns and sheds with well-thatched roofs, storerooms with iron doors protecting bolts of canvas, spinning wheels, new sheepskin coats, harness plates, and barrels bound with copper rings. Their sleds and gates had crucifixes burnt into their wood. There was a time when I found nothing more alluring than the life of a *mouzhik*. Riding through the village on a sunny morning, you'd think, how good to take a scythe into the fields, to thresh the wheat, to sleep on sacks of straw on the threshing floor, to get up with the sun on holidays as church bells ring, their weighty and melodic notes pouring through the village. How good to wash from a barrel, dress in a shirt and pants of simple linen, wear those indestructible boots with steel along the heels. And if you add to this a pretty, healthy wife dressed in holiday attire, a trip to Mass, then lunch at the home of your bearded father-in-law—a lunch of hot mutton served on wooden plates with sifted-flour bread, with honey from the comb, and homemade beer—one could wish for nothing more.

Until quite recently (in days that even I recall), the rural household of an average noble family resembled that of the wealthy peasants in its economy, prosperity, and rustic, old-world charm. Such was the estate of my aunt, Anna Gerasimovna, who lived twelve *versts* from Vyselki. . . . Riding at a walk to keep from wearing out the dogs you take along, you never reach her house much before midday. . . . And you don't want to hurry—it's lovely in those open fields on a cool and sunny day! You can see far into the distance across the level plains. The sky is light—a deep, expansive blue. Carts and carriages have smoothed out the road since the rains, and now its oily-looking surface gleams like metal rails in the bright sun that slopes across it. All around you spreads the winter wheat in triangulated fields of rich, green shoots. A small hawk rises out of nowhere, hovers over something, fluttering its small, sharp wings in the transparent air. Telegraph poles lead far into the clear distance; like silver strings their wires curve along the sloping edge of the sky. Merlins perch on them in rows like sharp black notes written on a sheet of music.

I never knew or witnessed serfdom, but I remember feeling it, somehow, at Aunt Anna Gerasimovna's. As soon as you ride into the courtyard, you feel it there—feel it vividly. The estate's not large, but all of it is aged and solid, surrounded by willow trees and birches that are at least a century old. Many buildings stand inside the courtyard, small and neat, with uniformly dark oak walls and roofs of thatch. Only the servants' house, its walls going black with time, stands out from the other buildings because of its size—or more precisely, its length. The sole remaining household serfs of Russia peep out from its entrance like the last of the Mohicans: a few decrepit men and women, and a retired, senile cook who looks like Don Quixote. They draw themselves up very straight, then bow low, almost to the ground, as you ride into the yard. Coming for your horse, the grey-haired driver removes his hat while still beside the carriage house, then passes through the entire yard with nothing on his head. He was once my aunt's postillion, but now he drives her to church in a covered sleigh in winter, or a rugged little trap with metal bracing—like those preferred by priests—in summer. My aunt's garden is well known for its neglected state, its nightingales, its turtledoves, and its apples; her house is famous for its roof. The house stands at the top of the courtyard, just before the garden, encircled by the limbs of linden trees. Its walls are thick and rather small, but the roof—a hardened, dense, and blackened layer of thatch that had been pitched at an extraordinarily steep angle—gives the house an air of indestructibility: it seems impervious to time. I always had the sense it was alive: the front façade resembled an old face staring out from under an enormous hat with sunken, nacreous eyes—years of rain and sun had made the windows iridescent. Two porches jutted out from either side of that façade—large, old-fashioned porches with tall columns. Well-fed pigeons squatted on their pediments while thousands of sparrows moved like sudden bursts of rain from one roof to another. . . . It's comfortable there, in that nest beneath autumn's turquoise sky.

You notice first the scent of apples as you go into the house, and then the other smells: old furniture made of mahogany, dried-out linden flowers that were scattered on the windowsills in June. . . . In all the rooms—the entranceway, the drawing room, the dining hall—it's dark and cool, for the house is surrounded by the garden, and the windows' upper panes hold glass that's colored blue or violet. The rooms are quiet and clean, though you have the odd impression that all the armchairs, the inlaid tables, the mirrors in their narrow, twisted frames of gold might never had been moved from the places they now occupy. You hear someone coughing, and your aunt comes in. She's small, but, like everything around her, solid. She wears a large Persian shawl around her shoulders. She approaches you with both formality and friendliness, and soon, amid the steady stream of talk about bygone days and legacies, she begins inviting you to eat: pears at first, and then four kinds of apples—*antonovkas, plodovitkas, borovinkas,* and *belle barynyas.* All of this is followed by a remarkable meal: pink ham with peas, stuffed chicken, turkey, pickled vegetables, red *kvass*—strong, sweet *kvass.* The windows are open on the garden. . . . The cool and bracing air of fall drifts in. . . .

III

The spirits of the disappearing, landed gentry have been buoyed by just one thing in recent years: hunting.

In earlier days, estates like Anna Gerasimovna's were no great rarity. And there were noble families with larger holdings—huge manor houses, fifty-acre gardens—who kept on living lavishly even while descending toward bankruptcy. To be sure, a few of these estates still exist today, but all of them are lifeless now. . . . There are no *troikas*, no Kirghiz saddle horses, no borzois or hunting hounds, no household serfs, no owners to command it all—no landed devotees of hunting like Arseny Semyonych, the late brother of my wife.

At the end of September our threshing floors and gardens emptied out, turned bare; the weather changed dramatically. For entire days the wind battered and tore at the trees; rain poured down on them from morning until night. Sometimes toward evening the low sun's trembling, golden rays broke through the gloomy clouds in the west; then the air seemed particularly sharp and clear, and the light was blinding when it fell among the last few leaves and branches, which jumped and twitched like nets the wind had brought to life. The sky's damp blue shone cold and clear above leaden clouds in the north while white clouds slowly surfaced from beneath them like a snowy mountain crest breaking into view. . . . Standing at the window, you think that with a little luck it may turn clear. But the wind does not subside. It harries the garden, tears apart the ribbons of smoke rising from the servants' hall, drives together ashen, ragged, and foreboding clouds that sail in low and fast and soon obscure the sun—blot its light like heavy smoke, close that little window of blue sky. . . . Once more the garden seems abandoned, sullen. . . . And then the clouds begin to scatter drops of rain. . . . Quietly they fall at first, uneasily. . . . Then steadily they gather weight, turn into a driving stream, a storm that shakes the trees and makes the sky go even blacker. A long, uneasy night begins.

After such a thrashing, the garden trees are almost bare, quiet and resigned among the wet and scattered leaves. But how beautiful they are when clear weather comes again, when those cold transparent days begin October, that final marvel of the season. Any leaves remaining on the trees will now last until the first snow. The black garden will shine beneath a cold and turquoise autumn sky while waiting peacefully for winter days and warming itself in the distant sun. And already the fields are turning black beneath the plows or green with brilliant shoots of winter wheat. . . . The time for hunting has begun!

And so I see myself at the estate of Arseny Semyonych, in the dining hall of his large house. It's filled with sunlight and smoke from countless pipes and cigarettes. All the people in the crowd have tanned and wind-chapped faces, wear warm vests and high-cut boots. They've just had a filling lunch. They're flushed from loud and animated talk about the coming hunt, and though they've finished with their food, they make a point to drink until the vodka's gone. Someone blows a horn outside in the courtyard; dogs begin to howl in varied tones. Arseny Semyonych's favorite dog, a black borzoi, climbs onto the table and begins to eat leftover rabbit meat and sauce from the plates, but then lets out a terrified yelp and scrambles from the table, turning over plates and glasses: carrying a pistol and a hunting crop from his study, Arseny Semyonych deafens the hall with a sudden shot. Even more smoke fills the room as he stands before the guests and laughs.

"Missed. Too bad," he says, his eyes flashing.

He's tall and lean but broad-shouldered, graceful, strongly built. He's dressed comfortably in a shirt of crimson silk, tall boots and wide-cut velvet pants; he has a handsome gypsy's face. Something wild gleams in his eyes. Having startled his dog and all his guests with the pistol shot, he begins to recite in a deep baritone, his voice both earnest and amused:

Let us saddle now our waiting horses,
Sling our horns across our shoulders . . .

And then breaks off, says loudly: "But let's not waste our time—the day is short!"

I still remember how greedily I breathed, how capaciously my young lungs inhaled the cold and damp, clean air as I rode late in the afternoon with Arseny Semyonych's noisy hunting party, excited by the scattered barking of the dogs set loose to rove through some stretch of land known as Red Knoll or Rustling Copse, place names that alone could stir a hunter's blood. . . . You ride a Kirghiz saddle horse; he's powerful, thick-set, ill-willed, and you keep the reins in tight; it feels as if your body's almost joined to his. He snorts, urges you to let him trot, his hooves loudly stirring loose beds of blackened leaves, their rustling rising sharp and clear in the empty, cold, damp woods. A dog yelps somewhere in the distance, another answers it with anguished zeal, a third—and suddenly the woods resound as if they're made of glass with shouts and fervid baying. A shot rings out amid the uproar, and everything breaks loose, goes tearing, rolling off into the distance.

"Look sharp!" someone shouts through all the woods in a despairing voice.

"Look sharp"—the words pass through your mind like a drunken thought. You let out a shout to the horse, go flying through the woods as if you've snapped free from a chain, discerning nothing in the blur but trees that flit before your eyes and mud that flecks your face from the churning hooves. You burst out of the woods and see a mottled, strung-out pack of dogs running through the plains, and spur the Kirghiz even harder, race to cut the quarry off, storming over plots of plowed-up earth and stubble, fields of new green wheat—and then plunge into another woodland, lose the pack and all its frenzied noise. You're damp with sweat; your body trembles with excitement and exertion as you rein in the foaming, wheezing horse and breathe the icy dampness of the forest valley. The baying dogs and hunters' shouts drift off into the distance: dead silence spreads around you. The forest floor's uncluttered; the tall trees stand motionless: it's as if you've entered some forbidden hall. The heavy scent of mushrooms, rotting leaves, wet bark rises from the gullies. And the dampness rising with that scent grows ever more perceptible. . . . The woods are turning dark and cold. . . . It's time to find a place to spend the night. But gathering the dogs is hard. For a long time the horns blow forlornly in the woods; for a long time yelps and shouts, curses drift among the trees. . . . And finally, already in full darkness, the hunting party streams into the estate of some bachelor you barely know, the riders' noise filling up the courtyard, which now is lit by lamps and candles carried out to greet the guests.

Sometimes a hunting party would stay for several days in the home of a generous host. At early dawn the hunters would go out again in an icy wind and the first wet snow, ride through the forests and fields, and then, as dusk approached, return, covered in grime, red-faced, smelling of their horses' sweat and the hide of the slaughtered prey. Then the drinking bouts began. The bright and crowded manor house was always warm after a full day spent in the open cold. . . . Everyone wanders from room to room with their thick vests unbuttoned. They drink and eat without ceremony, noisily exchanging impressions of the slain, full-grown wolf that now lies in the middle of the hall, its teeth bared and its eyes rolled back, its thick and airy tail lying to one side, its cold, pale blood darkening the floor. After vodka and a meal, you slip into a state of such sweet somnolence, such languid, youthful drowsiness, that all the conversations seem to drift to you through water. Your face burns from the wind. If you close your eyes, the earth begins to float beneath you. And when you finally lie down in some corner room in the ancient house—a room with icons and icon lamps and a soft feather bed—a horse still seems to run beneath you, all your body aches, and dogs with flaming coats drift before your eyes. And yet you don't notice that you're drowsing off with these strange sights and feelings, don't realize that you're slipping into a healthy, restful sleep, forgetting even that this room was once a chapel for the owner of the estate, an old man whose name is bound to grisly legends from the days of serfdom, and who died here, in this room, quite likely in this very bed.

Sometimes it happens that you oversleep and miss the hunt. And then your rest is particularly pleasant. You wake up and lie in bed for a long time. All the house is quiet. You can hear the gardener as he walks from room to room, heating up the stoves; you can hear the pop and sputter of the burning wood. The estate's been boarded up for winter, and now a completely idle day spreads before you in the silence. You dress slowly, wander in the garden, find a cold, wet apple that's been forgotten among the leaves. For some reason it's remarkably delicious; it seems unlike any other apple. . . . And then you settle down among the books—books from our grandfathers' days, with thick leather bindings and little gold stars on their Moroccan spines. How wonderful they smell! Like prayer books from a church with their yellowed, rough, and heavy pages! A pleasant, slightly sour mustiness laced with old perfume. . . . And how good it is to see the notes written in their margins, a gently rounded script from a goose quill pen. . . . You open up a volume, read: "An idea worthy of ancient and new philosophies, the light of reason and true feeling . . ." And inadvertently you find yourself caught up in the book—*The Gentleman Philosopher*, an allegory printed some hundred years ago by the state board of charity with funding from "a highly decorated citizen." It tells the story of a gentleman philosopher who, "possessing time and the ability to reason well, set out to construct a model of the universe on his land and test the heights to which human reason might ascend. . . ." Then you come across the *Satirical and Philosophical Writings of M. Voltaire*, and for a long time relish the quaintly mannered style of the translation: "My sovereign lords: Erasmus was pleased to compose a tribute to buffoonery in the 16th century [semi-colon—an affected pause]; now you command that I extol reason and its virtues here before you. . . ." Then you move from Catherine's time to the Romantics, to almanacs, and finally to long and sentimental, slightly pompous novels. . . . The cuckoo darts out of the clock and sings above you with a mix of ridicule and sorrow in the empty house. A strange, sweet sadness starts to gather in your heart.

Here you come across *The Secrets of Aleksis*; then it's *Victor, or a Child in the Forest*. You read: "The clock strikes midnight. A sacred silence takes the place of the day's noise and the peasants' happy songs. Sleep spreads dark wings above the surface of our hemisphere, shakes dreams and darkness down from them. . . . Dreams. . . . How often are they a mere continuation of suffering for the forsaken. . . ." And your favorite, time-worn words begin to flash before your eyes: crag and oak, pale moon and loneliness, spirits, specters, *eroty*, roses and lilies, "the pranks and gambols of misbehaving youths," arms as white as ivory, Lyudmilas and Alinas. . . . And here are journals with the names of Zhukovsky, Batyushkov, Pushkin in his student years. With sadness you remember your grandmother, how she played a polonaise on the clavichord, how she languidly recited lines from *Evgeny Onegin*. And that dreamy, antiquated world rises up before you. . . . How lovely they were, the women and girls who lived on those estates! Now they look down at me from portraits on the wall: aristocratic, beautiful, their hair arranged in old-world styles. With diffidence and grace, they lower their sad and tender eyes behind long lashes. . . .

IV

The aroma of *antonovkas* is disappearing from estates and country houses. We lived those days not long ago, and yet it seems a hundred years have passed since then. All the old people of Vyselki have died off. Anna Gerasimovna is dead. Arseny Semyonych shot himself. Now begins the age of petty farms, owners on the verge of abject poverty. But even those impoverished lives are good!

And so I see myself once more in the country. Deep fall. Cloudy, dove-grey days. Mornings I ride into the fields with a dog, a gun, a hunting horn. The wind blows hard, head on, whistling and humming in the barrel of the gun, dry snow swirling in its stream at times. All day I wander among the empty plains. . . . Hungry, chilled to the bone, I return toward dusk, and when the small lights of Vyselki begin to flicker in the distance, when I smell the smoke of kitchen fires from the manor house, happiness and warmth begin to rise in me. I remember how they liked to sit and talk with the lamps unlit, watching the dusk fade away as evening spread throughout our house. Coming inside, I notice that the double panes have been put back in all the windows in anticipation of the growing cold, and this adds even more to the mood of quiet winter calm. A worker is heating the stove in the hall. I squat the way I used to as a child beside a mound of straw, smell its winter freshness, watch the blazing fire, watch the window where the bluing dusk is sadly dying out. Then I walk into the servants' kitchen. Here it's bright and crowded: girls are chopping cabbage. I listen as their flashing knives tap out a fast and friendly rhythm, and they sing their poignant village songs in harmony. . . . Sometimes the owner of a small estate comes to take me to his farm for several days. . . . And the life of the petty landowner is also good!

He wakes up early, stretches soundly, rises, rolls himself a cigarette of cheap tobacco. The pale November dawn reveals a simple study; other than a pair of stiff and yellowed fox hides nailed above the bed, the walls are bare. A stocky figure in wide-cut pants and a long, unbelted shirt stands before the mirror, his sleepy face with slightly Tatar features hanging in the glass. Dead silence fills the warm and half-dark house. The old cook who's lived here since her childhood lies snoring in the corridor beyond the door, but this does not prevent my host from shouting in a hoarse voice that penetrates every corner of the house:

"Lukerya! Samovar!"

Having pulled on boots and wrapped a vest around his shoulders, he walks out to the porch, the collar of his shirt still unfastened at the side. It smells heavily of dogs behind the closed door to the *sentsy*. They rise lazily and stretch when he comes in, yawn with little squeals, smile, crowd around his legs.

"Go on, go on," he says in a slow, indulgent, low-pitched voice and starts walking through the garden to the threshing barn. He draws deeply into his lungs the dawn's sharp air and the smell of the bare garden under frost. His boots pass noisily through fallen leaves, black and curled with rime, as he walks along his avenue of birches, half of which have been chopped down. Jackdaws doze on the barn roof's ridge, their ruffled feathers sharp and clear against the low sky's gloomy backdrop. . . . A fine day for hunting! The owner stops in the middle of the avenue, looks for a long time at the autumn fields, the abandoned plots of green winter wheat where calves now roam. Two hunting dogs whine at his feet, but Zalivai has already raced beyond the garden: leaping over plots of sharp stubble, he seems to plead and beg to go out on a hunt. But what can you do with a pack of hunting dogs at this time of year? The quarry's in the field, keeping to the open spaces and the plowing, too frightened by the rustling of wind-blown leaves to go into the forest now. . . . Without borzois you won't catch a thing!

Threshing has begun in the barn. The drum drones as it slowly gathers speed, and the horses lazily pull their traces, swaying as they walk a circle strewn with their own droppings. The driver sits on a little bench at the center of the wheel, turning as the horses walk and shouting at them in a monotone, his whip falling constantly on the same brown gelding, which moves more sluggishly than all the rest: his eyes are covered; he might well be walking while he's sound asleep.

"Well, now—girls, girls!" sternly shouts the operator, a staid man wearing a wide sackcloth shirt. The girls scatter with their brooms and barrows, hurriedly sweep up the threshing floor.

"With God's grace . . .," the operator says, releasing a small, test bundle of rye. It flies into the buzzing, squealing drum, then rises up and out of the machine like a tattered fan. The drum drones more and more insistently, the work begins in earnest, and soon all the separate noises merge into the pleasant, even sound of threshing. The owner stands in the entrance and watches as hands and rakes, straw, red and yellow headscarves flicker in the darkness of the barn, and all the bustling movement's made rhythmic, measured by the drone of the drum, the whistling and monotonous shouts of the driver. Clouds of chaff drift toward the door and cover the owner in grey dust. . . . He glances at the fields again. . . . Soon, soon they'll be white. Soon the first snows will cover them. . . .

First frost, first snow! Without borzois it's impossible to hunt in November, but when winter comes, the real work starts with hounds. And as they did in earlier times, the owners of small estates go to visit one another, drink away the last of their money, disappear for entire days in the snowy fields. And on some distant farm the lit windows of a hunter's hut burn far into the dark winter night. Smoke fills the hut; the tallow candles burn wanly. Someone tunes a guitar, begins to sing in a deep tenor:

> *At dusk a violent wind began to blow,*
> *It flung the garden gate wide open . . .*

And the others join in clumsily, with sad and hopeless bluster, pretending that it's all a joke:

> *It flung the garden gate wide open,*
> *And buried all the roads with drifting snow . . .*

[1900]

Notes to the Stories

MITYA'S LOVE

One could almost believe that the larks had returned, bringing warmth and joy: Larks are often associated with warm weather in Russian culture. A familiar proverb advises: "Warm days come with larks, cold days come with finches."

In the distance Pushkin's statue rose, pensive and benevolent . . . : A monument to A. S. Pushkin (1799–1837), Russia's greatest and most beloved poet, stands at the intersection of Tverskaya Street and Tverskoy Boulevard in downtown Moscow. It was erected in 1880, paid for with donations from the Russian public.

Kuznetsky Most: Literally "Ferrier's Bridge," this is still a major street in downtown Moscow.

Mitya accompanied Katya to the actors' studio at the Moscow Art Theatre: The theatre was founded in 1898 by Konstantin Stanislavsky and Vladimir Nemirovich-Danchenko. A young actress like Katya would have attended drama classes at the studio.

The spring fast: Similar to Lent, the spring fast lasts for seven weeks, usually beginning in March.

Domostroy . . .: Written in the late sixteenth century, the *Domostroy* offers instructions for daily conduct in keeping with principles of Orthodoxy. It states that a husband should maintain strict rule in his household, beating both his wife and children as necessary.

"Junker Schmidt, it's true—summer does return": From a poem by Kozma Prutkov.

The Asra: An operetta by Anton Rubinstein (1829–1894), based on the poem by Heinrich Heine (1797–1856); said to have made a deep impression on Bunin.

"Oh darling, live and laugh," she said, quoting Griboyedov with a timid smile . . .: From Aleksandr Griboyedov's masterpiece, *Woe from Wit*, a play in verse written in 1822–1824 and considered one of the greatest plays in Russian.

mouzhik: A male peasant; plural, *mouzhiki*.

Tulsky Pryanik: A large, sweet, rectangular cookie, sometimes compared to gingerbread or spice bread.

My God, how forlorn he looks on the platform, the worker waiting for the owner's son—for me, the *barchuk*—to arrive . . .: The original text uses only the word "*barchuk*," which literally means "little *barin*" or "little landowner." A Russian reader would understand immediately that this must be Mitya. I've added the words "for the owner's son, for me" to try to make it completely clear to an English reader that the *barchuk* is Mitya.

Maslenitsa: A weeklong celebration that precedes the spring fast, traditionally marked by eating *blini*, Russian crepes.

A *sych*: Literally translated as "little owl" in most dictionaries. I have chosen to leave the Russian name here as the English equivalent would be unintentionally comic.

drozhky: A light, four-wheeled, open carriage in which passengers sit on a thin bench.

. . . It was so close; its call was so distinct, so sharp and startling, that Mitya even heard the wheezing and the trembling of its small, sharp tongue as the cuckoo began to wail: A cuckoo's song is an important and frightening omen in Russian culture. The number of calls the bird makes is believed to equal the number of years remaining in the listener's life.

Faust: Charles Gounod's opera, based on Goethe's version of the famous legend, debuted in 1859.

Leonid Fyodorovich Sobinov (1872–1934) and Fyodor Ivanovich Chaliapin (1873–1938) were two of Russia's most acclaimed opera singers. They sang together in 1899 at the Bolshoi Theatre. Chaliapin left Russia in 1921; Sobinov remained in the country and supported the Bolshevik government as a performer and briefly as an administrator.

"There was a King of Thule . . .": The Ballad of the King of Thule is sung by Margaret in *Faust*. His dying mistress gives the king a golden chalice, which he keeps faithfully for years, weeping from the memory of his lost love whenever he drinks from it. His last act before dying is to drink from the cup and throw it into the sea.

verst: Russian measurement of distance equal to 3,500 feet.

He was riding down the main avenue, known by the local *mouzhiki* as Table Road: The word "table" in English is misleading here. The Russian word *tabel'ny* probably refers to a government registry rather than a piece of furniture. The idea, apparently, is that the (private) road on which Mitya is riding is actually large enough to be listed among the country's major thoroughfares.

Sevastopol: A major city in the Crimea, founded in 1783 as a military port and fortress.

The Baidar Gates: The gates mark the chief pass through the Crimean Mountains to the Black Sea

The gardens of Alupka and Livadiya: Elaborate estates and gardens built in the early nineteenth century on the Crimean coast of the Black Sea.

Mitry Palych: Mitya is a short form of the name Dmitry. The full, formal name of the story's hero is Dmitry Pavlovich. The steward shortens this to "Mitry Palych."

kvass: A dark, fermented, nonalcoholic drink made from rye or barley.

salo: Pork fat, sometimes salted or smoked.

Aleksey Feofilaktovich Pisemsky (1821–1881) was a Russian novelist and playwright. He wrote extensively and sympathetically about the peasantry.

CLEANSING MONDAY

"Cleansing Monday": In Russian Orthodoxy, the longest of the three major fasts lasts for seven weeks, beginning on a Monday, usually in early March. This first day of the fast is known as *Chisty Ponedelnik*, or, as I've translated it, Cleansing Monday, and could be likened to Ash Wednesday, the first day of Lent in Western Christianity. But Cleansing Monday is not strictly a religious term; it apparently refers to the widespread practice of cleaning house on the first day of the fast. The week before Cleansing Monday is known as *Maslenitsa* and is traditionally celebrated by eating Russian pancakes, known as *blin* (plural, *blini*), similar to crepes.

Hugo von Hofmannsthal (1874–1929), Austrian playwright, essayist, and poet, probably best known for his collaborations with Richard Strauss.

Arthur Schnitzler (1862–1931), Austrian short-story writer, novelist, playwright, and critic.

Kazimierz Tetmajer (1865–1940), Polish romantic poet.

Stanislaw Przybyszewski (1868–1927), Polish symbolist poet, critic, and writer of fiction.

Andrey Bely: The pen name of Boris Bugaev (1880–1934), one of Russia's leading symbolist poets. Bunin detested the symbolists' aesthetics.

The Fire Angel: A novel by Valery Bryusov (1873–1924) about black magic in sixteenth-century Germany. Like Bely, Bryusov was a major figure in the symbolist movement.

Cathedral of Christ the Savior: Originally conceived by Aleksandr I to mark Russia's victory over France, the huge cathedral took several decades to build. It was completed in 1883. In 1933 Stalin leveled the cathedral and built in its place a large heated swimming pool for public use. The cathedral was later rebuilt from 1995 to 2000. Ironically the narrator's complaints about the building are voiced by many Muscovites today.

"Platon Karataev says that to Pierre": A reference to Tolstoy's *War and Peace*.

Sunday of Forgiveness: The last day of *Maslenitsa* and the day before Cleansing Monday. Traditionally a day when one asks forgiveness for transgressions.

St. Yefrem Sirin's prayer: The first line continues (roughly): "Lord and Master of my life, do not let come to me the spirit of idleness, despondency, domination, and vain talk. . . ."

Schismatics: In 1650 the Russian Orthodox church altered several of its religious rituals to correspond more closely to Greek Orthodox practices. The changes, which included altering the number of fingers one uses to make the sign of the cross, triggered a violent schism. Those who refused to accept the changes came to be known as Old Believers; many fled to remote areas of Russia or committed suicide. If Peter the Great is seen as the chief force of Westernization and modernization in Russia, the Old Believers could be said to represent the forces of mystical, archaic, non-Western Russia.

Ripida: A round, wooden icon of a cherub, waved by a deacon over the sacraments.

Trikiry: A candelabrum holding three candles, used in rituals involving high church officials.

Peresvet and Oslyabya: Monks remembered for battling fiercely against the Tatars in the fourteenth century.

kryuk: An ancient system of writing music in the Russian church, beginning in the eleventh century.

Aleksandr Ivanovich Ertel (1855–1908): Russian writer exiled to Tver for political activities. His work was highly esteemed by Tolstoy, Chekhov, and Maksim Gorky.

"The Moscow Art Theatre and a saccharine Russian style," she said, shrugging her shoulders. "What an irritating mix": The plays of Anton Chekhov (1860–1904) were first successfully produced by the Moscow Art Theatre. Although often critical of the theatre world, Bunin was fond of Chekhov and generally admired his work.

"Let's drive around a little more," she said. "And then go to Yegorov's for our last *blini*. We'll take it slowly, though, all right, Fyodor?": The speaker refers to "our last *blini*" because the Great Fast begins on the next day, Cleansing Monday.

Aleksandr Griboyedov (1725–1829) is best known for his play *Woe from Wit*, a satire of Moscow society written in verse.

The Virgin with Three Arms: According to legend, St. John of Damascus (676–754?) was once falsely accused of a crime, for which his hand was cut off. When the appendage miraculously grew back, John made an icon depicting the Virgin Mary with a third arm. A copy of the icon hung in a Moscow monastery. Apparently the speaker sees a similarity between this image and the Hindu God Shiva, who is often portrayed with four arms.

"You, my dear friend from the nobility—you cannot begin to understand this city the way I do": As a member of the merchant class, the speaker is a descendant of peasants while the narrator comes from the gentry. She implies that only the common people can fully understand Moscow's spirituality.

Zachatyevsky Monastery and Chudov Monastery: Founded in the sixteenth and fourteenth centuries respectively.

Sakhalin: An island for convicts in the Sea of Okhotsk, some four hundred miles north of Japan.

kapustnik: During a *kapustnik* (derived from the word for cabbage), actors and students would sing, dance, and perform informal skits that they themselves had written, often making fun of their colleagues and other artists.

Konstantin Stanislavsky (1863–1938): One of the founders of the Moscow Art Theatre. His "method acting," which emphasized a performer's identification with the character, influenced modern drama throughout the West.

V. Kachalov: An actor in the Moscow Art Theatre.

Leopold Sulerzhitsky (1872–1916) worked closely with Stanislavsky in the Moscow Art Theatre.

Shamakhanskaya: Probably a reference to a khanate in the Caucasus, controlled by the Tatars. Kachalov presumably alludes to the young woman's striking dark features.

"The Grand Duchess Elzavet Fyodorovna is there, sir, with Grand Duke Mitry Palych": The groundskeeper condenses both names. Elizaveta Fyodorovna (1864–1918) was the sister of Tsarina Aleksandra (wife of Nicholas II); she was killed by the Bolsheviks after the revolution. Dmitry Pavlovich (1892–1942) was one of the few Romanovs to survive the revolution. Due to his involvement in the plot to murder Rasputin, he was sent abroad before the Bolsheviks came to power.

THE ELAGIN AFFAIR

"Op. Pulv.": powdered opium.

"*Quand même pour toujours*": And still, it is for eternity.

Alfred de Musset (1810–1857), French romantic poet and playwright credited with writing France's first modern dramas.

Zygmunt Krasinski (1812–1859), Polish poet, considered one of the country's most important Romantic writers.

Aleksandr Pushkin (1799–1837), Russian poet and prose writer, probably the single most important author in all of Russian literature.

Mariya Bashkirtseva (1860–1884), Russian painter and writer who lived in France and Italy. She is probably best known for her diary, which describes her thoughts and feelings with unflinching candor and was translated into several languages after her death from tuberculosis.

Mariya Vechyora: In 1889 the bodies of eighteen-year-old baroness Mariya Vechyora and Rudolph von Hapsburg, crown prince of Austria-Hungary, were found in a hunting lodge outside Vienna. It is believed that the prince shot Mariya Vechyora, his lover, and then himself. "Dear mama, forgive me for what I have done," Vechyora is said to have written in a note. "I could not overcome my love. . . . I will be happier in death than I was in life."

And so the prosecutor read from the testimony of the accused, selecting those passages he wanted most to keep alive within our memories: It is not entirely clear why the prosecutor wants this passage to stay fresh in the court's memory, as much of it supports the defendant's claim to have only carried out Sosnovskaya's wishes. Perhaps all that matters to the prosecutor is that Elagin here admits openly to shooting the murder victim.

TANYA

Kazakova: The feminine ending ("a") on this name would immediately inform the Russian reader that the owner of the estate is a woman.

Petrusha: an affectionate, intimate form of Pyotr, the name of the male protagonist.

They had forgotten to give him everything necessary for the night: a chamber pot.

Barynya: A *barin* is a male member of the gentry, comparable perhaps to a lord in English. "*Barynya*" could be translated as "the wife of the *barin*" or "a female *barin*." It is often used by peasants to refer to the female head of an estate. A *baryshnya* is a young, unmarried noblewoman. When Tanya later says, "I'm not a *baryshnya*," she means she is not a member of the upper classes (who know how to kiss with their mouths open).

Toward evening he passed her on the porch as she prepared the samovar: Coals would have to be lit inside a small chimney that heated the water in traditional samovars. A servant would prepare kindling and light the coals outside, then bring the samovar to the table.

Well dressed for the city, she walked behind the stationmaster, who addressed her formally as "thou" as he carried her two large sacks of goods: There are two forms of "you" in Russian: roughly speaking, *vy* (thou) is used to address formal associates and to show respect. *Ty* (you) is used when speaking to close friends, family members, and children. It was also customary for members of the upper classes to speak to menials and peasants with *ty* while servants and workers always addressed their superiors with *vy*. The stationmaster would ordinarily speak to Tanya with *ty*, but he has evidently mistaken her for a member of some class other than the peasantry because of her packages and good clothes.

Tanechka: an affectionate form of Tanya.

Bolshoi Moskovsky: an expensive, popular restaurant for Moscow's upper classes, literally "The Big Moscow (Restaurant)."

Pyotr Nikolaevich: the first name and patronymic of the male protagonist.

SUKHODOL

Sukhodol: The name combines two words that would convey to a Russian reader the idea of "Dry Valley."

Natalya: Her first name can be shortened to Natasha or Natashka, as it often is when the narrator speaks about her in her youth.

Her mother was my father's wet nurse: It was customary for a serf to breast-feed the offspring of nobility. Wet nurses were generally well treated as their health directly affected that of the owner's child. The use of wet nurses continued in Russia long after it had ended in Western Europe.

Could she be the witch Baba-Yaga?: A popular figure in Russian children's stories.

In the servants' quarters hung a large dark icon of St. Merkury—the same saint whose iron sandals lie before the iconostasis in the ancient cathedral of Smolensk: The Bunin family reportedly had such an icon, passed down from Ivan Aleksandrovich's grandfather. But the story behind the icon, as told in "Sukhodol," seems to combine the histories of two separate martyrs. According to legend, St. Merkury of Smolensk heard a voice from an icon that called on him to fight the Tatars in 1239. He defeated them but was killed in battle. The people of Smolensk buried him in the city's main cathedral, where his sandals remained on display before the iconostasis. An earlier St. Merkury lived in Rome in roughly 249 A.D. He won a major victory over the barbarians but then declared himself a Christian before the emperor and refused to accept the pagan gods. He was tortured cruelly for several days and eventually killed by decapitation.

"Ou etes-vous, mes enfants?": "Where are you, my children?"

Nyanechka: an affectionate, diminutive form of the word for Nanny.

odnodvortsy: A class of free people who enjoyed limited privileges, including the right to own serfs, but who were often only slightly better off than the peasantry. Odnodvortsy were often settlers in outer regions of Russia, particularly in borderlands with Ukraine. Still, it is surprising that Natalya, a serf, would imply that she is more frail than they.

"Maître corbeau sur un arbre perché": Raven, perched in a tree . . .

sentsy: a small room without insulation leading to the entranceway or vestibule of a house. Used for shaking off snow and dirt before one enters even the outermost part of a building. Comparable perhaps to a "mudroom" in English.

She lived in a daze, stunned by her crime, spellbound by her terrifying secret and her treasure, like the girl in the tale of the scarlet flower: A reference to the story by Sergey Aksakov (1791–1859), in which a girl asks her father to bring her nothing but a scarlet flower from his journeys while her sisters plead for expensive gifts. The flower turns out to be magical.

kalach: a kind of white-meal loaf, similar in shape to a soft pretzel.

The Nogais: an ethnic group residing primarily in the Caucasus and some areas of the Crimea. Traditionally nomads who survived by fishing and raising cattle.

Oginsky's polonaise: M. K. Oginsky (1765–1831), Polish composer.

The Feast of Pokrov: Held on October 14 (October 1 old-style calendar), it celebrates the appearance of the Virgin Mary before the Holy Fool Andrew in Constantinople in the tenth century. According to legend, the Virgin appeared holding a veil (*pokrov*). Peasants traditionally sought to complete their harvesting and other preparations for winter by the time of this holiday.

Aunt Olga Kirillovna: Olga Kirillovna is the aunt of Pyotr Petrovich and Arkady Petrovich. This would make her the great aunt of the narrator and his sister, but in Russian tradition they refer to her as grandmother.

"Your sacred word has bound you to a dead man": an inexact quotation from Mikhail Lermontov's "The Dead Man's Love."

"Martyn Zadeka already predicted this in my future": a reference to a well-known book for the interpretation of dreams.

Crimean War: Fought between 1853 and 1856, the war pitted Russia against the Ottoman Empire, France, England, and Sardinia. It stemmed in part from disputes over the Palestinian holy lands.

"No, Uncle Yevsey. I won't ever go to the altar": Here "uncle" is used as a term of respect and affection.

She crossed herself and bowed to the icon in the corner, then to the mistress and Miss Tonya, and stood waiting for questions and instructions: In pre-revolutionary Russian houses, one corner of each room was dedicated to an icon; it was customary to bow to this "beautiful corner" of the room upon entering.

Sometimes when she worked, she would narrow her eyes and sing in a deep, strong voice about the infidels laying siege to Pochaev, and the Mother of God defending the monastery as "the evening sunset burned above the walls": During the Tatar-Mongol invasions of Kiev, monks and priests took refuge in the Pochaev Mountains beginning in roughly 1240. According to legend, the Virgin Mary appeared in a column of flames in that year. A church was built on the site where the vision was said to have occurred.

In the fall, Russian peasant women from Kaluga were brought in for the harvest and the threshing, but Natashka stayed away from them: Because they are Russian (as opposed to Ukrainian) it would have been natural for Natashka to strike up a friendship with the women from Kaluga. In the Russian text they are given the nickname *raspashonki*, a word for a loose-fitting jacket for small babies that can be easily removed.

"Holy Saint! Pray to God for me, a sinner, Mariya of Egypt!": St. Mariya of Egypt led a young life of promiscuity in Alexandria toward the end of the fifth century. She traveled to Jerusalem with a group of pilgrims and was prevented by an invisible force from passing with a crowd into Christ's tomb. She repented and began a life of solitary fasting in the desert for fifty years.

"So I headed home, to Rus. . . . I'm not going to waste away, I told myself": The Kiev Monastery is in Ukraine; Yushka returns from there to Russia (Rus), his original home.

It was the eve of St. Ilya, the ancient fire-thrower's day: celebrated on August 2. St. Ilya is associated with thunder, lightning, and rain as well as fertility.

They took Aunt Tonya to a saint's remains in Voronezh: The remains of saints were believed to have both physical and spiritual healing powers.

Various rumors came about emancipation, triggering alarm among the house serfs and the field hands: Serfdom would be abolished in Russia in 1861.

THE SCENT OF APPLES

babye leto: Literally "the women's summer," this term signifies the last warm days of September before the onset of fall. Often translated in English as "Indian summer."

odnodvortsy: a class of free people who had the right to own serfs as well as other limited privileges, but who were themselves often no wealthier than the peasantry. The word literally means "one yard," a reference to the limited landholdings most *odnodvortsy* were able to amass.

barchuk: the word might be literally translated as "little master." In *Mitya's Love* the protagonist is also referred to as *barchuk.*

It wasn't customary for married sons to split off land from their fathers' plots in Vyselki: In much of Russia it was common practice for peasant sons to divide evenly their fathers' land. This resulted in ever smaller plots being held by different members of a single family, often making it impossible for anyone to farm effectively.

The Gentleman Philosopher: An anti-utopian novel by Fyodor Dmitriev-Mamonov (1728–1805). The author later used the title as his pseudonym. The novel tells of a landowner who builds a model sun and solar system on his estate.

The Secrets of Aleksis; Victor, or a Child in the Forest: Novels by the French sentimentalist François-Guillaume Ducray-Dumenil (1761–1819).